GAME BETWEEN SPIES

GAME BETWEEN SPIES

BY

ELIZABETH J. JUNG

This is a book of fiction. All the characters and incidents portrayed in this book are fictitious; any resemblance to real people or events is purely coincidental. All characters have no existence outside of the imagination of the author and have no relation whatsoever to anyone bearing the same name or names.

1stBooks - rev. 12/29/00

ACKNOWLEDGMENTS

This book is dedicated to my late husband, Bob, who was my inspiration and my best friend. Also, for my family who offer encouragement and assistance. To all my friends who gave the push, help and special words of wisdom; to Colette Eneboe for her patience and typing skills; to Carol Mills, Gladys Remillard, Dora Soria and Connie Luedtke for just being there; to Gary Schichtl for all of his help; and, especially to all my readers for reading my works.

OTHER NOVELS BY ELIZABETH J. JUNG

The Budapest Connection

CHAPTER ONE

"Can't you make this car go any faster?" Johnny Collins snapped. He sighed and pushed his weary body toward the edge of the seat and pressed his forehead against the cold windshield. The howling of the April wind sent a shiver throughout his body.

His eyes were red and itched from lack of sleep. Leaning back against the seat, he raised his arm and glanced at his watch. It had been over twenty-four hours since he had left CIA Headquarters in Langley, Virginia.

He was still upset over the string of "what ifs" left unanswered from the Zagreb assignment. It had been an agency disaster and a personal loss. Nothing had gone right. Even now, he had no idea who the woman was that had killed his best friend. Now, with Barr missing, it was two missing persons assignments, back to back. That was a bit much.

"If you want, I'll pull over and let you drive," Jim Swartz answered, breaking the silence. He spoke without moving his head; his eyes remained locked on the dark street ahead of him.

Swartz's remark broke Collins's concentration. He glanced at Swartz and sighed. Turning away without a comment, Collins glanced out into the darkness and adjusted his seat belt.

He kept silent for several minutes, turned and checked the speedometer again. "Damn it, Swartz. You're only going 30 miles an hour. You have diplomatic plates on this car, you could step on it, there isn't another car in sight."

Collins scratched his head and pushed several strands of dark hair away from his eyes. He pulled at the black turtleneck and felt the breast pocket on his jacket for the notebook he always carried.

Swartz glanced at Collins, muttered to himself and turned his eyes back to the road. He shifted in his seat, but, added no pressure to the gas pedal.

Collins stretched his neck back and forth and raised his shoulders up and down. He looked out the rear window. In an

1

exasperated tone, he said, "Come on, what are you afraid of? Get moving!"

Swartz looked at Collins for a split second and then squinted at the dimly lit road in front of him. He spoke slowly and louder than he had any time earlier in the evening. "There is no sense in killing ourselves, diplomatic plates or not. I'm not going to speed down these dark unfamiliar streets. I've never been out here in the dark and I can't judge which street goes where."

"I'm just anxious," Collins replied, rubbing his head with both hands. "I'd like to find Barr alive! I'm afraid every minute it takes us to get there, could be his last." Collins sat silent for several seconds and then continued. "Are you sure we're going in the right direction? What if we get lost? He'll be dead for sure."

Frustrated with the situation, Collins slapped his hand against the dashboard. A loud cracking sound vibrated throughout the car.

Swartz jumped and jerked the steering wheel. The car darted across the street. He tapped the brake slightly and brought the car under control.

"Hey, take it easy," Swartz said. "You damn near scared me to death. What's the matter with you?"

Swartz pushed on the brake, twisted the steering wheel sharp to the left and turned down a deserted street. He slowed down, almost stopping.

"Look, this is the right district." He pointed to a business address sign nailed to the side of a building. "Barr's already been missing several days. There's a slim to none chance he's even alive."

"But, there is always a chance," Collins muttered, rubbing the new growth on his chin. Once again, he pulled at the dark shirt that fit tight around his neck. He felt as if he were suffocating.

Swartz muttered, sped up and then slammed on the brakes. He turned the steering wheel sharp to the left, throwing Collins against the door. The tires squealed. Swartz pressed down on the gas pedal. As the car sped forward, he said, "What are the odds anyway? A million to one?"

Swartz's fingers gripped the steering wheel. He spun the late model black American Ford around the sharp corner and onto a narrow gravel roadway. Gravel sprayed up against the windshield. Loud cracking noises pierced the still night air.

Struggling to keep control, Swartz cussed as the car swerved onto the sidewalk. He twisted the steering wheel to the left, barely missing a tree trunk.

Collins gasped aloud. "Geez, that was close. Don't get us killed. That would be a hell-of-a-mess," Collins said softly, after the car came to a stop. He took a deep breath and exhaled.

"Do you see anything unusual?" Swartz asked, his voice quivering slightly. He inched the car forward slowly.

Collins squinted and replied, "Vienna is barely visible through the trees. I don't see anything usual or unusual. I haven't seen a living soul since we left the Gurtel area. Hell, it's the middle of the night, who do you think we're going to see? Sane people are home in bed."

Swartz steered the car through the long slithering shadows that swayed back and forth across the deserted lane. "What a place to be. It looks like a horror movie scene. What in the hell are we doing? Why would Barr be out here, miles away from anything?"

Collins rolled down his window and stuck his head out. There was a slight breeze. The cold wind was gone. He whispered, "Should we move closer? That looks like a large warehouse over there."

Swartz, the State Department Officer, answered, "Hell no, this is as close as we're going to drive. It doesn't look as if that is even a road over there. I'll park here and we can continue on foot." He turned the car toward the side of the lane and parked it under the shelter of a large elm tree, totally concealing it from any one driving past.

"This is fine," Collins whispered, motioning for Swartz to stop. "Are you going to carry the cell phone?"

3

Before Swartz could answer, Collins pounced from the car, quietly closing the door behind him. He stood silently for several seconds, taking time to get his bearings.

Swartz crept out of the car and walked around to the trunk. "Maybe not," he whispered when Collins joined him. "Let's leave the cell phone in the trunk. I'd hate like hell to get in there and have the damn thing start squawking."

Before leaving the Embassy, they had rummaged through the closet. They had changed to black turtleneck long sleeve shirts, black jackets, black docker slacks, black rubber sole shoes and dark socks.

Swartz quickly opened the trunk and took out a small bag and two black backpacks, which were each filled with small tools, rope, smoke bombs, medical supplies and a pair of handcuffs. Silently, he handed Collins a backpack and one each of the larger items. He put the rest either in his pockets or held them in his hands.

Each man now had a pair of Bausch & Lomb Night Ranger, night vision glasses around his neck, and a flashlight. Collins had a night light compass and Swartz had an emergency flare stuck in his waistband. They each carried a weapon of their choice.

Collins preferred a knife. It was hidden in a holster on his left leg. Swartz first resisted the idea of carrying a weapon but finally settled for a small black pistol. He placed it in his belt, against the small of his back.

Pausing for a moment, Johnny Collins reviewed the reason why he was in Vienna. Alan Barr, an Embassy communicator, had never returned to work after a routine vacation. The Embassy had no idea why.

A phone call to the Embassy, just an hour earlier, was their only lead. An anonymous caller had left a simple message that Barr could be found in the warehouse at 20 Muthgasse.

The Danube River was directly behind the men as they stood in the darkness. The musty smell of damp papers and the stifling odors of floating oils filled the air.

An uncanny feeling saturated the night. Periodically, the slapping of the water, hitting a retainer wall, broke the silence.

It was an industrial neighborhood with no private residences, just large dirty gray block buildings, surrounded by wire fences with gravel walkways and parking lots. The small pathways, driveways and parking areas were lined with a wide assortment of wood and metal storage containers.

No lights were lit in any of the neighborhood buildings. A single street lamp, hanging in the middle of each block, swayed back and forth from the soft night breeze, casting a dim, narrow, hazy beam. The dirty, weak bulb offered little comfort or assistance.

Collins adjusted his clothing and glasses one final time. He took a deep breath, looked around and asked, "Ready?"

Swartz nodded and stepped behind Collins. Collins moved cautiously several yards. He stopped, turned and motioned. He believed the address was directly in front of them. He bent down and took a handful of moist dirt.

Swartz did the same. They smeared the dirt on their faces and hands. Adjusting their night vision glasses in place, they moved forward.

A ten-foot high wire security fence completely encircled the warehouse grounds. At first glance, the fence posed a huge obstacle. They separated to locate an entrance, making hand signals to one another as they moved.

Silently, they made their way around the fence toward an open makeshift gate. Stopping for a moment, they listened to the night. Nothing stirred.

Collins raised his arm as a signal to advance forward. After sprinting across the lot, the men froze in place, listening for any sound before they went into the building. Convinced they were alone, they proceeded.

A small sign, nailed to the side of the building, read Mobel Transport, 20 Muthgasse. They both nodded. This was the right warehouse.

A side door was ajar. A broken light bulb, hanging from an exposed wire over the entrance, swayed with the breeze.

The agent signaled. He was going inside. Swartz, providing backup cover, ran toward the door holding his gun ready, crouching in a ready-to-fire position, prepared for the unexpected.

Collins crept inside and moved around to the right side of the building, using his instinct to guide him. With his night vision glasses on, he stopped and looked around. At first, the warehouse appeared completely empty except for several pieces of discarded trash. Packing papers and cartons laid ignored, crumbled and torn, against the walls and littered the floor.

With Collins safely inside the building, Swartz crept in and cautiously closed the door. He stood near the door, then crept slightly to the middle of the room.

Collins moved toward the back of the space. He reached his arm up to switch on a hanging light bulb. Warnings flashed through his mind as he remembered his CIA bomb training classes.

Large sweat beads covered his forehead and began creeping toward his eyes. His fingers shook. He held his breath and turned the switch.

A dim haze filled the building and the tall man sighed with relief. The smell of sweat, dirt, grease and neglect filled his nostrils. The odor in the closed building was somewhat familiar. It was sweet and musty, almost overpowering. Pushing the night vision glasses from his eyes, Collins studied the vast warehouse.

Standing back, Swartz put his hand over his nose stopping a sneeze. Following Collins's lead, he also pushed his glasses off his eyes. Carefully, Swartz moved across the warehouse floor toward Collins.

They both crept forward, heading to the warehouse office in the back against the far wall. Maintaining silence, they slowly searched the interior of the building. The beams of their flashlights moved up and down, swaying as they stepped.

They glanced at one another and shook their heads. They were almost convinced the trip had been for nothing. Collins motioned and they began retracing their steps.

They went slower this time, moving their flashlights over the floor, examining the building foot-by-foot, inch-by-inch. Each taking opposite walls.

Suddenly, Collins stopped and cried out in a penetrating whisper, "Here! Over here!"

The beam of Swartz's flashlight swung around trying to find Collins. He called, "What is it?" and ran toward the light.

They stood rigid with their eyes fixed on Collins's light. It was shining on the wooden pillars that supported the building. As Collins held the beam of his flashlight on the spot, Swartz moved his light up and down the framework.

Halfway up the support, two rafters crossed each other forming the shape of a cross. It was here they saw what they had been dreading. Exactly where the wood was nailed together, six feet off the floor, they found Alan Barr, the missing American Embassy communicator.

CHAPTER TWO

The man was dead. He hung naked. His eyes were closed and his head bent forward in an awkward, unnatural position. A dirty, smelly rag dangled from his mouth.

The men stared as they followed the beams of their flashlights. Someone had taken a white thin rope and tied it to the hanging man's penis and testicles.

The rope was then attached to a small metal pot, and in the pot were several small rocks. The weight from the pot had caused the penis and testicles to rupture. A small pile of stones was on the floor at the base of the support. The stones were covered with blood.

It was obvious that the man had bled to death. A long painful, excruciating death.

His legs were straight and rigid. They were streaked with dried brownish-caked blood. Blood had dripped into the pot and onto the ground below him.

Collins ran his light up along Barr's arms, they were caked with streaks of blood and dirt. Small flies were swarming around the entire body.

Collins said, "Look at those arms. Looks like the poor guy was injected. We need to make sure that Langley gets a chance to check those puncture wounds."

Swartz muttered, "I don't feel so hot. My stomach is churning." He began moaning.

Collins stepped back and put his hand over his mouth. The scent of death was overwhelming. "Should we cut him down?" Collins asked.

"No," Swartz gulped. He ran toward the door and rushed out into the fresh air.

Collins followed cautiously, weaving as he ran, trying to hold the flashlight steady in his trembling hands. He knew if he didn't take deep breaths he would begin vomiting. He could already taste the bitter bile in his throat.

"What a hell of a way to die," Swartz muttered, leaning against the side of the building, gasping to get fresh air into his lungs. A pile of vomit lay on the ground beside the side of the building. "We'd better get our butts back to the Embassy and call Security and get someone out here and get poor Alan down. Someone will have to call his wife. Geez, someone will have to call the Ambassador, and the Duty Officer. Hell, half the Embassy will have to be called out tonight before we're through. Can you imagine what Greenly is going to say when he hears about all of this?" Swartz kept shaking his head and rubbing his fingers across his mouth.

Collins shuddered as he walked back and shut the warehouse door. Pulling the door tight, securing it, he hoped to offer the dead man some dignity. He briefly considered returning to turn off the light but decided against it.

"What a shitty world," he muttered to himself. He took out the notebook from his pocket and quickly made notes. "What day is it anyway?" he asked. "The days are all running together."

Swartz looked at the sky and said, "It's Friday morning now."

Streaks of sunlight were breaking through the slight fog cloud overcast. The men hurried toward the car.

After retrieving the cell phone, Swartz started the ball rolling. He called Bob Blinksdale, the State Department Security Officer, and asked him to meet them at the Embassy and to alert the doctor and the Ambassador. He stated simply that Alan Barr had been found dead.

CHAPTER THREE

"Did they find the body?" the older man asked the young couple. He was dressed in a large bulky white terry cloth robe and brown leather slippers. His dark damp hair glistened in the light. He twisted himself around in his leather desk chair to get a better look at the newcomers.

"You may go to bed now, Sarah," he said. He motioned toward the white haired woman that had escorted the couple into his room. He watched and smiled as the old lady, still dressed in her uniform black dress and white apron, shuffled out of the room wearing her bright red fuzzy slippers.

Turning back to the couple, he waited for an answer to his question. He had placed his disfigured right hand over the telephone receiver, making sure that the person on the other end couldn't hear what was being said in the room.

"Yes, they're back at the Embassy," the younger man answered. He closed the door after the old lady left. He waited until his partner had taken a place directly in front of the big walnut desk, then moved forward and stood beside her.

George Haddah, the ruddy faced Lebanese, smiled and nodded. He turned his back to the couple, spoke softly and finished his phone call.

Patiently, the couple stood at military attention and waited. Their eyes were fixed on the oil painting behind the older man's desk. It was a huge winter mountain landscape scene that almost covered the entire back wall.

"So?" Haddah questioned impatiently, once the phone was back on the cradle. His dark piercing eyes darted from one to the other.

Mehmet Gadhafi and Gabrielle stood straight and erect. Their eyes shifted from the painting and locked onto Haddah's face.

Gadhafi spoke first. "I called the American Embassy as you had instructed. We stood in the shadows by the warehouse. We

10

saw the two men arrive. With our night vision binoculars, we tracked them until they entered the warehouse. Once they were inside, we backed away closer to our car and watched and listened to them with our heat sensor equipment and listening devices. We could follow their steps inside the building. When they were back outside, one of the men became sick." Gadhafi looked at Gabrielle and grinned.

Gabrielle straightened, held her head high and said, "We knew they had found the body. We continued watching until they started walking back toward their car. We started our car and kept the lights off until we were safely away. Then, we drove straight back to the American Embassy."

Holding her head stiff, she shifted her eyes from the older man back to her partner. As if rehearsed, she continued, holding the tempo of the conversation without taking a breath. "We knew it would be just a matter of time before they arrived back at the Embassy. We were lucky to find a parking place within a block of the front door. Actually, it was almost the same place where we had parked earlier in the day. We sat and watched until we saw both men enter the Embassy. Then, we drove here."

Haddah inched forward in his chair and asked, "Who seems to be in charge? Is it the CIA or the State Department?"

Gabrielle looked at Gadhafi. She answered, "That CIA agent, Collins, appears to be the one in charge. We were watching when he first entered the Embassy with Swartz earlier this afternoon. He apparently had just arrived from Langley."

Gadhafi nodded in agreement. He glanced at Gabrielle and then at Haddah. He said, "Yes, she is right."

Haddah rubbed his injured hand, a smile filled his face. He watched the couple for a few seconds and then said, "Yes, I received a call from our "watcher" at the airport when Collins arrived today." He leaned back in his chair continuing to rub his hand. After several seconds of silence, he said, "Now we are ready to proceed. Are you firmly established in the American school, Gabrielle?"

She nodded, reached up and removed her black knit ski cap, releasing her long shiny brown hair. She smiled and took a deep breath. Her large breasts pressed firmly against her dark shirt.

Haddah smiled. She looked beautiful in the soft light. But, he knew that when she dressed in bulky men's clothing, her disguise was perfect. Without makeup and with her slim firm body even he had trouble telling if she were male or female.

This was only the second time he had even worked with Gabrielle. He was extremely careful not to offend her. It was well known that her loyalty was shared between the Russian and the Arab worlds. Also, he had recently heard that she had taken a lover.

Haddah suspected her lover was the Russian, Colonel Nikolai Golodin. Unfortunately, it was Golodin who was in charge of their present assignment, and it was the Russians that were providing all the financial support.

Haddah smiled and said, "That is fine. You both have done your jobs. Gabrielle, someone will be in touch with you regarding your role at the American School. Sleep well."

He continued rubbing his injured hand, which was a constant reminder of his dedication to his country. "The Americans will soon understand the agony they have caused the Arab world. It's payback time."

Smiling, Haddah walked his guests to the door. He watched as they crossed to a dark sedan parked on the corner. Moving to the side of his doorway, he checked to see if any strange cars were parked in the neighborhood. Confident that no one was watching, he sighed with relief and walked back into the house.

He double locked the door and pushed against it with his hip to make sure the catch was secure. Taking his time, rerunning the events of the evening in his mind, he returned to his office.

The flicker of his computer screen caught his attention. For a brief moment, he considered finishing the Free Cell game that was still on the screen.

Instead, he turned, reached for the cordless phone and dialed the Russian Colonel's private number. He sat back in his comfortable leather chair and looked around his room. He knew Colonel Golodin was waiting for his report.

CHAPTER FOUR

Colonel Nikolai Golodin had spent the evening reading in his apartment just blocks from the American Embassy. After checking his watch several times, he no longer could concentrate. The words were blurred. If nothing else, his years of directing Barr and the other American agents had taught him patience.

He knew that Americans were always quick to react when one of their own was in trouble. It was just a matter of time before the CIA would send an agent to find Barr.

Golodin expected Melvin Hubert, the Director of the CIA European Division, to send Johnny Collins. The Soviet Embassy in Washington,DC had already informed him that Collins was back in Virginia after his assignment in Zagreb had failed.

Now, Golodin just needed confirmation either from Washington or from one of his Viennese agents that Collins had actually departed for Vienna. Hopefully, Haddah would know if Collins had arrived. He had followed Collins's career during the cold war days and knew that Collins was one of the CIA's most experienced men.

The message Golodin had received earlier in the day, from one of his agents within the Langley CIA Headquarters building, was still on his desk. The report stated simply that Collins had been called into Melvin Hubert's office.

The agent wasn't able to verify exactly what was discussed, but confirmed Collins left Langley with a plane ticket to Vienna in his hand. The agent also verified that Mrs. Collins had been summoned to Dulles airport.

Golodin hoped this time he would have the chance to meet Collins face to face. Over the years, he had only been able to observe the CIA agent from a distance. Never up close and personal, as the Americans would say. Now, Golodin felt it was time to have the personal satisfaction of playing against an equal.

Daydreaming was a favorite pastime for Colonel Nikolai Golodin since his beloved wife passed away from cancer. He felt old, although he had just celebrated his fifty-sixth birthday. He still had a full head of dark hair and was able to wear the same size clothing he wore when he was thirty.

His only son, a doctor, was married and living in Moscow. They rarely communicated. Now, his work was his only family.

Glancing at an old worn picture of his wife and son on the end table, he remembered the good times. As if his arm were mechanical, he brushed a tear from his eye.

Silently, he sat remembering his earlier days with his beloved GRU. Recalling each moment as if it were only yesterday. Over the years and with the fall of the iron curtain, things changed, but they remained the same.

The day he was recruited into the organization was a major highlight in his life. He clearly remembered the first time he learned of the Glavnoye Razvedyvatelnoye Upravleniye, the division of the Russian Intelligence Service, whose responsibility was to carry out military intelligence work for the Russian Army throughout the world. He had known from the beginning, he wanted to be a member. His heart quickened as he recalled the thrill of hearing he was to be one of the chosen few.

Studying hard, he learned all the rules and memorized the regulations. He knew that GRU members were assigned within the Russian Foreign Ministry, the Ministry of External Trade, Aeroflot, the Academy of Sciences, and around the world on Embassy duty. Even after the dramatic changes in Russia, the GRU continued to be the eyes and ears of the Russian military as modern day spies.

Fortunately, Gabrielle had added a spark to his daily routine, but he was no fool. He knew she was only using him and would leave when she thought he could no longer help her. He smiled and knew that two could play that game.

"Hello," Golodin answered quickly, immediately after the first ring.

"They have found the body. Everyone has returned to the Embassy. Will we meet tomorrow?"

Golodin smiled and tapped his fingernail on the tabletop. "Yes, in Turkenschanz Park. Near the duck pond. About five in the evening. Has Langley sent anyone?" He could feel his heart racing.

"Yes, they sent Collins."

Golodin quickly hung up the phone, not giving anyone time to trace the call. His heart was beating frantically against the walls of his chest.

Golodin had been taught early in his training that being a spy was like playing a child's game. Except in the real world spy game, each country raced against the clock, the prizes were bigger and failure was often deadly.

The Russian GRU Colonel was finally able to relax. He had returned home earlier and had washed the dried blood off his shoes. He had tried to stay away from the body, but something compelled him to visit the warehouse. Although, he trusted George Haddah, Golodin still had reservations and had to see for himself. Rubbing his forehead, he frowned.

Why couldn't Barr just do as he had been instructed? What had happened to him? Why had Barr jeopardized everything that they had so carefully planned?

Golodin sat quietly as he thought of the alternatives that had been available to him. It was crystal clear, he had done the right thing.

Golodin smiled as he thought of the agents still in place. He was sure the Americans didn't know about them. And, with his new diversion plan, the Americans would shift their focus.

He walked slowly to a small closet outside of his office. Pushed back the accordion folding door and turned on the computer. Within seconds, he clicked with his mouse on a red star icon in the top right hand side of the screen. An E-mail form instantly appeared. "The Game has started," he typed. He clicked on the send button and smiled.

CHAPTER FIVE

Wednesday started like every other normal workday for CIA agent, Johnny Collins, when he was home in Fairfax, Virginia, living the American Dream. He lived with his wife and 3 kids, 2 boys and a girl, in a two story split-level home in a safe neighborhood away from street gangs and the homeless. The children went to public school, took part in school activities and had all the electronic gadgets like their friends. None of the children were old enough to drive, so the family only had two vehicles, Mom's and Dad's.

Dressed in a pair of dark brown dress slacks, a tan short sleeve shirt, a brown tweed jacket and a soft blue tie, Johnny kissed his wife as he walked out the door on his way to work. He whispered to remind her to arrange for her parents to baby-sit for the Saturday night office party.

He knew his teenaged kids loved spending time with their grandparents and sharing pizza. There were too many wild parties and drugs in Fairfax to leave them home alone.

When Johnny passed through the security check-in and entered the CIA Headquarters building in Langley, Virginia, the sun was bright in a cloudless sky. After a long cold winter, the slight hint of spring was welcome.

He swelled with pride as he walked down the main hallway past the United States seal. His step grew brisker as he continued walking with thoughts of the weekend party. He had to remember to find his darts. He couldn't remember when he had used them last.

Turning the corner toward his office, he heard his boss's baritone voice bellowing through his closed office door. He crept past and wondered what had gotten the old man so excited so early in the morning.

Sue, the beautiful, middle-aged department assistant, was standing in the hallway outside Johnny's office, obviously waiting. Her eyes flashed when she saw him.

Johnny smiled and admired Sue's long bright green form fitting dress and trim body. For a moment, he wondered, was it St. Patrick's Day? As he stepped near her, he bent his head close to her ear and asked, "What the hell's going on?"

"I've been standing here waiting for you for fifteen minutes. About time you arrived," she answered sharply, shaking her finger at him. Putting her finger to her lips, she whispered, "Johnny, better keep your voice down. There's a big stink in Vienna. The proverbial shit has hit the fan. The Man is foaming at the mouth. He ordered me to call an all department team meeting for ten this morning. Just now, he finished with the Austrian Desk Officer. Got the poor guy out of bed before five this morning."

"What's it about?" Johnny asked, stepping around Sue and trying to turn into his office.

Sue continued to whisper, "I only know bits and pieces. Johnny, he has been asking for you. I'm to let him know as soon as you arrive. He wants you in the "igloo.""

"Damn, just when I was adjusting to the states. Wouldn't you know it?" Johnny muttered aloud, walking away from Sue and down the hall toward Hubert's office. He took a deep breath before knocking on his boss's door.

"Come in! Collins, it's about time you got in this morning," a harsh voice roared from within the room as soon as the door opened.

The door squeaked when Johnny closed it. Casually, he strolled across the office toward his favorite soft leather chair. It was hidden from the direct line of vision of anyone entering the room, and kept him downwind from the foul smell of the after-shave cologne his boss always wore.

"Sue says you want to see me," Johnny said before he sat down.

Hubert, a white haired man with thick glasses, heavy eyebrows and deep laugh lines, stared at Collins and said, "Since the Lonetree incident in Moscow and Vienna in the 80's, how many times have I issued specific orders to keep me informed?"

Collins just nodded and shrugged his shoulders. He had no idea what Hubert was referring to.

Hubert continued, "The need for good agents, the problems with Congress, budget cuts, the national debt and the changes in the White House made all of us older agents wonder if all of this is worth our efforts. Maybe, I should retire."

Melvin Hubert, a seasoned officer, had risen to a director position after twenty-five years of climbing the rank ladder. Recruited after graduating from the University of Iowa, he had taken field assignments all over the world. Most of them, he openly described as "hell holes."

Collins made himself more comfortable in his seat. He had listened to many of Hubert's sermons and knew it was going to be a few more minutes before Hubert said anything new.

Without taking his eyes off of Collins, Hubert said, "Now, for the past five years, I have been in charge of this office. Wouldn't you think that our people knew what I did here? Don't they know what the CIA does?"

Johnny knew that in training, all CIA agents memorized the original purpose of the CIA. They were required to read the papers, which outlined the National Security Bill of February 1947. This bill was the authorization to coordinate and evaluate foreign intelligence from all sources outside the continental United States.

Hubert moved several manila files around on his desk. Most of them had a big red CLASSIFIED stamped on the front. "I'm getting tired of all the changes, all the shuffling, reorganizing and renaming we have gone through after the discovery of moles in the 1980's and 90's. This is the new millennium. Things are supposed to be better."

"Do you want to tell me what this is all about?" Johnny asked, glancing quickly at his watch.

Johnny didn't know what to expect but he knew it wasn't good. He recalled the hell the department paid the night the wife of a London agent got drunk in a packed restaurant and started spilling everything she knew about the CIA. He sat and watched a promising young agent and his family transferred within hours of the incident.

Also, he remembered the time when the teen-aged kids of the Paris Station Chief began experimenting with drugs. Collins met the Station Chief's family, with suitcases, the next day at Baltimore Washington Airport. Melvin Hubert was tough, but Johnny respected him.

Hubert stood, put on his dark blue sports jacket that was hanging on the back of his chair. He adjusted his tie, which was brown with star designs and looked as if it had been rolled up in a ball before he put it on.

Hubert walked around the desk and motioned for Collins to follow. The two men went halfway down the long hall. Collins stood back as Hubert stopped beside a tall plant, faced the wall, pushed aside a false light plate and pressed a combination of numbers onto a keypad.

Instantly, a concealed door swung open and the two men entered a small room. Within the Agency and the intelligence community, this type of room was known by many names: "Igloo," "Cone of Silence," "Tank," "Bubble" or "Security Briefing Room." It had been specifically designed to neutralize any type of listening devices.

The room, Johnny Collins and Melvin Hubert entered resembled an Eskimo Igloo. It was a room within a room.

As they entered they passed through one of the most advanced electric eye sensor machines. This machine had the ability to distinguish various metals and would beep if anyone were carrying some device, which was not allowed in the rooms, such as a tape recorder, camera, phone or computer equipment. It also took measurements of the men and could detect if anyone had a fever or physical ailment.

Both men turned and looked toward a camera, which monitored all such rooms 24 hours a day. They knew that their visit would be taped and logged into an agency record book.

The structure of the basic room was similar to every other room within a secure environment: no windows, one entrance door, no external outlets for air conditioning or heating. A room totally containing another complete room built within its four walls. A steel-encased room especially designed to prevent electronic penetration because of its electromagnetic producing field.

The inner room was erected within the initial structure's walls. Collins always thought it reminded him of adults building a huge see-through tent within a room. All inside walls of the inner room were made of a sophisticated, indestructible plastic.

Between the walls of the rooms were sets of complete ventilation and electrical systems controlled by the entry room structure. Although the room was spacious, it provided an overwhelming feeling of claustrophobia.

Turning on the electricity, which turned on both the lights and strong air conditioning system, Hubert paused by the door allowing Collins to enter first. The room contained one large gray metal ten foot long conference table and twelve gray metal chairs. All furniture had been cleared through detecting devices before being placed in the room.

Off to one corner of the room hung thick, maroon floor to ceiling curtains, which could be pulled to close off the area, should complete secrecy be required.

Within the Agency, every secure room was swept daily for "bugs", more often if needed. Being cautious, Hubert waited for the air conditioning to reach its maximum speed before he began talking.

"Collins, I have one hell of a problem for you. Last night, our office in Vienna contacted me. It seems they have a 'situation.' Within the past several weeks, sensitive information has been showing up in newspapers in Vienna, Moscow, and some of the Arab countries. Our in-house agency Embassy staff translators have alerted us, and sent the papers. We don't know who's behind it or even the department. Some think it came from the Defense Attaché Office or from an Embassy Political Section. Have you heard any rumors about this?"

Collins looked confused. "No, this is new to me," he answered. "Please, continue."

"Now, Vienna is telling me, they have reason to suspect the person passing the information is one of our communicators at their Embassy. They suspect it's Alan Barr. It seems Barr spread the word he had information to sell."

"How did they learn about this?" Collins asked.

Hubert waved his hand. "It doesn't matter. Now, it appears this "nice gentleman" has disappeared. Needless to say, I'm a bit upset to find this out now, after the fact."

Collins slid his chair back and sighed. He rubbed his face several times. Finally, he leaned forward, put his hand together on the table and made a tent. "Which means?" he asked.

"I've also discovered our field station in Vienna had suspected Barr for some time, and sent the information back to me by routine routes," Hubert continued. "But to this hour, I've not received it. Some son of a bitch clerk is probably sitting on it and hasn't even opened the pouch."

Hubert stood and walked around the table. He rubbed his lips together and said, "I've called a ten o'clock meeting this morning with the Agency's Section Chiefs to find out what the hell's going on." His voice became softer and softer as he spoke.

Johnny knew from experience that when Hubert began speaking softly it was only because he was trying to control his temper. Holding his breath, Johnny strained to hear Hubert's soft voice over the humming of the loud air conditioning. He didn't want to further upset Hubert by asking him to speak louder or to repeat himself.

"And, to add to the situation, Greenly, Vienna's Chief-of-Station, and Swartz, State's Chief Communicator, both approved Barr's leave papers. They knew about the suspicions and told me they were going to talk to Barr when he came back from vacation. Vacation! Can you imagine them approving a vacation for a man that they suspected was leaking sensitive information?"

Collins shrugged and raised an eyebrow but didn't say a word.

Hubert added, "Who in his or her right mind would approve a vacation for someone who could be a possible double agent? Stupid bastards! What in the hell could they have been thinking? Sometimes I think the people in the field are way out in outer space. They just don't have their heads screwed on straight. They're so damn afraid of what someone will think or say. They sit in their big Embassy houses, with their hands glued to a damn wine glass rather than going out and doing a little bit of investigative work. And that, by the way, is what they are supposedly getting paid for!" Hubert's face began to get red. The veins on his neck were enlarged.

Collins put his hands flat against the table and asked, "What do you want me to do?"

"Well, now they called me and asked what they should do. I'd really like to tell them what they should do, but I know that our telephone lines are not secure, no matter what the scientific department says. If I had anyone to replace them both, I'd haul their sorry butts back here to Washington. They'd be pushing papers in the archives department for the rest of their work days. But, I'm stuck with them. So, now it comes down to you."

Collins said, "And?"

"I want you in Vienna, NOW. Get everything you need from Sue. Collins, find out what in the hell is going on! Find Barr. Find out where the leak is and stop it. I don't care how you do it. You have complete authority."

Collins turned and followed Hubert as he walked around. The words "complete authority" made him shutter. He hadn't been issued those words since he had to deal with a double agent in Romania. Having a "wet" assignment always meant big trouble.

Hubert walked toward Collins and stared down at him. "Johnny, be sure you go in and introduce yourself to the Ambassador and keep him informed. He knows about the "situation". We don't want him pissed off at us."

"This sounds too much like the Zagreb assignment. After that fiasco, are you sure I'm your man?" Johnny questioned.

Hubert looked at Collins and ignored what he had just said. "The Ambassador's a political appointee and sometimes they're not as keen regarding our associations in a country as a career Ambassador would be. All facilities will be open to you. Just don't make more enemies than necessary."

"Do you have any hunches what country might be behind this?" Collins asked, knowing he was going to Vienna whether he wanted to or not.

"Johnny, you know how it is? It could be anyone. We've had reports that the Abu Nidal, Hizballah and Popular Front for the Liberation of Palestine - General Command, also the reorganized KGB are in Vienna. Then too, the Russian GRU is active throughout Austria. Since the division of the KGB into separate sections, who knows. We now have a group in Russia called the SVR or the foreign intelligence section as well as another splinter group called the FSB or the internal intelligence sector."

Johnny stood, took a deep breath and straightened his jacket. He turned toward Hubert. "I thought the reports from the field said that the Russians were cooling down."

Hubert laughed. "Don't tell me you believe everything you read. Now, our sources in Russia tell us that although they have different areas to cover, they often overlap. Hell, it could be your friends, the Serbs. Who knows what other small terrorist groups could be there? Everyone knows Austria is neutral, but as we learned during the Badder Meinhof days, Vienna is a great recruiting spot. The Hamas have been known to openly recruit there as well as the Algerians. It's anyone's guess as to who wants us to look bad. Hell, it could be the French or Brits! Especially the French. I wouldn't put anything past those bastards. Since the peace talks in Bosnia, word is that several of the off-the-wall solders of fortune groups are looking for new members and some action."

"Have there been any recent threats or events happening in Austria that might have some bearing on the case?" Johnny asked. "Maybe there is some small splinter political faction group waiting to flex its muscles and make a name for itself?"

Hubert pulled a small pocket size calendar from his pocket. He flipped through several pages. "Well, the Secretary of State is going to pay a visit to Vienna in a week or so. He's going to address the United Nations Headquarters. The Vienna Station Chief can fill you in on his schedule. Then, OPEC might be meeting for their annual spring meeting but I can only guess. The Sikhs are wandering around in Hungary and Romania. They could be staying in Vienna and recruiting. Could even be a splinter of the PLO. One never knows with that group. They usually work in the Middle East but they could be looking for support in Vienna. Vienna's so close to the Eastern Countries, any of the breakaway countries from Russia might be trying to make contact. Hell, it might even be the Russian Mafia. As I said earlier, it's anyone's guess. Let's go to my office and I'll give you what little information I have."

Walking back to Hubert's office, Johnny knew what was facing him and he didn't like it. This type of disappearance could be anything from a defection to a simple running away with a lover. One thing, Johnny knew for sure, it would be sometime before he'd be home with his wife and kids. He definitely wouldn't be attending the office party on Saturday night.

CHAPTER SIX

Waving a large sealed manila envelope, Sue was waiting patiently for Johnny Collins outside her boss's door. Smiling, she said simply, "Visit the Dirty Tricks Department and cashier before you leave the building. You're all set. There's a business class ticket, your diplomatic passport and a State Department Identification Card in this envelope. I called your wife. She's adding clothes to your bag and will meet you at Dulles. Enjoy." She turned to walk away and stopped. "Don't forget this time you promised to bring me back a real Sacher Torte. I want one of those you buy at the Sacher Hotel that come in the wooden cases. Okay?"

"Sure, I'll get you one," Johnny answered. He remembered promising her the last trip to Vienna and had completely forgotten about it. He walked into his office and immediately made a note regarding the Sacher Torte in his notebook. Then, he opened the envelope and spilled the contents on top of his desk. He checked the paperwork to see what name he was going to use this trip. A big smile crossed his face when he found out that he wasn't going under a cover.

Johnny glanced at the items, stuck them back in the envelope, stuffed the envelope in his jacket pocket and walked out the door. Without thinking, he headed down the hallway.

Officially, the "Dirty Tricks" department is called the "Research and Development Section" and it is a vital part of CIA's Technical Services Department. Johnny always felt like some type of a James Bond character when he punched in the seven digit combination that gave him access to that section of the building.

Upon entering the visitor room, a small space which consisted of four gray straight back plastic chairs, he was happy to see that no one was waiting ahead of him. In that department, he knew he was treated like everyone else. No favorites.

When a clerk came to the glass window, he nodded at Johnny. Nodding back, Johnny pushed his CIA identification card through the metal tray slot and waited for the door to open.

Walking down the hallway, he was pleased to see some fresh yellow color had been applied to the drab walls. There were also new light fixtures, which gave the hallway a bright cheery look. Walking by the newly painted doors, he muttered the names he had for the different sections; explosives, toxic agents, flaps and seals, disguises, photography and imagery, electronics, and new tricks.

It was the new trick section he wanted. That department worked with all the other technical departments as a research and development lab. The rooms resembled a "mad scientist" laboratory.

Objects were hung, piled, displayed, and stacked around the room in every possible space. Some looked destroyed, while others looked as if they had just arrived off an assembly line.

This area was where all the "new toys" were tested and kept until they were either ready for production or storage. During his years as an agent, Johnny had shared the responsibility of testing many of the new "toys." Most had proven to be very effective, while a couple had almost cost him his life.

After pushing the buzzer, a scientist engineer, a short little man, wrapped in a dingy white lab coat several sizes too big for him, opened the door and nodded. The man, looking like the typical "mad scientist" with long gray rumpled hair and wire framed bifocals, grunted a good morning.

"I've been waiting for you," he muttered giving Johnny a passing glance. He walked back into the lab and expected Johnny to follow.

Among other things on the long white laboratory table in front of them was a small silver tube-shaped object. The scientist placed the cold metal object in Johnny's hand.

"This appears to be nothing more than a basic flashlight. It's smaller than most but very effective. The solar energy battery provides an energy supply, which has never failed. The ray produced is so bright you can see an area a half block away. Its light is small and direct but it has a very powerful steady beam. It's small enough to fit into a shirt pocket or pants pocket without feeling clumsy or bulky."

He waited for Johnny to take the item. "Now, unscrew the end, remove the first battery. That battery is a dummy. Its ends can be easily removed. Take off the end and remove the small piece of gummy substance. The gum is actually a piece of plastic explosive similar to Pyrenol. It can be used for several purposes. You could put a tiny bit over a door latch to gain entrance. It could be used to make a key imprint, or when combined with direct heat, it will ignite in seconds and becomes a powerful explosive."

Johnny nodded and asked, "Any warnings on it?"

The scientist looked at Johnny seriously, "Agents already using it have found many other uses for it. One agent said he added boiling hot water to it and placed it in coffee. Although, it doesn't dissolve completely, he used the runoff fluid. He reported the recipient died within minutes. It causes a sudden heart attack."

The scientist scratched his head and looked at Johnny. He continued, "Can't quite decide what kind of poison it becomes, but I do know it killed lab mice. Also, when empty, the shell could be used to conceal a computer chip or piece of film, should you run into such an antiquated item and need storage."

"Don't plan to," Johnny answered, fingering the flashlight, turning it off and on and pointing the beam toward a distant figure.

"Remember, if you use the substance as an explosive," the scientist warned. "A little dab will do you" and it must have direct heat, such as a lighter flame placed directly on it. Only takes a bit more than ten seconds to go boom. So you want to make sure you are out of reach." The scientist pushed his glasses back from the tip of his nose and rubbed his beard stubble absentmindedly.

"Sounds good to me," Johnny said.

The lab scientist walked to a different area of the lab and continued, "Now, over here we have a belt buckle that we adapted from one we acquired from the Israelis. Our belt buckle is in the form of a "X." The top moves independently of the bottom part. Just hold it and I'll walk you through its uses."

Johnny set the flashlight on the table. He took the belt buckle in his hands and listened attentively.

"Now, when pulled out , it forms a knife which can be used in case you don't have your Swiss one handy. That's right, just pull that part." The scientist watched and then continued, "Now, the bottom part pulls apart, and hidden inside is a very thin strong wire that can be used for multiple purposes. It's similar to piano wire but more flexible. I'm sure you can think of your own uses. It will hold up to 300 pounds."

Johnny pulled it out and ran his finger over the wire. He ran a finger down the line.

"Hey, be careful, that's sharp," the old man said. "We've made the belt easy to operate with only one hand, just in case the other hand is busy. Let's practice with it. Take this and move it like so." He showed Johnny where to put his fingers. "Now, pull this section back, take the wire out and pull it tighter. See how it stretches. It can extend about ten feet and then will recoil by pushing that part of the buckle."

Johnny pushed the buckle and the wire snapped back making a whizzing sound. He jerked with surprise.

The old man laughed. "I told you to be careful, see how it moves back into the holder? It's razor sharp when recoiling. It could cut your finger to the bone."

The two men walked over to the middle of the room. "Anything else you might need?" the older man asked.

"Do you have any gas acid vials? I want the small ones that you just snap the top to activate and can be used close up."

The old man scratched his head. His eyes went wide. "Got some over here. Be careful with them. These are not something you carry around in your shirt pocket." He opened a cabinet and

29

handed Johnny one. It was in a clear plastic case completely encased in foam.

Johnny motioned for one more. The man handed him another one without a question.

"But, I insist that you take a couple of these antidotes also," the old man said, taking a card out of a case. There were six pills attached within a bubble. "Sometimes, one has to get too close for comfort and these antidotes can prevent something from going deadly wrong. You do know how to work them, don't you?"

Johnny nodded. He thought for a moment and then asked, "Do you have any of those new silencers that can adjust to almost any type of a gun?"

"Are you talking about the plastic ones that you can cut off the end to fit both pistols and rifles?"

Johnny nodded. "Right, I guess they are plastic. I've been told they're marvelous, but I've never used one."

The scientist scratched his head again and sighed. "They are good but they do have their drawbacks. They can't be used for a long period of time, I think we say five or six shots max. Also, they won't fit on any of the ceramic style guns that some of our people use to pass through airport security. They work best on the metal weapons but you do have to cut off the end to use them with pistols. They come in the longer length already fit for rifles."

"That's the one. Can I take a handful?"

The older man reached into a drawer and pulled out a handful, wrapped a rubber band around them and handed them to Johnny.

"These look like metal cigar holders. Why the design on the side?" Johnny asked.

"Silly man, they were specifically designed to resemble the imported cigar holders. Less questions are asked. Some of the agents are carrying them in shirt pockets."

Within minutes, the scientist was escorting Johnny from the room. "Have a safe trip. Remember, if you need anything special, just contact me and I can send it in a diplomatic pouch. You can usually have it overnight. I already sent a "survival kit" to Vienna for you. It left an hour ago," the old man said as he closed the door.

Yes, Johnny knew exactly what he meant. The usual necessities for surveillance such as: code books, inks, cameras, tear gas, bugging devices, laser communication receivers, night vision equipment, laser microphones and the inevitable heart attack capsules. He would see if any other special equipment was in the pouch when he arrived in Vienna.

Sue, the Director's secretary, was running down the hall as Johnny stepped out into the main hallway. Johnny stopped and waited as she rushed toward him. Her blonde hair swayed back and forth with her movement.

Sue had only worked in the CIA Headquarters for a couple years. Rumors circulated that she had been married to a field troubleshooter who had been killed in the line of duty. To help the CIA cover the scandal of an assignment gone bad, the Director had personally offered her a job.

Breathless, Sue spoke as she neared Johnny. "The boss wants you to take these on the plane with you. We've declassified them but don't let them out of your sight, even if you go to the bathroom on the plane. Read them and shred them when you're finished. He wants you to know whom you'll be working with and against. Are you about ready? The plane leaves in a couple hours." She handed Johnny another manila envelope, fatter than the one she had given him earlier.

"Thanks. I'm going to put these things in my briefcase, stop at the cashier and then I'll go right to the airport. I'll let you know when I arrive in Vienna and I won't forget the Torte. See you when I get back. I'll be in touch." He turned and walked down the hallway without looking back.

CHAPTER SEVEN

After returning from the warehouse, neither Johnny Collins nor Jim Swartz spoke a word until they were safely within the walls of the Embassy and back in Swartz's office. Both men were having their own problems coping with what they had seen in the warehouse.

"Bob Blinksdale should be here soon," Swartz stated, sitting in his big chair behind his desk. "It's been over thirty minutes since he received my call. Dr. Clark should be arriving any minute, too. Wonder what Blinksdale told Ambassador Latham? He's probably climbing the walls. He doesn't like anyone or anything that makes waves. This sure as hell is going to make big ones. Maybe even cause a flood."

Swartz sounded upset. His voice quivered when he spoke.

Johnny walked back and forth in front of Swartz's desk. He said, "Well, he has to take some of the blame. If he had called us right away, we could have had a couple days head start. These political appointee Ambassadors are so unrealistic. Although, I don't know him, he appears to be one of those Ambassadors that honestly believes the cold war is over. In his thinking, it would be unrealistic to think that anyone would ever want to recruit one of our people to spy against us."

"He's a pretty good man, just a bit unsure when it comes to embassy rules and regulations. He was a college professor and all of this is a bit overwhelming for him at times," Swartz stated simply.

"Hell, every nation in the world is trying their best to recruit our people," Johnny said, obviously upset. He went back and sat at the chair he used earlier in the evening, and slipped off his shoes. "They always have and always will. France, England and Israel have openly admitted trying to recruit our people. Look at all the South American countries, especially Columbia. It's spy heaven down there. Services are sold to the highest bidder."

"Here comes Blinksdale now. That's the doctor with him," Swartz interrupted, looking down the hallway.

"Wait!" Collins called, putting his shoes on and stretching his long legs out in front of him. "First let's call Greenly. After all, Barr is or was a CIA employee. Greenly should take control of the situation now. Hand me the telephone and his number."

Swartz nodded his head and handed Collins the cordless phone. He pointed to the paper that contained all the Embassy employees' home phone numbers. While Collins dialed, Swartz walked out the door and hurried toward the two men who were rushing down the hallway.

After completing his call, Collins waved at the three men to join him in Swartz's office. Swartz walked back to his desk chair.

"Johnny, this is Bob Blinksdale and Dr. Gene Clark," Swartz said, pointing to each man as he said their names.

Neither men had taken the time to shower nor shave, and looked as though they still had their pajamas on under their clothes. Both seemed to be fairly alert, in spite of their rumpled appearance.

Bob Blinksdale, pulled a chair from the corner and sat down. He pulled his long legs back and hooked each foot behind a chair leg.

He was a tall, extra large muscular looking man. He wore a navy blue two piece jogging suit, and a dark blue windbreaker. With the jacket zipper partially down, a gun holster could be seen under his left arm. His short brown military style haircut looked fresh, but there was a days' growth of heavy beard on his face. His features were sharp. He reminded Johnny of a life size G.I. Joe.

Johnny glanced for a moment at the doctor. Doctor Gene Clark, was dressed in a faded red Yale long sleeve sweatshirt and loose fitting blue jeans. He was without a doubt the oldest man in the room. His hair was snowy white and his face was heavily wrinkled. But, his bright blue eyes looked alert and ready for action. Around his waist, he wore a black fanny pack. A piece of gauze was sticking out through the zipper.

Collins began the briefing. After hearing the details of how Collins and Swartz had found Barr's body, the four men discussed what would be needed to get the body down from the rafters.

Checking their watches, the men knew the sooner they retrieved the body, the better. Blinksdale ran to the back parking lot to get an Embassy station wagon. As he rushed past the Marine at Post One, he asked for a sharp knife and a blanket.

The doctor went to his office to collect several containers so he could take samples of the death scene. Never having done anything similar, he didn't know what might be needed, but wanted to be prepared.

Once the car was parked in front of the Embassy, the men loaded a metal six-foot step ladder on the roof and rope and other supplies into the back of the wagon. Finally, loaded and ready to leave, Swartz ran back into the Embassy to borrow another flashlight from the Post One Marine guard. Although it seemed to have taken hours for the men to get ready to leave, in reality it was less than an hour.

The men were getting into the wagon, when Chief-of-Station Roy Greenly parked. They turned and watched Greenly as he stepped out of his car.

After being called, Roy Greenly had taken time to shower and shave. Every piece of his hair was perfectly groomed. It was almost six in the morning and he was ready for the day. Greenly looked as if he had just stepped out of a man's fashion store compared to Blinksdale and the doctor.

Greenly, a short man, in his mid to late forties was slender, with blond hair and light features. Johnny thought he couldn't have weighed one hundred and sixty pounds soaking wet.

Collins scrutinized Greenly's clothes, noticing how they fit. His gray suit was perfectly tailored and his shirt and tie were coordinated.

As Greenly moved closer, Johnny shuddered. Greenly was too polished, too poised and too perfect. Something about him didn't fit. Greenly stood facing Johnny and Johnny recognized something in Greenly's eyes that alarmed him.

It was the look of burning zeal, the strange overwhelming need to "get-ahead." The same look Collins had seen so often in the eyes of the modern day Station-Chiefs. The look of ambition, the uncontrollable desire to succeed, no matter what the cost or who had to be stepped on while climbing to the top.

Collins thought Greenly looked more like a young doctor or lawyer than a CIA Chief-of-Station. Greenly was an outstanding example of the textbook version of a true "yuppie." He was a member of the new breed of government agents, properly educated, polished, and conditioned.

Johnny smiled and was thankful that he didn't have to work for him. He knew that since the early 90's, it had become a requirement for all Embassies to publicly declare their assigned CIA Station Chief. In Austria, Greenly was listed on all official records as being with the CIA. His official Embassy title was as a special political advisor to the Ambassador. He operated in the open.

His name, title, position, and address were public knowledge within the entire Diplomatic community. He was listed in the Diplomatic Register, an official handbook, available to anyone who requested it and had the money to purchase a copy. Some things changed, but as things changed, things remained the same.

Johnny remembered meeting Greenly during a session at the CIA Farm at Camp Peary, near Williamsburg, Virginia. Johnny didn't particularly like him then, now he remembered why.

Quickly, Blinksdale introduced Collins and Greenly as a point of formality, and Swartz brought Greenly up to date on the details of the body. Greenly listened and nodded when appropriate.

"Blinksdale, why don't you, Swartz, and the doctor retrieve the body as you planned. We'll be here waiting for you,"

Greenly directed, giving orders as if it were the most normal thing in the world for him to do.

Collins wished the men good luck and asked, "What has happened to Barr's car? Does anyone know where it is?"

The men all looked from one to the other shaking their heads "no". Blinksdale finally answered, "I don't think any of us know anything about it. We did ask the Austrian police to watch for it but I've not heard that they've found it. When I get back to the Embassy later this morning, I'll look into it."

Johnny frowned, "That would be great. It might have something to tell us. We need to find it as soon as possible and have it checked over. Do we have any Sea-Bees assigned to the Embassy?"

"Yea, we have one, but he's in Budapest until next week. What is it you want?" Greenly questioned, tilting his head slightly to get a better look at Collins.

"Well, I just thought that he could look over the car. Most of those guys know a bit about everything. Do you know how to check a car for fingerprints and evidence?" Collins snapped back rather sarcastically.

"No, I don't but I am sure that I can get someone down from Frankfurt that could, if we needed to." Greenly snapped back.

Johnny was upset with Greenly's attitude and spoke softly in reply. "Well, as I asked earlier, if we had a Sea-Bee here, we wouldn't have to get one of our people down from Frankfurt."

The three men waiting in the car looked at each other. Finally, the car started and they drove away from the Embassy.

A chill ran through Johnny's body. He knew this was only the beginning and asked himself, "What else am I going to discover? Was Barr a double agent? If so, are there any more? Are the Russians behind this? Or, is it another one of those Middle-Eastern groups out to make a name for themselves?"

CHAPTER EIGHT

Once the three men had left to retrieve the body, Collins followed Greenly back to Swartz's office. Not wanting to cause any further bad relations with Greenly, Collins headed for the comfortable chair arrangement he had created earlier in the evening. He took off his jacket and rolled it into a ball. Remaining silent, he spent a couple minutes molding his exhausted body into a restful position with his jacket as a pillow.

Greenly walked around the room muttering to himself, adjusting his coat and tie as he moved. Finally, Greenly broke the silence. "Good to see you again, Collins. Sorry you had to be the one chosen for this job. When I talked to the home office they thought it best to bring in someone, instead of using one of my people here."

Collins glanced up, stretched his shoulders and grunted.

Greenly continued. "I'm inclined to agree with them, it would have blown what little cover we have here. I think the other countries know all about us, no matter how hard and cleverly we try to hide. How's the coffee?"

Greenly walked to the coffee pot, looked at it, shook his head and looked back at Johnny.

Collins muttered, "It's probably pretty strong by now." He turned his head sideways and closed his eyes.

Greenly replied in a low tone, "Huh, it smells bad." He flipped off the switch and closed the office door.

Collins knew he wasn't going to get any sleep and uncoiled from what little comfort he had found. He was feeling irritable, and didn't feel like humoring anyone, especially the Station Chief. Putting his feet on the floor and trying to stand up, took all the concentration he could muster.

"Tired, old boy?" Greenly muttered as he moved to Swartz's big desk chair. He pushed most of Swartz's paper work into a pile, making a big production out of his movements. Having made a clean space on the desk in front of him, Greenly took out a pen from inside his suit jacket, tapped it several times on the desk top, and asked louder than necessary with a puzzled expression on his face. "Well?"

Collins adjusted his dark top and slacks as he walked over to the coffee pot. It was obvious that Greenly wasn't going to make a fresh pot, so Collins picked up the pot and walked toward the door. Looking back over his shoulder, he answered in response to Greenly's question. "I can't do anything without a good cup of coffee. Just a minute while I get some cold water and have a few seconds to collect my thoughts. It's been a long twenty some hours."

Johnny took the time away from Greenly to splash his face with cold water and comb his hair. He felt better when he walked back into the room. Glancing toward the desk, he walked over to the coffee pot and switched it on, but didn't say a word. He spent a few minutes inserting a clean filter and adding fresh coffee grounds. He could feel Greenly's eyes watching him.

Once Johnny had turned back toward his chair, Greenly said, "Johnny, I've just been thinking. With the doctor, Blinksdale and Swartz retrieving the body, we can't do anything but wait. I think we should have a game plan. The Ambassador has a breakfast with the Russians this morning, so we'll talk to him when he gets back. When the body arrives, the doctor is going to check it, then we'll have to arrange to send it back to Washington. Don't you agree?"

Johnny didn't feel like patronizing Greenly, so spoke very matter-of-fact, completely ignoring his question. "We couldn't reach Barr's wife earlier this morning. Swartz tells me he sent a guy to wait at their apartment for her to show up. No one is even sure where she is. All I've been able to learn is that they both came back from their vacation on Friday. Mrs. Barr then went to visit her sister in Frankfurt, and according to her sister was supposed to have been back in Vienna by now. Do you have anything else?"

Johnny glanced at his notebook where he had made notes earlier in the evening before finding Barr's body. He glanced at Greenly and waited for some type of answer.

"I don't know anything different," Greenly answered. He looked down at the clean space in front of him and continued, "I think the message to the home office should request any background information on similar murders on file. Especially those with the same torture M O. Did you hear anything back at headquarters?" He took a piece of clean paper out of the computer tray and began drafting a cable to Virginia.

"How long did you suspect Barr was the one leaking classified information?" Johnny asked, while he stirred some sugar and powdered cream into the cup, he watched Greenly out of the corner of his eye.

"I didn't suspect anything, nor did we hear anything down the pipeline directly linked to Barr," Greenly answered, still writing on his paper. "Barr transferred in this past summer from Moscow. He was scheduled for annual leave. His leave request was routine." He stopped talking and looked directly at Collins.

"Hubert told me before I left the home office that you suspected Barr," Collins said after pouring the coffee into the cup, he turned and walked back to his chair.

"Hell, we suspected everyone," Greenly sighed. "We knew someone was leaking information, but we had no real proof against Barr. For months, Barr and his wife had planned to tour Italy and Switzerland. Both liked to hike and were learning mountain climbing. It doesn't seem logical, if Barr were the double agent, whoever he was working for would kill him. It would be like killing the goose that laid the golden egg."

Johnny was tired and didn't feel like tiptoeing around the real problem. He knew Greenly should have known if Barr was in trouble. As the boss, it was his job.

"Alan and his wife left for vacation a week ago. Alan was scheduled for work this past Monday," Greenly said. "When Monday came and went and Barr never reported for work, I talked to the Ambassador about him being late. I thought Barr might have had an accident or had trouble crossing the borders. The Ambassador was the one who suggested we wait before notifying Washington. I had someone call Barr's house, but no answer. Late Monday afternoon we sent someone out to check with the neighbors. They were all as surprised as we were that the Barrs hadn't returned as scheduled. One neighbor was watching their cat. They told us the Barrs were scheduled to be back Saturday, because Alan liked to have a day to rest before he went back to work."

"Did they have a history of returning late?" Collins asked.

"No, I don't think so," Greenly answered. "I have never heard anything about them being unreliable. Monday, we also checked with border officials and found Barr and his wife crossed the border from Italy into Austria last Friday by car. Finally, after talking to the Ambassador again, we reported to Washington that Barr was missing. I guess it was then, everything hit the fan in DC and Virginia, and you were contacted."

"That's about right," Collins said. "I saw in Barr's bio that they didn't have any children. Was there anyone special that Barr was close to at work?"

"No one special. He was rather a loner. That's very normal after a reassignment. I think they got along with their neighbors alright," Greenly answered. He took a small notebook out of his suit pocket and flipped through several pages. "From my notes I see that the airline records show that Mrs. Barr took a late flight to Frankfurt by herself Friday afternoon. Tuesday, we found out from the neighbors that Mrs. Barr has a sister living in Frankfurt. So we called her. The sister, a Mrs. Eva Metcalf, confirmed Mrs. Barr had been in Frankfurt, but was already on her way back to Vienna. Mrs. Metcalf didn't seem to think her sister's visit was unusual."

Johnny frowned and replayed what Greenly had just said, "What makes you suspect Barr now?"

"Just a hunch, now that he's dead. We had no proof that Barr was the one behind the leaked information. The only thing we know for sure was that Barr was on duty when some of the information arrived and he had access to it. We have no substantial proof pointing only to Barr. There were other communicators that also had access to the released information."

Johnny emptied his cup and got up and poured himself another one. For only a brief second, he thought of offering Greenly a cup, but fixed his own and went back to his chair.

Greenly pushed the cable he had written across the desk toward Johnny. "I've started a cable to Washington. Do you want to read it? Once, it's ready, I think you should go check in at the Hilton. You might want to shower and get something to eat."

For the next several minutes, they discussed what to say in the message, taking special care with the wording. They decided to go ahead and send the message now that Barr's body had been found, but agreed to follow up with more information as the day progressed. Checking their watches, they realized the six hour time difference would make it still the middle of the night in the states. They were sure the message would get sent right away, even with the time difference.

When Greenly left to send the message, Johnny sat reviewing the events of the day. Years of CIA agent experience had taught him to look outside of the immediate circle for the answer to pressing problems. However, this time, he had an uncanny feeling the problem was within the agency, and that one, if not more, CIA employees were operating as double agents. Barr had been one of them, otherwise, why would he have been killed so brutally? Whenever a double agent problem was suspected, it almost always took the Agency years to catch the renegade agent in the act. Johnny vividly recalled the Adams affair.

CHAPTER NINE

After gathering his bags from behind the front desk, manned by the Marines, Johnny Collins waited for a taxi by the heavy metal doors inside the Embassy's main entrance. His mind was reviewing what he had learned since arriving in Vienna. It totaled a big fat zero. He was no closer to knowing what happened to Barr than before he left Langley. The only thing he'd been successful in doing was finding Barr's body.

However, he knew he had nothing to do with its discovery. The body would have been found if he were in Vienna or not. Now, he had to find out why Barr was killed, and if he were a double agent, and if there were other double agents within the Embassy?

Looking out toward the street, Collins watched as a late model blue Volkswagen car drove pass the Embassy entrance. An Austrian police officer, standing guard by the small guard shack, also glanced up at the passing car.

The car was moving very slowly. The light from the street, mixed with the early rays of sunlight, landed directly on the face of the man sitting in the passenger seat.

Johnny opened the Embassy door and quickly stepped out into the brisk air to get a closer look. Looking through the car window glass, the man's piercing eyes stared directly at Johnny.

With a glance, Johnny felt a cold chill as if he were having sudden recognition. The man's head was bald, and he had a large gray mustache.

Although, Johnny was unable to see the driver, he had the distinct impression it was a woman. Suddenly, the car accelerated and roared down the hill on Boltzmanngasse. The sound of screeching tires echoed through the early morning hours.

The police officer ran to the street as if trying to read the license plate number, but the car was out of sight. He shook his head.

"I didn't get the number. I thought it was just a tourist going by. We have casual lookers all the time," the police officer apologized in perfect English, as Johnny ran toward him.

"It probably wasn't anything important. Don't worry!" Johnny answered as his taxi arrived. "But, if that car happens to come by again, see if you can get a license number. It might be a good idea if you also ask your replacements to watch for the car. I think it was a dark blue color, but those VW models all look about the same. Could you tell if a woman was driving?"

"Yes, it definitely was a woman driving, and a bald headed man on the passenger side. Did you know them?"

"No, but they might have known me. Thanks for your help," Johnny answered, picking up his suitcase and holding his briefcase close to his body.

"I'll pass on the information to my superiors. We'll keep close watch if the same car should go by again. Good morning to you, sir."

Johnny nodded and walked to the taxi that was just parking in the restricted parking zone.

"Take me to the Hilton Hotel, please," he asked, when the driver got out and placed his suitcase in the trunk.

Johnny's eyes scanned the scene, reacting naturally, trying to spot anything out of place. Convinced all was in order, he opened the taxi door and got in for the trip downtown.

CHAPTER TEN

As the driver moved in and out of the early morning traffic, Johnny looked out the taxi window, noting the growth of the city. It had been five years since his last trip to Vienna. Ring Street looked the same.

The main change, he saw instantly, was that some of the majestic government buildings had been sandblasted and were considerably cleaner. Although the smell of heavy traffic was noticeable, the morning air seemed to have a crisp freshness to it.

The lobby of the Hilton Hotel was almost bursting at the seams with Japanese tourists. Four empty busses were parked in front of the hotel. The passengers were waiting among a muddle of confusion, noise and suitcases. Excited voices drowned out the words being spoken by overwhelmed clerks behind the security of the reservation desk.

Johnny Collins, well over six feet tall, felt totally out of place among the group. His eyes overlooked the many baseball caps, suitcases, and cameras, which were blocking his path. As he moved back and forth among the crowd, he kept getting in the midst of yet another picture taking session.

Finally, with his suitcase placed firmly between his two legs, and his brief case on the counter under his arm, he leaned over the reception counter toward a frazzled receptionist. After three unsuccessful attempts at trying to give his name, he extended his long arm over the counter and found a pad of paper. Slowly, he printed his name in big bold letters.

The receptionist simply shook her head, took the paper and quickly exited the area through a door on the left of the reception area. Within seconds, she returned with a card in her hand.

Moving to the computer terminal on the counter, she expertly punched keys and a paper spurted forth. Handing the paper to Collins, the receptionist seemed to have gained her composure. With a smile, she asked Johnny for his passport while signaling with her hand for him to sign and initial the paper on the lines near her finger.

Smiling back, Johnny signed the paper. He took the black diplomatic passport back and the small folder, which contained his room card from the top of the reservation counter. Almost immediately, another group of twenty or more Japanese tourists ascended on the reception area.

Immediately, a bellboy, dressed in a red suit, ran to Johnny and reached for his bag. Johnny motioned him away and said, "I can handle them both."

The boy shook his head, extended his hand for the suitcase and room key. He replied in excellent English, "Mr. Collins, I can carry your larger bag for you. I believe you have messages waiting for you. All our rooms are equipped with the latest state-of-the-art communications. You can retrieve your messages from the television monitor, which also acts as your computer screen. I'll show you how to operate it. Your room number is 420. Please follow me."

Without another thought, Johnny followed the bellhop as he expertly maneuvered his way through the crowd toward the elevators. Within seconds, the elevator whisked the couple to the fourth floor. The attendant opened the door, entered the room and opened the curtains. The bellboy had the suitcase on a stand and the television turned on as Johnny walked through the door.

With the same efficiency, the attendant showed Johnny how to use the television remote to retrieve his messages. After continuing to check the room and the bathroom to make sure all was in order, the bellboy walked toward the door.

"Just dial seven for room service. There's a list of services and their phone numbers on the telephone. Call the receptionist if you have any questions. Will there be anything else?" the bell boy asked, with an outstretched hand.

"No. That's fine. Thank you." Johnny smiled, grateful for the efficiency and offered an American five-dollar tip. He remembered he'd have to change some of his American money for Austrian Shillings later. When he had paid the taxi cab driver, he had used his last ten dollar bill. However, neither the cab driver nor the attendant complained at being tipped with American dollars.

Locking the door after the boy left, Johnny laid the room key card in plain sight on the television. Since the hotels and motels had modernized and converted to using key cards, Johnny was always having trouble remembering where he placed the small thin plastic card.

Taking a moment, he read the messages on the television monitor. One was from the Embassy saying he was going to be late arriving. Another was from his wife. She said she was just calling to make sure he had arrived safely. Another was from the hotel inviting him to a cocktail party. Johnny looked at the date and realized it was for last night. He had already missed his free drink.

Next, he went to his suitcase and began unpacking. He hung his suits and slacks in the closet and put the rest of his things in a drawer. Listening to his stomach growl, he dialed "7" for room service and ordered an American style breakfast.

Following procedure, he took a small black Sony cassette recorder out of his bag along with his shaving items and set everything on the desk. Before he did anything else, he turned on the small cassette player, checking first if it was operating properly. Then he held it securely in his right hand, about a foot straight out from his shoulder in a position easy for his eyes to see the revolving of the tape inside the recorder.

Holding it steady, he began walking slowly around the room. He knew it was the only way he had to personally check for illegal listening devices. Later, if it was necessary, he could always ask someone from the Embassy to sweep the room.

Attentively listening for squealing sounds, he walked carefully around the room, holding the player closer to obvious hiding places for "bugs." Moving from one area to another, he covered: the lights, telephone, pictures, electric outlets, grates, drawers, window sills, and bed. As he neared a small potted plant on the desk, the recorder gave off the tattle tale warning signal. Looking into the plant, he probed with his free hand and uncovered a very small microphone hooked to a stick supporting the plant. Smiling, he carefully put the microphone back, placed the plant on the window sill and pulled the curtain around it.

He knew a good agent always planted listening devices in pairs, so he continued his search. Without a great deal of effort he found a second microphone. It was in the entrance hall, fastened to the leg of the small table on which he had placed his briefcase.

It was all very clever, he thought. The listeners would get first comments and reactions of anyone who walked into the room.

He didn't take time to examine the devices to see if he could learn who owned them. If it proved to be necessary, he would have the Embassy check the room later and take pictures of the microphones. However, he knew with the way sophisticated electronics were selling in today's market, it would be hard to tell who was buying what from whom.

Pleased he had found both transmitters, but being cautious, he finished checking the bathroom and closet. Finding nothing else, he smiled and prepared for a leisurely shower. Glad at last to get out of his black attire.

Stepping back into the room with a towel wrapped around his waist, the door buzzer rang. Barefooted, he walked to the door and looked through the peephole. Opening the door, he smiled and stepped aside. A boy pushing a meal cart entered. Relaxed, Johnny picked up the New York Herald Tribune and settled down with an animalistic attack on his breakfast.

After finishing the toast and bacon, Johnny wheeled the cart into the hallway. He moved the coffee pot and cup to the nightstand.

Still wrapped in a towel, he laid on the bed, poured a cup of coffee and reached for the paper. Settled comfortably, he drank more of the coffee. As his eyes closed, the paper slid through his fingers and fell silently to the floor. The coffee cup dropped to the floor with a thud, spilling what coffee remained but not breaking the cup.

CHAPTER ELEVEN

Within seconds, the door to room 420 opened, and a tall, bald man dressed in a European cut light gray suit walked into Johnny's room. He held a room card in his hand and a small magnetic tool, which he had just used to lift the door lock.

He walked with certainty and authority. A passerby would have thought he belonged in the room. The door closed without a sound.

Glancing around the room, the man walked to where Johnny was sleeping on the bed. Johnny's towel remained wrapped around his waist. The intruder picked up the coffee cup and carafe and went to the bathroom and rinsed them out.

After replacing the dishes exactly where he found them, the man stepped back and smiled. loosening the towel carefully, the man exposed Johnny's body. He reached into a small black bag that he had set on the floor and pulled out a purple silk ladies flimsy nightgown. He placed it carefully by Johnny's side. Then, he reached into his pocket and took out a small camera and took several pictures of the sleeping man. Carefully, he retied the towel, put the nightgown back into his bag and placed the newspaper back over the sleeping body. He took care to position it as if it had just been left there.

Without a sound, the intruder searched the room with an expertise that would have impressed the CIA Director himself. Checking the plant in the window, he left it sitting on the window sill. The intruder looked around the room with a smile on his face, but the smile instantly was replaced with cold professional determination.

He walked to the entrance hall table. He took a sharp knife, and with a flick of the wrist he meticulously cut a small incision in the binding of Collins's briefcase. After placing a very small transmitter into the cut, the intruder took a tube of super glue from his pocket.

Expertly, he ran the tube over the incision, blew on it, and waited a few seconds for the glue to dry. Rubbing his finger over the leather, he was unable to detect the cut. A look of satisfaction and accomplishment filled his face.

Before replacing the briefcase exactly as he found it, the bald man opened it, inspected the contents and carefully took pictures of each piece of paper. Glancing toward the bed, he closed the briefcase without the least interruption of movement.

Softly as a cat he walked toward the door, touching the furniture with the surgical gloves he was wearing. Out of habit, he ran his hands over his bald head, as if he were straightening his hair. Glancing back at the body on the bed, he smiled, picked up his bag and let himself out of the room, taking care to click the lock of the door behind him.

Once the door was closed, he reached into his right suit pocket and took out a small white folded calling card. He had already written on the card. Taking off his right plastic glove, he purposely took the card and held it with his middle finger and thumb of his right hand. He pressed the card hard. Still holding the card with the two fingers, he bent down as if he were picking up something he had dropped. Carefully, he slid the white folded card underneath the door to room 420.

Standing upright, he smiled. Removing his other surgical glove, he placed it in his coat pocket. Humming to himself, he strolled away from the room and down the hallway toward the elevators. He was sure no one had seen him go into or leave the room.

CHAPTER TWELVE

The Hilton Hotel lobby was almost deserted. There was no indication that it had been a mad house just a couple hours earlier. The coffee shop was open and several customers were sitting around the glass topped tables drinking the strong Viennese morning coffee and eating pastries.

One of the customers was holding the latest edition of the *KURIER* and appeared to be completely engrossed in the printed pages. However, he glanced up occasionally when someone got off the elevator just to the right of him.

When Johnny Collins stepped from the elevator and crossed the lobby to go to the taxi stand, the man dressed in a stylish European gray suit called for his check and put his paper down on the table. He quickly paid his bill and headed for the door, seconds behind Collins.

As he turned to leave the restaurant, the waitresses commented to one another that he had drunk a lot of coffee that morning. They also joked he could well afford it because he never had to spend money on haircuts. Laughing at their own jokes, they turned and went about their business. They had completely forgotten all about the man as the day progressed.

CHAPTER THIRTEEN

The ride to the Embassy gave Johnny time to think. His head hurt and he still felt tired. He had slept longer than he had planned and wondered if he might not be coming down with a cold.

Finally, he admitted to himself, that being overtired, combined with the hot shower and the heavy breakfast could have been contributing factors to his extra hours sleep. Lastly, he attributed his pounding headache to jet lag and hoped someone would give him an aspirin when he arrived at the Embassy.

The street in front of the Embassy was jammed with Embassy staff and personal cars. The number of the Austrian police officers had also increased. He wondered if that was usual for a normal working day, or if something had been leaked about Barr's death.

Entering the Embassy, he discovered that a different Marine was on duty. He had to go through the usual procedure of showing his State Department Identification and diplomatic black passport. After checking the records, the Post One Marine Guard handed Collins a Visitor ID card, which allowed him unrestricted access throughout the building.

Heading toward Swartz's office, Collins saw Greenly standing in the hallway. Greenly didn't say a word but motioned for Collins to follow him.

Once inside Swartz's empty office, Johnny, irritated at Greenly's attitude, turned to Greenly and spoke sharply. "I don't know what the hell your problem is. I'll only be here long enough to help clear up this mess, and then I'll be out of your hair. Until then get used to me, because I'm here and there's nothing you can do about it."

Unable to hide his resentment over the whole situation, Greenly barked back. "I just don't know what to make of this whole deal. Seems everyone wants to find out from you what's going on. And, of course, you were no where to be found. You were off sleeping."

"You knew I was going to the Hilton and check in. I didn't get a chance to do it earlier and I had to pay for last night, even though I didn't use the bed," Johnny snapped back.

Greenly adjusted his suit jacket, turned his head sideways and glared at Collins. He said, "I resent them asking for you personally, and not going through me. I'm the ranking person here. Swartz didn't want to say anything until you got back. He went home and showered and changed and got in a few minutes ago. Doc Clark has finished checking the body and wants us together before he leaves. He has to go to Moscow."

"What's going on in Moscow?" Johnny asked, trying to ignore Greenly's comments. He could only picture another dead agent.

Greenly shook his head and waved his arm and answered, "He didn't say, only that there's some problem there. Then, too, the Ambassador has been asking for you. His office has called three times already this morning. I didn't know what else to tell them other than you went back to the Hilton to shower and change."

"Well, it was the truth," Collins said, looking at the coffee pot, which was still turned on and the coffee in it looked like thick mud.

Greenly took a deep breath. He said, "Man, you could have at least called if you were going to be this long. Well, now that you're here, is it okay with you if I call everyone for a meeting?"

"Sure, that's fine. But first I need to talk to you." Johnny decided to just ignore Greenly's attitude as much as he could. He reached into his pocket and carefully extracted the white folded note card he found on the floor in his room. "I found this after I woke from my nap. I want to know if you have any way of checking it for fingerprints."

"Yes, we've just received a can of that presto print that's supposed to be so wonderful. You just spray it on whatever you want to check and if there is a print it will pull it up. It's supposed to be a thousand times better than the old powder. I'll have one of my people run the paper through one of our new black light scanners. The scanner will take the print from the paper and put it into the computer. We can send the print back via e-mail to Virginia. We should have a report back on whose print it is within minutes or hours. Depending on whose working in Langley and their backlog. Do you have any idea who left it?" Greenly asked, his voice still sharp.

"No, but the words printed inside say, WELCOME TO VIENNA. HOPE WE HAVE A CHANCE TO MEET FACE TO FACE. ADVANCE TO GO. It could be from almost anyone," Johnny answered shrugging his shoulders.

"Did you touch the paper?" Greenly asked as if he were talking to a new recruit.

"Very, very carefully. I put it in one of these plastic bags I carry in my briefcase. My prints are on file, so they should be able to disregard them," Johnny answered.

"I'll drop it off in my office before I get in touch with everyone regarding the meeting. I'll tell them we'll meet here in Swartz's office in ten minutes." Greenly started to walk away.

"Roy, I also want you to put out feelers to your contacts," Johnny said. "See what they know. My guess is that one of them knows something about Barr's death. I'll authorize payments if you need a small cash incentive. I'll go now and personally contact the Ambassador. I'll tell him we're meeting in a few minutes and ask if he wants to attend, or if he'd like a report."

"Great! Then I can begin arranging for the body. I don't like it being here in the Embassy," Greenly said. He turned and hurried from the room.

After talking to the Ambassador, Johnny went back to Swartz's office and sat and thought of what the Ambassador had just said. The Ambassador explained he was going to a luncheon, and would like an updated report when he returned. He had nothing new to relate from his early morning breakfast with the Russian Ambassador. The Ambassadors hadn't discussed anything other than the usual topics. Such as the reduction of arms throughout Europe, Russia's right to protect her borders, the Serb's right to protect their borders, and the existing restrictions being enforced against certain Arab countries. Same old problems both nations had been battling over for the past several years.

While the office was empty, Johnny made a new pot of coffee and borrowed some chairs from an empty office. He arranged the chairs in a semi circle around the desk. He wanted to watch everyone's face when he talked.

Within minutes, Swartz entered his office to find Johnny deep in thought sitting in his desk chair. Johnny glanced up and nodded.

Swartz was now stylishly dressed in a three-piece gray suit, and his hair and face looked as if they had been freshly washed and polished. He wore glasses with a slight tint that hid the color of his eyes and made him look younger than his thirty six years.

Swartz poured himself a cup of coffee, and said, "Good morning, I feel better since I cleaned up a bit. Do you?" He pulled a chair around to the side of the desk and sat down.

Johnny smiled and answered, "Almost human."

Within seconds, Blinksdale and the doctor arrived together. Both still looked as if they had just gotten out of bed, neither had changed their clothing. They looked more awake than when Johnny had left them earlier in the morning. They walked toward empty chairs near the coffee table, leaving one chair empty for Greenly, who arrived almost immediately.

All seated, they looked at Johnny waiting for him to begin. Greenly grunted to everyone, sat and made a big production of taking out his pocket watch and checking the time.

Johnny was sure Greenly was making a mental note of the time to use it against him later. *What an ass,* Johnny thought to himself.

"Well, let's begin with the doctor. Then we can go around the circle and get everyone's input since I haven't had a chance to talk to any of you since early this morning," Johnny said.

The doctor sighed, took a deep breath and said, "Well, it was after six by the time we arrived at the warehouse. We ran into very heavy morning traffic, and there was an accident on the Gurtel, which also complicated things. It took all three of us to get Barr down from the rafters. We laid him on the floor on a sheet of plastic that we took with us. We all three checked him over as best we could there in the warehouse. While I examined the wounds and arm punctures, Blinksdale and Swartz went around the building. I'll let them tell you what they found." He looked at both of the men, paused for a moment and then continued.

"The man died from a couple things. The pot's weight on his private parts caused them to rupture. The loss of blood, stress and maybe even whatever was pumped into his system all contributed to the heart failure. I couldn't find any fractures, anything out of place, or anything abnormal except the obvious signs of torture. His fingernails were intact. They weren't broken, nor was anything driven under them. His eyes and ears appeared normal. His lips were slightly cracked and dry, but this could be due to dehydration and the extended period of hanging."

Johnny asked, "Any idea of time of death?"

The doctor shook his head. "I can only estimate the time of death to be early last evening, but its only a guess. It's my belief, Barr had been tied in that position for a few days. Probably Friday evening or early Saturday morning."

"What makes you say that?" Greenly asked in a doubting tone.

"When I checked him in the warehouse, I thought from the way the hands were tied, it looked to be at least three or four days, maybe longer by the stiffness and swelling. Also the amount of blood, shows that he was killed while he was hanging. Otherwise, there wouldn't have been so much blood on the ground below him. However, I could be wrong. An expert will have to be consulted."

"Do you think anyone would be able to get fingerprints from the body?" Collins asked.

"Maybe they can in DC. I bagged his hands, feet and arms the best I could. When we returned I preformed the standard exams and found he hadn't eaten anything, except bread, for the last couple of days. He didn't have anything except a little bread and fluid, probably water, to prevent dehydration. I didn't notice anything strange about the body. He hadn't have any other strange cuts or such. He did have a mole on the underside of his knee, which looked as if it should have been examined, but nothing else. Now, it really doesn't matter if the mole is checked or not."

"What are you going to state in your report?" Greenly asked.

Johnny looked at Greenly and could almost read his mind. He knew Greenly didn't want anything in the report that would look bad regarding him.

The doctor, took a notebook out of his pocket and glanced at it for a couple seconds before he said, "In my opinion, he was captured and taken where we found him. Then, each day, more weight was added to the pot until he eventually died. It was a very painful torture. He suffered a great deal. Although, I believe the pain would have been so intense he would have passed out from time to time. His eyes were closed, but I'd guess someone else closed them. I don't think they were closed when he died." He looked at Johnny and nodded. "I'll make a note that they check to see if they find any fingerprints on them. I saw what I believed were bruise marks high on his cheeks, as if someone applied pressure to them. Could be it took a great deal of effort to close his eyes? But, we all know that a body rarely bruises after death."

"It could be that the bruises were made trying to get him to regain consciousness," Johnny said.

"Could well be," the Doctor answered. "We took scrapings from the floor and from the pole where he was hanging. They're being sent back to the states by courier this morning. I'm having my secretary type up my report. His body is ready to be released and, with that, I need to run home and pack." He glanced at his watch. "I've just enough time to catch my flight to Moscow. Anything else, gentlemen?" the doctor asked politely, and when no one responded, he hurried for the door.

"What do you think, Swartz?" Johnny asked after the men, in unison, wished the doctor a safe flight.

Swartz helped himself to a refill of his coffee. He said, "Blinksdale and I went over the warehouse for anything that might have been there that could help us. We only saw the papers and trash that you and I saw earlier. We have the Embassy checking ownership of the warehouse. The windows in the building were so covered with grease and dirt that light barely came through. I don't think, in that neighborhood anyone would notice if something went on inside the building. I took several pictures. We'll have copies made for all concerned parties."

"That's great," Johnny said. "Did anyone check outside the warehouse?"

Swartz nodded and said, "We walked the grounds outside and didn't find anything out of place. The rope they used was the kind that can be purchased anywhere, and the pot was similar to others from the million homes in the city. The rocks can be picked up anywhere around town. I don't know what else to say. We did bring back the rope and pot and rocks if anyone else would like to take a look. I don't know, but shouldn't we send them back to the states, too?"

"Yes, we should," Johnny said. "Greenly, will you take care of shipping them back? Anything that you want to add, Blinksdale?"

Blinksdale shifted in his chair. "No. It's a lot like Jim just said. It wasn't a very pleasant sight, and I don't think I'm going to sleep easy for a while. I can't believe someone didn't hear him screaming. We know he had the rag in his mouth, but at sometime it must have been out. At least it must have been taken out when he was eating. They wouldn't have drugged him or they wouldn't have killed him in such a painful manner. I'm sure they wanted him to know what was happening. We didn't even find a step ladder. The people who killed him must have carried one back and forth with them."

"I never thought about that, but you are right," Johnny said. "They would have had to drive a car big enough to fit a ladder in it. Were there any tire tracks?"

"Nothing that we could make out," Swartz said. He frowned and continued. "You know something, I remember reading about a killing similar to this. Let me see, I believe it was thought to be an Arab means of disposing of double agents. I'll have to review my files, but I think that's what it meant. You might have your office check that out, Johnny."

Johnny answered, "I already did. I don't think we have an answer yet. I'm sure they'll let us know when they can. So, what the doctor said was that he was captured probably Friday or Saturday, taken to this warehouse and left to die slowly. Today's Thursday, so he died Wednesday night. Probably a few hours before we found him. Maybe that's when they called us. Say, do the Marines tape any of their incoming calls. Would they by chance have a copy of the caller's voice?"

Blinksdale, the Embassy Security Officer, shook his head in disgust. "No, we aren't that modern here. I have asked for such equipment, but with budget cuts we don't even have an answering machine."

Johnny shrugged his shoulders, "Well it was worth a thought. Anyway when we received the call, the caller already knew Barr was dead. They simply wanted Barr's body found, which means they didn't want him any longer. Don't you think that no matter what Barr might have said, the killers would have had to kill him? What could Barr possibly have known that threatened someone?"

Greenly said, "Whatever it was would have had to be major enough for them to go out there daily by car carrying a step ladder."

"Okay, where do we go now?" Johnny asked and looked to Greenly, who was still fiddling with his pocket watch.

Greenly looked up and said, "Well, I'm going to wait for the message from the home office on what to do about the body. Blinksdale, I'll work with you on contacting the Austrian police. They'll pitch a fit that we didn't call them to get the body down."

Blinksdale said, "I know Inspector Kuhner. Maybe we can get him to play along with us. I'll use some of my contacts in the police department to smooth things over. They'll be upset because it was not on Embassy property and it was their jurisdiction."

Greenly smiled for the first time during the meeting. He nodded his head and said, "See what you can do. The home office and the Ambassador will tell us what should be released to the Embassy and the papers, if anything at all. I'll leave you three to begin the questioning of the communicators and other Embassy employees. As for now, all we need to say is that Barr is missing, and we'll wait until we get the go ahead before we say or do anything else. Is that agreeable to all of you?" He put his watch back in his pocket.

After they all nodded to him, Greenly left the room to go and make arrangements for the body, promising to meet with Blinksdale in an hour to decide how to handle the local officials.

"Well, men," Collins said. "I guess we'd better start being detectives and do what has to be done. Jim, could you sit in with me and we'll begin asking some of the employees questions? Bob, will you follow up on whoever owns or is renting the warehouse? Find out what the latest is on Mrs. Barr. See if anything has come back from the check on their bank accounts. Keep us informed of what you find out. Then, Bob, you'll be with Greenly the rest of the day. Jim and I'll probably be here unless we get a chance to go to Barr's residence. We already know some answers but there are still many questions that remain unanswered."

CHAPTER FOURTEEN

After Blinksdale left, Jim Swartz left his office to round up any communicators who were available for questioning, leaving Collins all alone. Collins continued to have a nagging pain in his head just above his right eye. He had forgotten to get something from the doctor, so began to look through Swartz's desk to see if he might find some type of a pain killer.

He searched through drawer after drawer. Finally, after opening the bottom drawer on the left side of the desk, he found a super large bottle of Bayer Aspirin and sighed with relief.

As he took the bottle from the drawer, he noticed a checkbook, which appeared to be hidden underneath the bottle. Thinking it was a strange place to keep a checkbook, rather than on his person, at home or in one of the top drawers, Johnny glanced at it. Moving it slightly with his finger, he saw two recent deposit slips for over ten thousand dollars each. One was made on the first of last month and another on the first of this month.

Quickly he put everything back as it was and made a note of the bank. He would have the home office check Swartz's bank account. It looked suspicious.

After shutting the drawer, Johnny took the aspirin with a drink of coffee. He set the cup down just as Swartz entered the room with one of the communicators.

"Larry Mason, this is Johnny Collins," Swartz said. "He wants to talk to you about the disappearance of Alan Barr. Get a cup of coffee if you'd like, and take a chair. I know I've already asked you a few questions, but maybe if we put our heads together, we can come up with something new. Okay?"

"Nice to meet you, Mr. Collins," Mason said. "Fine. I'll have a cup of coffee. I didn't work yesterday, but have been here since the early hours this morning." "Okay, if I call you Larry?" Johnny asked. He reached for a sheet of paper from the bottom of Swartz's printer tray.

Larry Mason was about six and a half foot tall and pencil thin. He wore dark docker slacks, a plaid cotton long sleeve shirt and a black necktie with a big red Woody Woodpecker on it. His dirty sandy colored hair was long and swept back into a ducktail in back, kept in place with heavy hair spray. He was wearing black highly polished cowboy boots. He wore a gold wedding band on his right hand.

Mason quickly helped himself to a cup of coffee and sat down directly in front of Collins. "Sure," he answered, looking straight at Collins.

"Larry, we're trying to learn everything we can about the last couple weeks or so Barr was at work. That would be the time before he left on vacation. We may even go back as far as when he transferred in from Moscow."

"I worked with him at various times. We work shifts so sometimes he worked different times than me. What kind of things are you looking for?" Mason asked. His eyes went wide and he spoke slowly, with a slight Texas accent.

"Anything you might have thought unusual," Johnny answered. He tapped his pen a couple times on the desk as if he were getting ready to take notes. "Did he have many phone calls? Did he make many phone calls? Was he gone for long unexplained periods of times from the office? Did he seem to have a lot of appointments, which might not have been appointments, such as doctors or dentists? Did his wife call him at work a lot? Did he get any mail that seemed to make him upset?"

"Whoa, take a minute, sir," Mason answered, putting both of his hands up in the air. "You're going a bit fast for me."

"That's all right," Johnny said. "I'm just going to run over the type of questions we are interested in. You don't have to answer each one now."

Mason laughed, "That's better. My mind doesn't work quite that fast."

"Now, did he talk to anyone else at the Embassy in a very friendly way?" Johnny continued. "How did he act when messages of a sensitive nature came into the center? Did he want to handle them all by himself? Did he show everyone the messages? Did he ever take a message without logging it in the book? Did he ever take sensitive material out of the room with him? Did he seem moody at times? Did he seem to keep too much to himself? Did he go out for drinks after work very often? With whom? Did he drink too much? Did he seem to have a lot of money? Had he bought anything recently that seemed to be expensive for his income? Do you have any idea how his marriage was? Did he ever mention if he and his wife were having problems? Do you know if he had a lover?" Johnny rattled off question after question.

"Wow, that's a lot of questions," Mason answered, when Johnny stopped talking. He rubbed his face a couple times and shook his head. "Now, I can't remember the ones from the beginning."

"That's all right," Johnny said. He started over with the questions, taking time to let Mason answer while he made notes.

After almost an hour, Johnny stood and walked to the door. He opened the door and thanked Mason for his help. As he watched Mason walk back to the Communication Center, he saw a woman come out of the Communication Center. He recognized Mrs. Swartz from the photo on her husband's desk.

Turning back to Jim, Johnny asked, "Does your wife work here at the Embassy?"

"Yes, she's a roving secretary and works whenever the Embassy calls. Today, she's working for the front office, helping out the Ambassador and DCM secretaries. Why do you ask?"

"I thought I just saw her come out of the Communication Center?" Johnny answered.

"You may have. She was probably picking up the incoming cables for the front office. She might even have been dropping off some out-going ones. Do you want to talk to her?" Jim asked with concern.

"No, but do all secretaries have such free access to the Communication Center?" Johnny asked.

"Johnny, come on. Everyone that works on these floors of the embassies have Secret or Top Secret clearances. Some of them have higher clearances than I have. And to answer your question, yes, they all have access to the communication center."

"Are they watched or observed while they are picking up traffic?"

"Johnny, there is no way my people can watch everyone coming and going. The Embassy employees go in and pick up the traffic. The combinations are suppose to be kept within their section, but occasionally when someone is sick, one of the secretaries will pick up traffic for another section. Sometimes, they will even ring that small bell and my people will get their messages for them."

"So what your telling me is that anyone that has access to pick up the cables could have given the information to someone outside the Embassy?" Johnny asked wondering if he wasn't chasing smoke.

"Actually, you're right," Swartz answered. "Any cleared American could have. It would be simple. They could have just put the information in their pocket and walked out the door."

"Well, that sure makes our job easier," Johnny replied. He knew there was no way in hell they could ever prove who had leaked the information. He was sure that in order to prove who actually had done it, he would have to catch someone with classified information on his or her person as they left the Embassy.

"Well, that certainly narrows it down," Johnny said. He glanced at the wall clock and after listening to the growling of Swartz's stomach, he suggested they break for lunch.

CHAPTER FIFTEEN

After lunch, Johnny stopped by the Ambassador's office to update him. Ann, the Ambassador's Secretary, told Johnny to have a seat and the Ambassador would be only a moment. Johnny glanced at his watch. Five minutes later, he looked up and saw the Ambassador by the doorway.

"Come in, Collins," Ambassador Charles Latham said.

He motioned for Johnny.

Ambassador Charles Latham was dressed in a three piece dark brown suit, white shirt with French cuffs, gold cufflinks with an initial on them, a brown and gold tie with matching tie clasp. He was in his late sixties, over six foot tall, short gray hair and looked the part of a college professor.

"Thank you for seeing me," Johnny said, sitting down after the Ambassador.

The Ambassador adjusted his gold wire frame glasses, slipped them on and looked at Johnny. He said, "Barr's body will be sent back to Virginia on the Delta flight this evening. The Austrian police agreed that getting the body out of the country as quickly as possible was best."

"That's good," Johnny commented, glancing around the room at all the pictures and awards.

"Unfortunately, the Austrian police have not found any trace of Barr's car."

"That's strange," Johnny said. "Was Alan the last to drive it or was Mrs. Barr?"

"I really don't know. But, what is really strange is a comment made at the late morning meeting that I had this morning. The Russian Economic Officer, Nikolai Golodin, made a statement about vacations that was totally out of context. No one was even talking about vacations when he brought up the subject. Golodin said something to the effect that more diplomats were going to Italy and Switzerland for vacations this year. He added that he had heard rock climbing was quite a popular sport but could prove to be very dangerous. I thought I detected sarcasm in his words. It was as if he were hinting something."

"Did anyone say anything about Italy or Switzerland? Did anyone else at the meeting think his remark was odd?" Johnny asked.

"No one seemed to," the Ambassador answered. "I don't trust Golodin. Greenly tells me Golodin is the GRU representative in Vienna. I don't doubt it. I notice every time Golodin enters a room, even the Russian Ambassador gets tongue tied."

Johnny smiled and tucked that bit of information about Golodin into his mental file. He would make a point of doing some checking with Langley.

When Johnny stood to leave, the Ambassador motioned for him to remain seated. "I forgot to tell you that Mrs. Barr arrived back in Vienna. Roy Greenly is with her at this very minute."

"When did she get back?" Johnny asked. He wondered why he hadn't been told.

"Just now. I got a call just as you arrived. I have given permission for her to go back to Virginia as soon as possible to make arrangements for her husband's burial."

"What?" Johnny asked, completely surprised. "Has or is anyone going to question her? She might know something about her husband's death."

"Greenly assures me that she doesn't," Ambassador Latham answered. "I have to allow her time to make funeral arrangements. It's the decent thing to do."

Johnny stood and walked to the doorway. He looked back at the Ambassador and said, "I will put in my report that I am against her leaving before I have had a chance to talk to her."

The Ambassador stood and walked toward Collins. With a stern look, he said, "You can report what ever you wish, but she is going." He turned to walk back to his desk but stopped. "There will be a short press release issued in the Vienna newspapers simply stating Barr has died, including a statement that a memorial service was held here at the Embassy."

Johnny opened his mouth and then closed it. He thought for a couple seconds and then asked, "When was the service decided upon? And, what do you mean "was held?"

"It came from the State Department in Washington," Ambassador Latham said. He walked back to his chair. "The press release would be through routine Embassy channels from the United States Information Service with no mention of Barr's Embassy position. It's the desire of the Embassy to keep the service small and quiet. It would be best if reporters and other curiosity seekers could be kept from the service if at all possible. We want as little publicity as possible. I have asked State to state the cause of death eliminating any need for the Embassy to disclose any facts."

Johnny understood Ambassador Latham's concern regarding any public reaction to Barr's death. He didn't like the way he wasn't included in any of the decisions.

"Collins," Ambassador Latham said. "I will take immediate action if anything else is leaked to the press from the Embassy or the Communication Center. Do you understand me?"

"Yes, I do, sir," Johnny said. "Is everyone in the Embassy aware of your feelings on this matter?"

"They damn well better be," Ambassador Latham said. "I do have the authority to ship anyone out that I wish. You do understand that, don't you, Collins?"

Johnny nodded his head in agreement and walked away from the Ambassador's office. He hurried down the hall wanting to get away as fast as he could.

He wondered how much money Latham had contributed to the Republican party in exchange for his appointment. He wished that Latham would have been a career appointment. They knew the workings of the embassies and knew how to work the system from within, not like political appointees who only knew how to assert political pressure.

CHAPTER SIXTEEN

On the way back to the Communication Center, Bob Blinksdale, the Security Officer, stopped Johnny. "I've found something out. Are you on the way back to Swartz's office?"

"Yes, I just left the Ambassador's office," Johnny answered as two secretaries walked past. "Let's don't talk here. Walk with me."

"I can't right now. I'm expecting a call any second from Greenly. He's at Barr's' apartment." Blinksdale whispered as one of the Marines walked pass.

"I'll be here the rest of the afternoon, either in Swartz's office or in the Communication Center. Come see me when you're free," Johnny answered, not breaking his stride.

The young Marine, looking neat and proper in his uniform, approached Collins as Blinksdale walked away. "I didn't want to say anything while you were talking to Mr. Blinksdale, Sir. The Austrian policeman just called from the guard shack outside and asked if you would call him or come out and see him as soon as you could."

"Thanks. I'll go out right now." Johnny turned and opened the gate that divided the Embassy hall from the entrance stairs and rushed toward the outside door.

With only his suit jacket on, Johnny shivered as he stepped outside into the brisk April air. He walked over to the guard shack and met the policeman who had been on duty during the early morning hours.

"Guten Tag, Sir," the policeman said. "I want to tell you the Volkswagen car that went by earlier has gone by two more times since we saw it this morning. Once just a few minutes ago, and about an hour earlier. Both times, a lady was driving. A bald headed man was on the passenger side. We've written down the license number. Our office is trying to trace the owner at this moment. It doesn't have diplomatic tags. It's registered privately. Is there anything else that we can do for you?"

"You've been most helpful. Call me on extension 2311 when you find out who owns it." Johnny shook the policeman's hand and with a shiver rushed back to the warmth of the Embassy.

CHAPTER SEVENTEEN

With the happenings of the day before and the circumstances surrounding the death of Alan Barr, it seemed to Johnny Collins that all the evidence pointed to Barr being a double agent. But, Johnny knew that since Barr wasn't alive to defend himself anyone could have planted that suspicion. Johnny knew that the former KGB, now the infamous SVR the Foreign Intelligence Division, or the Russian GRU, or maybe one of the radical terrorist groups was behind Barr's death. It just looked like their type of work.

Now, with the sudden interest in the American Embassy activities by unknown elements, Johnny couldn't help but think someone within the Embassy knew something regarding Barr's death. He was sure someone was keeping quiet either to protect himself, or Mrs. Barr.

During the walk back to the communication area, Johnny knew someone at Langley had really goofed when they approved Barr's reassignment to Vienna. He wondered who had been bought or bribed, knowing the Department of State and the Central Intelligence Agency usually were very detailed in checking such transfers. He could only speculate how far up the chain of command the request had been approved.

He knew either a routine polygraph or one of the debriefing sessions would have revealed something. He was sure someone, somewhere within the chain of command had been bribed or blackmailed into signing off on Barr's transfer. He made a mental note to have the facts on Barr's Moscow debriefing and his most recent polygraph results sent to him immediately.

As he turned the corner, Johnny saw Swartz and Blinksdale head toward Swartz's office. "Glad we're all back at the same time. Let's step into Swartz's office where we can have some privacy and go over what we've learned before we question anyone else," Johnny said when he joined the men.

Swartz headed directly for his desk chair. He looked tired. "Fine with me. I'm just glad to have the chance to sit."

"Well, I found out a few things," Blinksdale started, taking his notes from his pocket and glancing over the paper as he spoke. "I have the report on Barr's bank account in Virginia. Alan hadn't made any large deposits to their family bank account, and there's no record of his wife having a separate account either. All deposits have been through the direct deposit system from his normal pay." He glanced at his notes again and continued. "As far as withdrawals, there's no clue there either. The savings account looks normal. They sold a house before they went to Moscow, and the buyers are making a payment to the savings account on the first of each month. Nothing unusual."

"There's nothing at all?" Johnny asked. Still standing, he shook his head and glanced down at Blinksdale.

"Well, we did find out a bit more about Mrs. Barr's sister who lives in Frankfurt. Her husband works for a computer company in the states, and is their foreign representative. They've been in Frankfurt for over three years. The Metcalf's neighbors said that Mrs. Barr visits the Metcalf family several times a year. Mrs. Barr did the same thing when she was in Moscow. It seems last week was her niece's birthday. Mrs. Barr went up last Friday for the party which was held on Saturday. While there, Mrs. Barr ate some popcorn and broke a tooth."

Swartz exclaimed, "She broke a tooth!"

"Yes," Blinksdale continued. "Mrs. Barr has a friend who's a dentist in Munich, and made arrangements to go there to have her tooth fixed. He was going to work her in when she arrived. It all checks out. The tooth probably needed more work than he thought, so she stayed in Munich a bit longer."

"I can't believe she wouldn't try and call her husband," Johnny said. "If it were my wife she would have called."

Swartz laughed and added, "Mine, too."

Blinksdale just shrugged. He said, "Now, for the warehouse. It's owned and operated by a very reputable furniture company

71

here in Vienna. They use it to store goods while waiting for customs clearance in and out of the country. In case some shipments can't be delivered at once, it's not unusual for the company to put the shipments in that warehouse and leave it for a couple days, or even weeks. This furniture company also sells furniture to several of the embassies. They have a list of clients that runs from the American Embassy to the Russians, West Germany and several of the Arab countries."

Johnny pulled a chair closer to the desk and sat down. He looked at both of the men and asked, "Would they all know what is going on in the warehouse?"

Blinksdale answered, "It wouldn't be difficult for any of the embassies it works with to know this is a slow time of the year for the company. It's busiest in the summer and fall when the majority of new families are arriving at post. Also, at the first of the year when new furniture arrives. April is one of the in-between months. My contacts tell me, that on May 15 a new shipment is expected. The warehouse is to be cleaned before that in preparation for the new season. But for about six weeks from April 1 until May 15 the warehouse may not be checked at all. This doesn't seem to be unusual, for the company owns several such warehouses just like the one on Muthgasse. They only check the ones they are using at the time."

Johnny sighed, "That tells me that Barr's death is an inside job and not something related to a terrorist group."

Blinksdale shook his head. "Not necessarily. I also found out when I was checking with the company, that they usually let their people take vacations during this time frame, because they aren't busy. Nothing out of the ordinary there. Whoever was responsible for Barr's kidnapping was aware of this schedule. We checked the neighborhood as carefully as possible for anything out of the norm. Everything appears normal."

Blinksdale looked down and finished looking over his notes. Carefully stacking his notes into a small pile, he stapled everything together and put them into a manila file on Swartz's desk.

"Great. That helps a bit. Anything from you, Jim?" Johnny asked.

"I've checked the cable traffic for the past three months, that came in while Barr was on duty. We won't know anything for sure until we get an answer from Washington after they've had a chance to review what had been sent. If any other information was passed, I don't think it was anything but verbal, but then too maybe a copy was made. I just can't believe one of our communicators passed an original document. I know that's not much help, but it does show that whoever leaked the information took the time to make copies."

"Do you have a way of checking, was a copy made?" Johnny asked.

Swartz sighed and shook his head. "Not really, we have copying machines that are only used for classified information but no way to see what was copied. We do have a system that tells us which section used the machine because they have to put in a code. That's all."

Johnny answered, "Yes, we have the same system in Virginia. Anything else?"

"We're certain some of the material that appeared in the papers came directly from our office," Jim Swartz said. "We checked the messages, and the wording on a couple of the printed articles was identical. However, all the leaked original messages were logged. They had to have been copied and copies sent to the receiving parties."

"So you do have a record of who signed in the leaked information," Blinksdale asked.

"Oh, yes, we know that. But, it doesn't prove anything," Swartz answered. "Johnny, I've the last two communicators waiting for us wherever we're ready to begin questioning them."

"You might as well call them now, Jim," Johnny answered. "Then I think you should go on home and get some sleep. I believe a good night's sleep is what we all need. What do you say?"

Both men nodded in agreement. Swartz stood and said, "I think that's a great idea. I feel as if my batteries are running down." He walked slowly across the room to summon the next person for questioning.

CHAPTER EIGHTEEN

"Johnny Collins, this is Sue Farris," Jim Swartz said when he entered the room. He looked toward Blinksdale and Collins and nodded. "Sue, you already know Bob Blinksdale. He's going to sit in on the meeting."

Swartz walked around to an empty chair on the side of the desk, he pointed to a chair for Sue. He turned to Collins and said, "Sue knows Barr is missing, and she's ready to tell us anything she might know to help us. Sue's single and has only been in Vienna two months. She lives in the Rathaus apartment complex. She's worked with Barr on several occasions. He's the one who showed her around the office when she first arrived."

"Would you like a cup of coffee?" Collins asked. He was surprised to see that Sue Farris was so attractive. He had expected someone older and more plain looking.

"Thanks, but I'll pass," Sue answered. She looked around the room at all three men. Shyly, she said, "I don't know what I could tell you about Alan. Is it true that he is missing?" Her eyes grew wide when she mentioned Alan Barr's name.

Sue Farris was about six foot tall, with straight long blonde hair and big blue eyes. She was wearing a dark blue designer pants suit and a soft blue blouse. When she moved her head, Johnny could see large diamond earrings in each ear. He glanced down at her hands and saw that on almost every finger she was wearing some type of a gold ring.

"Yes, it's true," Johnny answered. He looked at the other two men in the room but neither said a word. He turned back to Sue and asked, "Where else have you been assigned?"

Sue smiled and counted on her fingers. "I have been in Africa, Saudi, Japan, Moscow and several other places."

Johnny was surprised to hear she had worked at so many embassies. He thought she was in her mid thirties but with that many assignments she had to be almost forty.

Johnny said, "Thanks. What can you tell us about the times you've worked with Barr? We're looking for anything that will tell us what might have happened. Just talk, and we'll listen and ask questions as you go. Begin with coming to Vienna and his showing you around the Embassy and office."

Blinksdale sat in the corner. He didn't say anything.

For several minutes, Sue explained what she knew about Alan Barr. The entire time, Johnny made notes.

When Sue stopped talking, Johnny asked, "When did you see Alan last?"

Sue chuckled. "That's easy. I went with them to a restaurant called Dubrovnik in the first district. Alan liked the food there."

Swartz suddenly became alert, moved forward in his chair and asked, "When was that?"

Sue looked at the wall and finally said, "I guess it was a day or so before they left for vacation to Italy. I think it was a Wednesday night."

Collins made another note, then asked, "Tell me about that night."

Sue shrugged. Her long hair fell across her face and she brushed it back. "There is nothing special to tell. We all had been there several times and knew it was a popular meeting place for many Embassies and their staffs. We were always running into people we knew."

"Where is this place?" Collins asked.

Bob Blinksdale answered, "The restaurant is centrally located on the Ringstrasse. It is around the corner from the Inter-Continental Hotel, and just a couple blocks from the British, Russian, and numerous other embassies. Actually, Johnny, it isn't far from the Hilton hotel."

"Oh, so it's downtown?" Johnny said. He turned back to Sue and asked, "Anything special about that night that you can remember? Did Alan Barr seem to be nervous, or short of money?"

Sue paused as if not knowing what to say next. "Not any more than any of us. We all complain about not having enough money. I think that comes with having a government job. It's the same at all the posts I've been. People are always complaining they never have enough money to do what they want. I think I'd have noticed if he had more money than normal. Which he didn't seem to. He was distant at times, as if he were out in another world, but sometimes we all are."

She stopped talking for a moment and then continued. "No, everything that night was normal.

Johnny glanced at both Swartz and Blinksdale. He turned back to Sue and ran through a long list of questions similar to the ones that he had asked Mason earlier.

When Collins was finished, Sue looked at all three of the men. She said, "He didn't seem to receive an unusual number of phone calls. His wife called every once in a while, but nothing excessive. The only thing I remember being strange, was one day a couple of weeks ago, I was with him in the cipher room and a message started coming across the wire. I believe it was from Langley. I do know it was classified "Top Secret." He asked me to go get him a cup of coffee. I left the room and when I came back, he was finished processing the cable and never brought up the message. I meant to check the log to see what it was, but it was almost lunch time when I got back and he told me to go ahead and go to lunch. He asked me to relieve him for lunch when I returned. By the time I got back from lunch, I got busy and never really thought about the message again, until now."

"Do you think you could find it in the log book," Swartz asked.

"Probably, I could look back on the log and see. I'd just logged in two messages from State in a row, so that would tell me the day, or about where to look. I'll look when I go back if you want me to."

"I think I'll walk back with you now and you can show me," Johnny said. "How did you like working with Alan? Was he easy to work with? Did he demand more from you than the others?"

"Oh, he was all right," Sue answered. "Oh, hell, I might as well tell you. I'm not sorry he's gone. Rumors have been flying around the Embassy this morning that he was found dead. He was a male chauvinistic pig! Every time we worked together alone, he made it a point to have me do the menial tasks. If the shredder needed emptying, I had to do it. If he wanted a cup of coffee, I had to go get it. Whatever he wanted, he wanted me to do. I hated working with him."

"Did anyone else know how you felt?" Johnny's voice was low. "Did Greenly know about it?"

"Greenly!" Sue stammered. "Hell, Greenly's too busy kissing up to everyone to worry about what any of us are doing. He's usually out with the diplomats doing the social thing. It's not his style to ask if any of the employees have problems." She wiped a tear from her eye.

Bob Blinksdale and Jim Swartz remained silent. They both looked at the lady mystified. It was very apparent by their looks that they knew nothing about this side of Barr.

Johnny thought over what Sue had just said. She sounded very convincing. She was an attractive lady, who dressed and appeared professional. He glanced at the two men sitting on the other side of the room and shrugged. "Do either of you have anything to ask Sue?"

Neither man spoke. Johnny continued, "We seemed to be finished here and I hate to keep you from your job longer than we really need. I'll walk back with you and you can show me what you were saying about the logged message. What's the name of the next one we're going to interview, Jim? I'll bring him back with me. Okay?"

"That's fine," Swartz said. "His name is Kevin Smith. While you're doing that, I need to check with my secretary and sign some papers. You can stay if you want to, Bob."

"No, I need to do a few things myself. I want to check at my office to see if I might have overlooked anything. I'll walk with you, Johnny. See you later, Jim. If you need me, call my office. They'll know where I'll be all day."

On the way back to the crypto center after Blinksdale left them, Sue Farris walked beside Johnny. Softly, only loud enough for her to hear, Johnny whispered. "Do you want to press any charges about the way Barr or Greenly treats you? You may if you'd like. I'll help you, if you want."

"No, it's too late now. One of these days I'll talk to Greenly about it myself. I love my job and I don't want to lose it. If I file charges I'll end up back in Langley doing a dead end job. The agency doesn't have the best reputation of taking care of sexual discrimination charges. I don't want that. I'll work it out myself, but thanks for asking."

CHAPTER NINETEEN

Bob Blinksdale was what most people would call the perfect example of an "All American-Man." His hair was cut short and neat. He was tall, muscular, pleasant and polite. He had entered the Marines right out of high school and had served twelve years with them. He left the service before retirement to accept a job in Security with the State Department.

Johnny had read a report about Blinksdale in his briefing papers during his airplane flight. Blinksdale had served in three two year postings in "hot" spots, and was considered the "cream" of the Security Department.

After Collins left Sue, he went searching for Blinksdale. He had a favor to ask. Johnny knew asking Bob Blinksdale to keep something hush-hush wasn't necessary. He just wanted to make sure Blinksdale didn't let it slip that he was working on a special request.

Collins found Blinksdale at the water fountain on the second floor. He stood beside him and in a low voice said, "Bob, I've got something special I need your help on."

Blinksdale stood up tall and straight and answered, "Sure, what do you need?"

"I want you to run a check on the background of all the people in the Communication Center. This is a request that I need in-house, not through any of the agencies. I want you to find out how many of them frequent the Dubrovnik restaurant. I also want to know if any of them have been flashing large sums of money or buying anything more than usual. Run a check on their bank accounts and look for anything uncommon, such as large deposits or withdrawals. And, be sure and include Swartz and Greenly in the inquiries. Can you do that?"

Blinksdale blinked several times, when Johnny mentioned Swartz and Greenly. He whispered, "Sure. I'll handle it myself and keep all notes on my person. When do you want the report?"

"Let me know as soon as the information starts to trickle in," Johnny said. "Remember this is just between you and me."

"Will do!" Blinksdale answered. He started to walk away, turned and went back. "Johnny, I'd also like to check up on Barr's wife. It doesn't seem right that she wouldn't tell him she was going to a dentist in Munich and when she was going to be back in Vienna. Something just doesn't fit. Is that all right with you?"

"Sure if you have a gut feeling on something, follow up on it," Collins answered. "I know my gut feelings often prove to be right."

"I will! See you later," Blinksdale nodded, walking toward the steps.

After Blinksdale walked away, Collins walked back up the steps and went into the Communication Center and shut the door behind him.

"Sorry I'm late, Sue. Did you find what you were looking for?" he asked walking over to Sue Farris.

Sue had already gone to her position in the corner of the room and was hard at work transmitting a stack of routine cables piled in front of her. She got up and walked over to the log book, as Johnny followed.

"Here it is. See where I logged the two messages together and Alan logged the next. This is it. This is the one."

Johnny's eyes widened as he read the note by the signature. The message was coded TOP SECRET DESTROY AFTER READING. It was for Chief-of-Station, Greenly.

Johnny knew all embassies had a Communication Center similar to Vienna's. The centers were situated in a secure restricted area, free from all types of exterior spying. Their location was only restricted by what space was available and how the space could be adapted for their specific needs. There was no general Embassy requirement regulating a special location such as on a certain floor. Although the centers were free from others spying into it, nothing could prevent those working within the center from spying from within.

Sue said, "The initial messages are transmitted in a specific code. The decoding and transmission is done by one of the station communicators. Messages arrive at the receiving equipment at various times. Normally, stateside messages arrived at an international destination during the down time of the receiving location. The receiving equipment is programmed to receive incoming messages, and store them in its memory until the computers are instructed to process the incoming messages. That's done during routine working hours."

"I understand," Johnny said.

She smiled and continued, "Every once in a while a special message arrives that requires a special decoding process. This simply instructs the receiver to notify the person with the required code number. That person is called and personally has to process the decoding."

"Are these type of messages frequent?" Johnny asked.

"No, not really," Sue answered. "It just depends on world events of the day. When cables or incoming traffic, as referred to by several agencies, is processed, copies are given to all addresses and a copy is kept in the reference file. All other copies are shredded, and a notation is made in the reference file log that the cable has been received. It's patterned on the same principle as a large business. Only those that have the need to know are giving copies of the information."

Johnny was familiar with the process and knew exactly how it should operate. Whether it was followed to the letter at this Embassy, he wasn't sure. He wanted to get a feeling of what she actually knew about her job.

"Something has been nagging me," Johnny said. "If someone receives a message and doesn't make a copy of it, is there any record within the Embassy that the message was arrived?" He wondered if Barr couldn't have received some messages and no one would have even known about it.

"No. I don't think there's any other record. Sometimes messages are on a disc but we clean them after so long and re-use them. Of course, the person that sent the message would have a copy and their sending office. They keep hard copy records of everything they send. But, no one at the receiving station would have any idea that such a message had arrived." Sue looked at Collins and frowned.

"Just wondered," Johnny said.

Sue said, "Once in a while, due to power outages, a receiving station might send out a general message to all units, requesting they re-transmit any messages during the down time. This isn't unusual, especially in the old, what was once, Eastern Bloc countries. Then, all interested stations would check their tapes and if they had sent a message during that specific time frame, the sending station simply re-transmitted the messages. Does this help?"

"Yes, please continue." Johnny answered, filing all the information away in his mind.

Sue went on to explain what happened the day in question. She said that according to the book, Alan had followed procedure. He logged the message as being received by Greenly.

Now Collins had to check with the home office, or Greenly to see what the message contained and if Greenly had actually received it. According to regulations, Greenly was supposed to come in, open the decoding machine himself and run the message. The original message would then be placed in the safe in Greenly's office. A notation was made in the reference book that Greenly had the only copy.

"Thanks, Sue," Johnny said. He turned to walk away but went back to the log book and asked, "Sue, do you know what these code numbers mean beside Alan's name?"

"Sure. Mr. Greenly had to come and get the message. Those are his initials."

"Did you see Mr. Greenly on the day we're talking about?"

"I don't think he was in the room when I came back," Sue answered. "But, he could have just left. It was over a week or so ago, and I never looked at the book again to see what the message was, so I don't think I would have noticed. He's in and out a great deal. If he'd been sitting over there in one of those chairs, I might not have noticed. I left almost immediately for lunch. I'm sorry I can't help you any further. I'm just not sure."

"That's all right." Johnny turned and asked, "Which one is Kevin Smith?"

"He's over there near the shredder," Larry Mason said. Mason had just walked into the Communication Center. "He does most of the pouching and makes the mail runs. I'll get him for you."

CHAPTER TWENTY

In the attic of the Russian Embassy at forty-five Reisnerstrasse, several blocks South of the Ringstrasse, the humming of electronic equipment vibrated off the walls and echoed through the classified area. The offices were constructed so that the most sophisticated spying equipment couldn't penetrate the lead lined walls. Although, the office was similar to the CIA cipher room on the fourth floor of the American Embassy, the Russian rooms were drab and badly in need of painting.

Since 1991, the Komitet Gosudarstvennoy Bezopasnosti, known throughout the world as the KGB, had gone through several name and organizational changes. Now, two major services had replaced the KGB and continued to monitor civilian intelligence around the world.

The Federal Security Service, presently known as the FSB dealt with counterintelligence, and the Foreign Intelligence Service, now known as the SVR, dealt in foreign intelligence. Members of the former KGB, that wished to remain active employees, were reassigned according to their previous experience and present wishes.

With the reorganization and blessing of President Boris Yeltsin, the SVR, became the controller of the largest sprawling network of intelligence gathering organizations known to man. Outside of Russia, the organizations to date remain the chief contact points for all terrorist groups and their intelligence agencies operating anywhere in the world.

The Vienna communications center served both the offices for the Foreign Intelligence Service and the Federal Security Service. The top ranking resident SVR/FSB agent was automatically appointed Director of the center. In Vienna, his name was Yuri Rubin.

Rubin was not only the SVR/FSB Director but also the senior agent of the Mokrie Dyela, the notorious death squad, "wet affairs" division which handled the dirty work. It is that unit that is responsible for carrying out termination by executive action, internationally known as the "black berets."

The office in Vienna was the European Regional Office simply because of its location in Europe. The information Vienna's SVR/FSB agents provided Moscow was enormous. It included everything possible regarding diplomats, political figures, noted personalities and international business men and woman. The files included their: food preferences, sexual orientation, reading materials, and any other bits of information that could be used by the Director's chosen few to develop psychological profiles.

The hub of the center contained the latest listening devices, computers, and decoding machines and equipment. The room extended the full length of the Embassy. The area, completely self sufficient, was kept alive with the generators, sophisticated antennas, air purification and cooling systems located on the roof of the Embassy building.

At various positions across the room, operators monitored the listening devices and sat in front of complicated ultramodern computer terminals, which resemble a modern airport control tower. The listening devices were constantly monitoring systems such as the American's latest Military Strategic Tactical and Relay System, known as "MILSTAR." MILSTAR provided satellite information to the US Military around the world.

At certain times of the day, the soviet's fine tuned equipment enabled them to hear what was being discussed within the Special Operations Forces Command and Control System. This command center was created prior to the American war with Iraq. Through this system, the Russians were able to monitor Omaha Command as well as the top military bases throughout the globe, including Bosnia and Serbia.

Although the Vienna center was interested in Americans, because of their location, they were also able to intercept incoming and outgoing signals from neighboring embassies. This included the Israeli military factions, as well as the well known militant groups such as the PLO and HAMAS. Like the Americans, the SVR/FSB and GRU were interested in all intelligence information, from South America to the struggling countries of Africa. Within the communication center, a shredding machine was placed every few feet to allow easy access. These machines take in all discarded papers and turn out small pieces of snow flake like confetti. This shredding process prevented anyone from reconstructing any of the shredded papers.

Large plastic bags of the shredded paper were stacked against one wall. When a large pile was made, the bags were sold to a paper goods store in Salzburg, Austria, under the name of one of the FSB's businesses. The shredded documents were ultimately packaged into small packages and sold around the world as confetti for party favors. This was one of the ways the new FSB used its cover businesses and it helped pay some of the costs for the intelligence network.

Two men sat in a small secure room within the communication section. The larger man, Yuri Rubin, sat behind his desk. He pounded on the desk top, and spoke in English. "What in the hell did you think you were doing?"

The shorter man was Colonel Nikolai Golodin. He looked at Rubin and answered, "I gave the Lebanese orders to pick up Barr and rough him up a bit. He was to ask Barr what information Barr had sold to other countries. We also wanted to know if Barr had learned anything else about the computer shipment. It was to be a basic pickup and question session. I never thought Haddah would go directly to torture."

"The Lebanese bastard is an idiot. He is out of control. What did you think he would do?" Rubin said. He stared at the shorter man. His eyes locked on the older man's face.

Golodin answered, "We hoped to find out if Barr had told anyone about his connection to us. Who would have thought it would go this far? What can I say, the Lebanese got carried away and went too far? Barr died."

Rubin slammed his fist on the desk top again. "You are an idiot, too! Barr's dead and now we have the American's all over the city."

Golodin laughed, "That's not all bad either. Besides, what choices did we have? We couldn't let Barr go back and spill everything he knew to the CIA or NSA, could we?"

Rubin sighed. He said in disgust, "You should have known better than to let an Arab do the questioning, especially Haddah. That man's crazy. His reputation is that he would kill his own mother for the right amount of money. I can't believe you never thought Barr would die? What did you think would happen when you started hanging things off his pecker and balls? Did you think he would get excited and spill his guts?"

Golodin threw both of his hands up in the air. "Now, that wasn't my idea. That was Haddah's. I think he read it in some Soldier of Fortune magazine."

Rubin said, "Why didn't you try and reason with him first? You could have offered him more money, some big incentive? Anything to get him to stay where he was and remain silent. Are you crazy, old man?"

Golodin stood, walked around the room, turned and looked at Rubin. He explained, "Barr was a loose cannon. Suddenly, he went religious on us. He said his conscience was bothering him. He complained of feeling guilty and not being able to sleep and eat. He never did say if he'd talked to his wife about how he felt. I have no idea what she knows about his decisions."

Rubin sat with his hands folded and made circles around with his thumbs. He said, "Are you telling me you don't know what is going on with Mrs. Barr?"

Golodin sat back down in the straight wood chair. "I don't personally. However, I do have one of my other agents watching her. Alan Barr was getting old. He was becoming weak and spineless. I had my orders from my home office and I followed them."

Rubin wasn't impressed. He couldn't have cared less if Colonel Golodin was a member of the GRU or not, or if he was only following orders. Indirectly, Colonel Golodin was responsible to him as long as he was posted in Vienna.

Rubin said, "We both know your direct mission in Vienna is to gather material, recruit, train, and employ people who would provide Russia with information about the western world, especially in the military field. You are not in Vienna to create a national incident by killing one of our double agents."

Golodin stood again. This time, he walked behind his chair and put his hands on the back of the chair and stared at Rubin. He said, "I didn't know Barr was going to die before we could get back to him. I had one of the drivers standing by, and then I got detained with a message from Moscow and didn't get back as soon as I'd planned. When I finally got back, he was dead. I didn't want to move him. Otherwise, I could have taken his body down and thrown it into the Danube. We could have made it look like a suicide."

Rubin rubbed his head. "Probably would have been better. Not much we can do now. The Americans have Mrs. Barr surrounded. I'll never be able to get in personally to see her. I'll have to send in someone else or wait until she's back in the states. My informer tells me the memorial service at the American Embassy will be in the morning."

Golodin smiled, "Is the service open to the diplomatic community?"

Rubin shook his head. "I'm not sure. I only know that the morning paper is going to carry a notice about Barr's death. It won't give any details. I tried to contact my other sources at the American Embassy, but they're not free to meet at this time. They fear everyone is being watched. It'll be tomorrow or later before I can make any contact."

Golodin asked, "Do you know any more about Collins?"

Rubin stood and smoothed his gray jacket. "I don't know any more about Collins than what we've already discussed."

Golodin smiled. He said, "We both know he's one of the best CIA troubleshooters in the business. I'm sure he wouldn't know me by sight. He's traveling under his real name and went straight to the Embassy, so he's not trying to hide anything. Langley sent him over before they knew about Barr's death. He was to check out the leaks. But, I must confess, I'm looking forward to working against him. As the Americans say, he should give us a go for our money. It's been many years since we've had someone to really offer us a challenge."

Rubin smiled and answered, "Yes, it has been years."

After pausing for a couple seconds to gather his thoughts, Colonel Golodin continued, "My directions are to work with you on finding out all we can, but I have been instructed to continue with my original orders. I still need up to date information about the arrival of the satellite computer system that the Americans are planning to give to Israel. I know the one message which Barr gave us said the delivery would be coming through Vienna as a shipment of building supplies. But we need more details. We still don't know when or how the shipment's coming and if it is still coming as originally planned."

Rubin snapped back, "You should have thought of that before you killed Barr."

Golodin glared at Rubin. "I'm the last person that wanted Barr dead. It would have made my work easier if he would have stayed as he was."

Yuri Rubin normally didn't have a day to day contact with Colonel Golodin. Although the two men were trying to achieve the same ultimate goal for their country, the two agencies they worked for were bitter rivals. Rubin discovered that rather than working with Golodin to gain information, they kept secrets from each other, creating problems as they pulled against one another.

Rubin walked to a file cabinet in the corner of the room. He removed a manila envelope with a large red "X" on it. He opened it, read a couple lines and then turned back to Golodin. "We must help each other now. What about our other agents within the American Embassy? Are they secure? And our agents in the states, will they feel any backlash from Barr's death? Our remaining Vienna agents still don't know about one another, do they?"

"I believe everyone is safe," Golodin answered. "The agents with the American Embassy are well hidden. No, there are only the two agents that you know about that know that others work for us. The other ones do not know anything about any others. I can only see one weak link with one of our Vienna agents. However, I feel that I can control that agent. The ones in the states should be fine. If we are able to divert the American attention as we plan, everyone should be able to continue as if nothing has happened."

"I certainly hope you are right," Rubin answered rubbing his bald head. "I left a message at the Hilton for Collins. I plan on contacting him later this evening. We might as well try and find out what he knows. When I checked his room earlier today, I didn't find anything interesting. However, I was successful in planting the microphone in his briefcase. My greatest wish now is that he carries the briefcase with him at all times. It could prove a blessing when he returns to Langley. I'm sure the CIA doesn't know what my true assignment is here in Vienna."

Golodin said, "I am willing to talk to him. Do you want me to see what I might learn from him?" His voice quivered slightly as he spoke.

Rubin shook his head. "No, tonight I plan to confront him with the computer shipment. I agree it'll add some spice to our job keeping a step ahead of a true professional. We can only hope that Collins will be a worthwhile competitor."

When Golodin left Rubin's office, Rubin couldn't help wondering why Colonel Golodin kept working. Although, he might have treated Barr in the same manner. After all, Barr was dispensable. The spy operations against the Americans were too valuable to risk discovery because of one person.

Rubin was also irritated for another reason. The latest transcript of Johnny Collins's briefcase transmissions was still sitting on his desk. He had only had a chance to listen to a few minutes, but it didn't seem very interesting.

The battery which activated the device was American made. A case of the batteries had been stolen during a raid on a Saudi Arabian military warehouse. Eventually, the batteries had found their way to Moscow.

Eventually, the powerful, long-life batteries, made in a small town in Iowa, in the middle of the US, had been sold to power medical units, weapons and equipment in the Middle East. Rubin smiled and sat thinking of the CIA and how an American battery was being used to power an electronic listening device against them.

CHAPTER TWENTY ONE

"How long have you been in Vienna, Kevin?" Johnny asked as they walked back to Swartz's office.

"I've been here two years already. I love it. The home office has just approved my extension for another year."

Collins nodded. "Yes, Vienna does seem to have an active night life. You'll have to tell me about some of the good restaurants. It looks as if I might be here for a while. I'm staying at the Hilton and I've been told there are several good places to eat within walking distance of my hotel."

"Yes, there's some special ones not far at all. I'd be glad to go with you if you'd like, or I can show you on a map," Smith answered eagerly.

"I think you should go home, Jim," Johnny stated as he walked into the room finding Swartz with his head on his arms. "You look dead tired."

"I will as soon as we finish with Smith. I guess I'm not as young as I used to be." Swartz sat up straight and ran his fingers through his hair.

"None of us are! Look at my gray hairs. We shouldn't be but another half hour or so." Johnny motioned for Smith to take a chair, then walked over and closed the door. He was also feeling the effects of the long night. But, was thankful his headache had finally disappeared.

"Kevin, what we're doing is trying to find out anything we can about Alan's last days at work here," Swartz stated simply.

"What is it you want to know? I didn't work with him a great deal, except for courier duties."

"Anything," Johnny answered. "Kevin, anything that would help us find out what happened to him. Just anything, no matter how small."

Kevin Smith shifted in his chair. He was over six foot tall and looked like a basketball player, tall, muscular and fast on his feet. He was the only black communicator assigned to the embassy. He wore his hair short and was dressed in a gray double breasted suit, soft yellow shirt and matching gray and yellow modernistic tie. His black loafers sparkled. His face was angular with gentle soft brown eyes.

Smith looked at the two men and said, "I don't know what I can tell you that you don't already know. I've been here two years. Barr came last summer. I helped show him around sometimes. I helped him and his wife get settled. They didn't have a car, so I lent them mine at various times so they could go to the commissary and do some shopping. They even borrowed my car one weekend to go to Munich when they first arrived. They wanted to buy a multi system VCR. They sold their old one before they left Moscow."

Collins frowned and asked, "Why did Barr have you show him around?"

Smith laughed, "I was his sponsor. You know the person assigned by the Community Liaison Officer to help new arrivals."

Collins smiled, and said, "Please, continue."

"I was a guest at their house several times. Since I'm single, Mrs. Barr tried to fix me up with dates."

Collins asked, "Did she fix you up with white or black girls?"

"Didn't make any difference to me," Smith chuckled. "A date is a date. Mrs. Barr was active in the American and the International Women's Clubs and had all sorts of contacts."

"Were the Barrs as friendly with other Americans here at the Embassy?" Collins asked. He was learning about a side of the Barrs that he was totally unaware of.

"Not any one special, I'd say. They went out with lots of different people. I went out to eat with them several times. Most of the time we went to a restaurant in the first district, called Dubrovnik. Have you heard of it?"

Johnny looked at Swartz and they both answered, as one voice, "Yes."

"Well, at work Barr was an okay guy. He was always willing to help me if I was running late for the couriers. Well, anyway, does any of this help?" Kevin looked from Swartz's eyes to Collins.

"Yes, that helps a lot," Johnny said. "Did you happen to notice if he had any more money than usual, or if he complained not having as much money as he should? Do you know if he had any problems working with any of the other communicators?"

"No. I don't think they had any money problems. They never talked about it. I think they saved in Moscow. From what they said of Moscow, there weren't many places to spend money. As far as working well with others, well, he had some problems."

"Would you tell me about them?" Johnny asked wondering what he knew and if it would collaborate Sue Farris's story.

"Well, he told me he didn't care for Sue Farris. I never actually heard him say anything to her face but I know he told me he thought she had gotten her job just because the State Department had a quota to make."

"Kevin, what do you mean by quota?" Swartz asked.

"Come on, you know? They had to hire so many women to be politically correct."

"Do you think Alan Barr thought Sue Farris had been hired because she was just a woman?" Collins questioned.

"Sure, she had two things going for her," Kevin said. "She was a woman and she was beautiful. Barr resented her. He used to say the person most discriminated against was the white male."

Collins thought for a moment and said, "It seems strange the Barr would tell you about Sue. After all, you're black. Did you think he felt differently toward you?"

"Alan," laughed Smith. "Heck, no. He wouldn't discriminate against me."

"Why not?" Swartz asked. He sat up straighter in his chair and leaned forward.

Smith looked at both of the men and said, "Come on, you're pulling my leg. Barr would never talk about me that way."

Collins said, "Kevin, tell us why. We really don't know."

"I thought you guys knew everything. Alan Barr had been married at one time to a black lady. Didn't you know that?"

Collins looked at Swartz. Both men shook their heads. "No, we didn't know that. Is this Mrs. Barr black?"

"Oh, good heavens no! He has only been married to this Mrs. Barr a couple years. His first wife died or he divorced her and he remarried when he was posted in Moscow."

Collins sighed, "Well, I'll be damned. Do you know who Mrs. Barr worked for in Moscow?"

"Sure, she was with the Embassy," Smith said. "She went into Frankfurt to do all the buying for the commissary and the embassy. I believe she made the trip once or twice a month. You know she has a sister living in Frankfurt?"

"Yes, we know about her sister. Is there anything else that you can tell us? By the way, Kevin, where do you live?" Johnny asked.

"I live in a one bedroom apartment on the side of the Barrs' apartment. First, there's the corner unit, which is Fisher's apartment. She's the lady who always watched the cat when the Barr's traveled. Then there is Barrs apartment, and then mine. There are three more apartments in that compound area. However, our three apartments share common walls."

"When you went out to eat with the Barrs, let's say that restaurant in the first district, the Dubrovnik, did you ever see Barr talk to anyone you didn't know, or to someone he never made it a point to introduce you to?"

Smith thought for a moment and then answered, "We were there the night before they left on their last trip. There were four of us. Mr. and Mrs. Barr, myself and a secretary who they knew from the British Embassy. I don't remember Alan talking to anyone in particular. Oh, now I do remember him talking to a fellow I'd never seen before. The only reason I remember him was that the man had no hair. He was bald. I also remember overhearing them talking, when I passed on the way to the men's room. I remember they weren't speaking German or English. I'm not sure what language they were speaking."

"Could they have been speaking Russian?" Collins asked.

"I really don't know. I don't think I heard any of it close enough to say. I just walked by them."

"Well, that helps some. Please, don't discuss with anyone what we've talked about here today. Is that understood? Also, I want you to keep an eye on the Barr apartment when you're home. Let us know if you see anything going on around it. Will you do that, and keep either me, Blinksdale or Swartz informed?" Collins got up and walked to the door. He held the door open. "Also, if you think of anything else that we might need to know, give us a call. Nothing is too small or too silly. Thanks for your help."

Kevin shook Johnny's hand and said, "Yes, I'll let you know."

Collins added, "Kevin, plan on going to the Dubrovnik with me one of these next nights. Sounds like a good place."

Johnny saw Kevin nod his head in agreement and stood in the doorway and watched Smith walk back toward the Communication Center.

"I think we could still have a double agent problem," Johnny whispered when Swartz joined him and they both started down the stairs toward the Marine desk.

"What makes you think so? I agree that Barr probably was one but with him dead, do you think we still have one?" Swartz asked as they neared the Marine Guard.

"I've a gut feeling. Things don't seem right. Farris didn't tell anyone about Barr's treatment of her. She must have told someone. I can't believe she wouldn't have."

"I don't know who it would have been, unless, it was Kay Blackburn. Kay's a courier from Frankfurt. She comes in weekly on courier run. Blackburn is due in tomorrow. You can talk to her then," Swartz answered. "I didn't know about the first Mrs. Barr, did you?"

Johnny made a face. "Hell, there isn't anything in any file that I read. I'll see you in the morning. If you need me, call the hotel." Johnny watched Swartz opened the gate and go down the steps and out the entrance door of the Embassy.

He waited for a few minutes by the Marine desk until Swartz was out of the building. He thought for a moment and then turned and went around the corner to Bob Blinksdale's office. Blinksdale was sitting at his desk and had several pieces of note paper in front of him. His eyes looked wary, and Collins noticed that the ashtray on the edge of his desk was full of gum wrappers.

"Have anything for me?" Collins asked with a surprising burst of energy.

"Just a couple things. The guards out in front of the Embassy are trying to locate you. You might want to call them from here. Greenly is back out at the Barr house. He wanted to look over the house before anyone else arrived. Mrs. Barr has packed and will be leaving for the states with the body. She won't be returning. They're going over things that she'll want shipped."

"Are they doing all that now?" Collins asked.

"I think just generally. Her sister from Frankfurt will be in sometime tomorrow morning, before the service. Mrs. Barr will have left by then, so her sister will represent the family. She'll be staying in the Barr apartment until the packers leave. I'm glad she's going to be there, I think someone might decide to take a look if we left the apartment empty. The family cat is going to be shipped out before Mrs. Barr's sister returns to Frankfurt."

Collins laughed and clapped his hand. "Well, that's a relief, I was really worried about that cat."

Blinksdale glanced at Collins and continued. "I sent out all the messages about the bank accounts. We should know something within the next couple of days, maybe sooner. I'm having someone in Washington do it without causing any waves. I think some of them may have hometown accounts in states like Texas or Illinois."

"That's good. May I use your phone? I'll check in with the guards in the front."

Blinksdale nodded his approval. As Johnny took the receiver, Blinksdale motioned that he was going to step out of the room for a moment.

While he was waiting for the guards to answer, Johnny glanced around Blinksdale's office. He noticed Blinksdale had pictures of his wife and children in various places. The children's pictures were of different ages. The one on his desk was apparently most recent. They had posed as a family picture and it included Blinksdale, his wife, two teenage children and a dog. Johnny smiled, it reminded him of his family.

In a few moments, the guard, Johnny had been talking too earlier, came to the phone. The guard explained the police were able to trace the license plate. The VW was registered to a Russian, a woman named Valentino Sergejevna Molkin. The address given was the Russian Embassy, 45 Reisnerstrasse.

Johnny thanked the guard and hung up the phone as Blinksdale re-entered the room.

"Bob, there's something I haven't told you that I think you should know. When I was leaving the Embassy this morning on my way to the Hilton, a VW car went by. The two passengers seemed to show an unusual interest in me. Then, when I came back this afternoon, the guards told me the same car had driven by the Embassy twice. I asked the Austrian guards to run a check on the license plate. The car belongs to a Russian woman by the name of Valentino Sergejevna Molkin. The car is registered under her name at the Russian Embassy address but it does not have diplomatic license plates. What do you make of it?"

Blinksdale pulled up a seat while Johnny was talking. "I think they would've used a car registered to Joe Blow with a false street address, unless they wanted us to know they were interested in us. The Russians aren't stupid. They don't play that openly without a reason. So, if the Russians are showing that much interest, it must be because the Barrs were in Moscow. Did you get a look at the people in the car?"

"The only one I saw clearly was a big bald headed man. He was on the passenger side. The driver appeared to be a woman. The car is registered to a woman, so that makes sense."

"I agree. Bald headed, you say? I just met a Russian at a recent cocktail party who had no hair. He was also big built. Seems he was assigned to Vienna sometime last summer. I don't remember his name, or what his title was, but I can check in the diplomatic book. It won't take me long." He walked to a bookshelf and took out a gray paperback book. He glanced at Collins and said, "You're beginning to look almost as tired as I'm beginning to feel. Are you on your way back to the hotel now?"

"Yes, I thought I'd go to the Marine desk and call a cab. You can let me know tomorrow what the man's name is. I think if I go back and take a shower and rest for a few minutes, I'd feel better. I just need to sort things out. What time is the service in the morning? I want to be here for that."

"I think it's at ten."

"That's good. I can get in early enough to read traffic and send a message back. Do you think it'll be crowded?"

"Yes. I look for it to be a full house. It'll be in the morning papers. I expect several of the embassies to send a representative. Alan was well known among the cocktail circuit, and knew lots of other Embassy people. We're already getting calls from the British Embassy. They must've heard a rumor, or they may have gotten a tip from the newspaper. The BBC is active here and they keep the Brits well informed."

Johnny said, "I know that Ambassador Latham wants to keep the service low key but I don't think it will be as low as he'd like it to be. I'm going back to the hotel now. If anything should come up that you think I should know about, be sure and call. I may go out for dinner, but I won't be gone long. All messages are posted on my television by computer so I can retrieve them at any time. See you in the morning."

Johnny walked out of the Security Office and down the hall to the Marine desk. The Marines had just changed duty, and the same Marine, from last night was back on duty.

"Nice to see you again. Could you possible call me a taxi for the Hilton?" Johnny asked the Marine as if they were old friends.

"Yes, of course, Mr. Collins. How have you been today? Will you want the taxi right away?"

"I'm fine. Yes, I'll be going as soon as it arrives. It's been a long day."

"Yes, sir. I'll tell him you'll meet him out front."

"Thanks."

Johnny went to get his coat and briefcase that he had left near a coat stand behind the reception area. When he was ready, Johnny walked out the heavy metal doors and down the steps toward the entrance door. He glanced out and didn't see a taxi waiting, so he walked over and sat on the bench the drivers used while they waited.

CHAPTER TWENTY TWO

It was late afternoon when Colonel Nikolai Golodin turned off the cross walk of Peter Jordan Strasse and walked through the entrance to Turkenschanz Park. As a precaution and a treat, he had arrived early and stopped at the Modul Hotel.

He relaxed in their second floor coffee shop and enjoyed a piece of excellent apple strudel and a cup of Irish coffee while he thought of his pending meeting. Upon his request, the waiter placed him at a table near the windows, so he could watch the people go in and out of the park.

Buttoning his overcoat against the cool wind, he walked slowly as he headed down the pathway toward the duck pond. His right pocket bulged with a bag of seed, he intended to feed the ducks.

He walked past a group of four old men. They were playing cards on one of the park concrete tables. They simply looked his way, and then returned to their game.

Taking his time, he glanced at the trees and noticed they were just starting to get new leaves. A wheelbarrow had been left along the side of the path. He stopped and walked toward it.

For several minutes, he stood beside the wheelbarrow and pretended to study the birds, plants and trees around him. Confident that no one had followed him, he walked back to the path.

As he continued along the twisting walkway around the closed snack bar, Golodin saw his Arab contact walk down another pathway several feet in front of him. The two men met where the paths crossed to the right of the small pool area.

Golodin asked in English, speaking softly, "So, have you found out anything more regarding Barr? Are there any rumors regarding the shipment to Israel?"

Haddah looked around and answered in English. "I thought for sure if Barr were supplying someone else with information, we would have heard by now. There's supposed to be a small paragraph in tomorrow's paper about his death."

Golodin nodded toward a bench. He walked toward it, brush the cement with his hand and sat down. He looked up at Haddah. "We can't let the shipment get through. Don't you agree?"

Haddah pushed his hands into his dark blue wool overcoat pockets. He looked around. No one was in the area. "We have no other choice. But, as we discussed, we have to take the focus off of the shipment. Taking the American bus hostage is the solution. It's bound to attract the attention we need. We have to cover up our real purpose."

He walked away from Golodin and moved toward the water where several ducks were swimming. He took a piece of bread from his pocket, broke it into several pieces and threw it on the water. After he watched the ducks retrieve the bread, he walked back to Golodin and asked, "Have you given any further thought about an attack on a social affair?"

Golodin looked at the man, nodded and asked, "Do you have anything specific in mind?"

After the two men talked for several minutes, they walked together down the pathway toward the larger duck pond. Haddah looked at the GRU Colonel and said, "We must go over plans in more detail at our meeting tonight. We will need some help from outside. I know a couple members of the Hamas that I can call. They would be happy to help. They're staying in a house over on Hockegasse. They need money."

Golodin nodded approval. "I was at our Ambassador's today. The American Ambassador was also there. He never made any comments about Barr. I was very disappointed. I look forward to reading the newspaper article. But, only one small paragraph. That hardly seems worth while." Golodin thought for a moment and then continued, "You say you know someone that could help us? How much money are we talking about?"

"The going rate for a mercenary in today's market is fifteen hundred a day plus expenses. I think I can make a deal with them to supply the equipment and do everything we need, plus help with the transporting of the computer equipment for an even fifty thousand. They need weapons. The Hamas are a bit more expensive than some of the other groups, but they are the most reliable. They rarely get caught and almost always are successful. Shall I call them and report back tonight at the meeting?"

"Yes, it doesn't hurt to check into it. If we decide to go ahead with it, we will do everything the same night. Each attack will be spaced so the police will not have time to think about one thing before another begins. I got the impression the American Ambassador is going out of country sometime next week to attend a conference in Paris. It will be to our advantage if we do something before he left. What do you think?" The Russian stopped, and rubbed his hands together and waited for Haddah to answer.

"We'll discuss more tonight," Haddah said. He stood and looked out toward the street and glanced at his gold Rolex. "It's too bad we can't protest how we feel about the Americans sending the spy equipment to Israel, but I am afraid it would just draw attention to them. Israel would only use the equipment against the Arab nations."

The Russian watched the Arab closely. He didn't trust him but what other choice did he have. Haddah was one of the best. The Russian knew that in today's political atmosphere, the logical place to hire a terrorist was within the Arab world. The Arabs were outspoken and freely admitted their hatred for Americans. However, trusting an Arab was risky. Golodin promised himself this would be his last mission with this specific Arab.

Golodin said, "I'll be home after our meeting this evening. I'll be expecting a guest. Remember you can always call me if you have any questions."

The Arab muttered to himself and walked down the path in the opposite direction of Golodin. Golodin watched him turn the corner and head toward Gersthofer Strasse.

Golodin turned back and walked to the large duck pond. For several minutes, he stood and threw food to the ducks. When the street lights turned on, he walked back toward the Modul Hotel on Peter Jordan Strasse and to the bus stop on the corner.

Completely absorbed in his thoughts, Golodin failed to look around the area and didn't see a blue VW car parked on the side street near the traffic light just off the corner of Gregor Mendel Strasse. The VW remained parked, with its motor idling, until the Russian walked up the steps to enter the bus.

Knowing the man was heading for his apartment, the driver turned right and proceeded down Gregor Mendel Strasse. The car drove slowly, giving the driver time to observe everyone walking on the sidewalks.

Turning left onto Gersthofer Strasse, the car sped in and out of traffic, causing several irritated drivers to honk their horns and shake hands and fingers in disgust. At last, the driver spotted Haddah walking toward a taxi stand.

The VW driver pulled over to the side of the busy street, pretended to look at a map, but watched the Arab. When the Arab entered a waiting taxi, the VW driver followed the taxi until it stopped in front of an apartment complex in the first district just south of Schottentur. The Arab paid for his ride, stepped out, crossed the street and entered a doorway on Teinfaltstrasse.

Earlier in the day, the VW driver had secured a sophisticated video camera to the VW's front dash. As she drove, the camera continued taping. The camera lenses moved in a rotating fashion, capturing everything within a 360 degree range.

Making a note of the address, the woman driver reached over and flipped a switch turning the machine off. Feeling very pleased with herself, she headed for the Russian Embassy knowing she had accomplished all she had been instructed to do.

CHAPTER TWENTY THREE

The city was in the midst of rush hour traffic, and the cars were moving at a snail's pace as the workers began their tiresome journeys back to their homes. When the lights turned green, tires squealed, and cars raced to the next light which was already red.

Sitting in the back of the taxi, Collins could not imagine why big cities, such as Vienna, didn't have all their lights synchronized to keep traffic flowing smoothly, in order to save gas and reduce pollution.

The Hilton hotel lobby was as busy in the evening, when Collins returned, as it was in the morning when he had first arrived. Several tourists were once again being assigned rooms, and the conversations seemed to be in a variety of languages.

Johnny waited near the elevator, behind an American couple who were touring Europe for the first time. He couldn't help overhearing their conversation and feeling sorry for them, because the couple didn't have the faintest idea about traveling. Just listening to them talk, Johnny knew the couple was much too trusting to survive their trip without an unpleasant incident.

Suddenly, Johnny remembered he needed to change money, in the event he left the hotel for his evening meal. He started back toward the cashier desk and when he passed the reservation desk, he noticed an envelope in the slot by his room number.

With the envelope in his hand, Johnny turned to the cashier and changed two hundred dollars into Austrian Schillings. Then, he walked back into the lobby and searched for an empty leather chair. He only wanted a moment to sit down, gather his thoughts and to read the message.

Carefully, Johnny inserted his ball point pen under the envelope flap, holding the paper away from his eyes. He pulled out the type written paper with two fingers. It read simply, "REQUEST A MEETING. WILL CALL LATER." Johnny frowned. He looked around the room to see if anyone was watching.

The large lobby was full of several small groups gathered together, as if they were planning their next activity. Johnny saw that the lobby could be entered from at least ten different entrances, several were outside exits. Finally, he decided it was useless to try and see who had sent the note. He crossed to the elevators. He only wanted the comfort of a shower and the peace and quiet of his room.

The room was as Johnny remembered it earlier. The only change was that the plant with the listening device was back on the desk. He had no way of knowing if the maid might have moved the plant, or if he might have had other visitors in the room while he was gone. After placing his briefcase on the entrance table, he walked to the desk.

Checking the plant carefully, he smiled when he found no one had removed the bug. He went back to the entrance hall and checked to make sure the device on the leg of the table was still in place. For a moment, he thought about going over the room once more to see if any more listening devices had been added, but he thought better of it and went for a shower.

Later, feeling refreshed, he put on a robe and stretched out on the bed to relax and think. He had opened the curtains, and as he laid on the bed, he gazed out the window and let his mind flow freely over the events of the last couple days.

Barr's death may revolve around his last assignment to Moscow. What had he done there? Why was the opposition so interested in him? What did he know? How was his wife involved? Was her sister in Frankfurt involved? Was Barr the one who had leaked the messages from the Embassy? His mind whirled as he thought of all the questions that needed an answer.

Finally, he closed his eyes for just a moment. He pulled a pillow over his head and fell asleep. It was almost seven.

CHAPTER TWENTY FOUR

Feeling a chill, Johnny rolled over almost falling off the bed. The sudden cold brought him back to reality. He sat up in bed and looked around trying to get a sense of awareness. Once the room and surroundings looked familiar, he got dressed.

His grumbling stomach was giving him a definite signal of hunger. He was still feeling very tired and decided he had only enough energy to catch a bite to eat in one of the hotel restaurants. Dressed in slacks and a sports shirt, he sat down to tie his shoes. The telephone rang.

"Hello," he answered with one hand holding the receiver and the other trying to adjust a button on his shirt.

"I left a message. I'd like to talk to you. Could you meet me in the city park, across from the Hilton? I'll be near the second bench nearest the water." The voice spoke rough, but with a touch of an American accent.

"How will I know you?" Johnny asked, trying to put a face with the voice.

"You'll know me."

"What time?" Johnny glanced at his watch. It was only a few minutes after seven.

"In twenty minutes."

With this, the phone went dead. Johnny stood up, and stared at the receiver in his hand. He had no doubt the man he had just talked to was Russian. Although his English was good, as if he were schooled in mid-U.S.A., he spoke with determination, in a demanding European manner, a tone Americans didn't use.

Deciding he had nothing to lose by meeting with the stranger, Johnny tested his belt buckle. He wanted to make sure it was working properly. He didn't want to be caught without something to help him should he need it. Out of habit, he patted his leg and felt the Swiss Army knife in a holder inside his left sock.

On the other leg, he quickly attached a Velcro small brown holster that held a long, thin knife with a very sharp blade. Usually this knife was kept concealed behind a secret compartment in his briefcase.

He put the small flashlight into his sports jacket pocket. The briefcase compartment held a couple other things, but as he glanced at them, he decided there was nothing else he might need for the meeting. He definitely knew he wouldn't need a starlight scope. He didn't have a gun, nor did he plan on doing any shooting. Looking around the room, he picked up his room card, secured his door, and walked out into the hallway.

He looked down the empty hallway, considered taking the steps, but headed for the elevator. With his back to the wall, he stood and waited. He saw a couple come out of the room next door to his.

They were a young couple, in their early to mid thirties. The woman was tall, thin and had long black silky hair. She was wearing a tight red jumpsuit and red leather boots. The top of her jumpsuit was decorated with hundreds of little colored beads. Her face was long and narrow with very high cheekbones. She looked disappointed.

Her husband was a plain nondescript ordinary looking man without strong features. He was an average height, weight, and common face, nothing that showed he had a special quality to attract such a beautiful wife. He was wearing a pair of faded blue jeans, a white shirt and a blue blazer.

Johnny thought, opposites do attract, as he watched the couple approach. He wondered if the man had money. They appeared to be arguing over how they were going to spend the evening. They were both carrying heavier coats. It was obvious they had decided to leave the hotel.

As they approached the elevator, Johnny overhead them mention the Dubrovnik restaurant. Johnny's ears perked up. He was amazed how many times since he arrived in Vienna he'd heard the name of that restaurant mentioned.

The elevator arrived, and Johnny held the door open for everyone to enter. He leaned over and pressed the button for the lobby. They rode down in silence.

The young lady left the elevator first, and walked toward the reception desk with her husband behind. Standing back, taking a minute to look over the lobby, Johnny looked around as if he were searching for someone. Then, he sat in a comfortable leather chair for a few minutes, checked his watch several times, as if someone were late meeting him. Actually, he checked to see who was in the lobby, so when he walked, the faces would be easy to recognize should anyone follow him.

After what seemed to be an appropriate time, he glanced at his watch again, shook his head, got up and walked out of the hotel through the area where the shops were located. He paused occasionally to look in the display windows, but checked the reflection for anyone behind him.

Slowly, he walked past the shops and the lot where the airport buses parked. He continued across the cement driveway past several empty tour buses, and toward the bridge that would take him into the city park.

CHAPTER TWENTY FIVE

Johnny Collins crossed the street and strolled along the path toward the entrance to the park. He casually glanced back toward the hotel and saw the young couple from the hotel. They were walking in his direction.

They were the only faces he recognized. He thought nothing of the fact that they were walking toward him. The path was a short cut to the inner city.

He continued slowly, turning onto the path that would take him to the small stream that ran through the park. Stopping for a moment, he put his foot up on the cement wall that ran around the length of the park, and adjusted the lace on his shoe.

As the couple drew nearer, they turned and walked down the path that led them thorough the center of the park and away from Johnny. Johnny watched them for several seconds, and then, continued on his way.

The evening was peaceful. The street lights were shining bright overhead. The cool night air was refreshing.

Several walkers and their dogs passed Johnny. He could hear the sounds of children coming from the playground behind him. He noticed the city workers had already begun working in the flower gardens. The park was clean and alive with the sounds of the city.

Johnny could hear the sounds of a Viennese Waltz coming from the Kursalon on the other side of the park. He was pleased to see the evening waltz performances had begun for the spring tourist season.

Walking casually, enjoying the night air, Johnny passed the first bench where two men and a child sat. The two men watched the small boy, and never looked up as he passed. One of the men was bald.

Johnny kept walking. Suddenly, he heard movement. Glancing back, the bald man stood, brushed off his coat, and started down the sidewalk behind him.

111

The stone pathway intersected with several other paths near the Johann Strauss statue. Near the statue, Johnny turned his head slightly and saw the man was still behind him. The second bench was directly in front of Johnny.

A lady occupied it. She was pushing a baby carriage back and forth with her foot. A newspaper had been spread out across the entire length of the bench. She never looked up as Johnny approached.

He wondered what to do next, so he kept walking. He crossed to a deserted path and continued walking until he came upon an unoccupied bench. His heart raced. The area was more deserted than he would have liked. The nearest street light was over a half a block away.

He brushed some twigs off the bench, sat down as if he were going to rest and watch the world. Within a few moments, the bald man, sat down on the bench beside him. The two men sat in silence for several minutes, both looked around as if enjoying the quiet of the evening.

"How did you enjoy your trip from the states, and how are you enjoying Vienna?" the bald man asked, with the mid-western accent that Johnny recognized from the phone call earlier.

"I love Vienna and the trip was fine," Johnny answered as if the man next to him were another tourist.

"You realize of course, we have known you were in the country from the moment you arrived at the airport?" the Russian stated with a sense of superiority.

Johnny laughed and answered, "Yes, I thought I saw one of your "watchers" when I arrived. I knew the boy, who looked like a college student, would be calling his superiors as soon as he recognized my face." Johnny turned, smiled and looked directly at the man sitting beside him. He asked, "You did show him a good picture of me, didn't you? I hope it was from my right side? After all, that's my best profile side." He turned his face so that his right side was toward the stranger.

"You Americans, always with the humor," the Russian said. "Come now. You could not have picked our man out so fast. Then again, maybe it is time we put some new ones at the airport." He shifted on the bench and glanced around. "At least ours aren't as obvious as some of yours at JFK. But that's not why I wanted to talk to you. I want to know if you want to trade or share some information?"

"How could you possibly know what I would want to know?" Johnny answered with a chuckle.

The stranger ran his hand over his face and put his hand flat on the bench and leaned toward Collins. "We know lots of things. We know all about your dead Mr. Barr. We know who's leaking information from your Embassy. We know why Mr. Barr was killed. We know many things of interest to you Americans. Do you not want to know about all these things that we know?"

"We know almost all of these things already," Johnny answered as if the Russian had nothing new to offer. Johnny was acting with a very positive attitude, trying to put the Russian off guard. Pushing his hands into his jacket pockets, Collins tried not to show his nervousness.

"But, you know something we would like to know. Aren't you even interested in knowing what it is that we want to know?" the Russian continued, beginning to show irritation with the American. As he spoke, he began to lose his American accent.

"My, my, your words are beginning to show your native tongue," Johnny teased, knowing it would make the Russian that much more upset.

"All I want to do is stop something that is about to happen which could cause a great discomfort to my country. I want to know about the satellite computer intelligence system that your president is sending to Israel," Yuri Rubin demanded, struggling to maintain his composure.

"I can't tell you about any intelligence system shipment," Johnny laughed. "Even you know I'd have to clear information like that with my superiors first. I'm sure you're aware that our

113

regulations have changed in the last couple years. When we're in the field, we don't have all the knowledge at our finger tips on every thing happening within our government." Johnny spoke slowly, hoping his companion would begin to loosen up and tell more than he had planned.

Rubin snapped back, "Don't treat me as if I am an idiot. I know all you have to do is get on one of the machines in the Communication Center of your Embassy. You simply call your boss, Melvin Hubert, at CIA Headquarters in Langley, Virginia. Relay details of this meeting and he'll give you his okay in exchange for information on who is feeding all the classified information to the press." Rubin looked at his watch and continued, "Let's see, you should have that permission by noon tomorrow. Then, I'll be expecting to hear from you. If not, I'll contact you personally." He stood and looked down at Collins, "Oh, by the way, Collins. I wouldn't move the plant in your room out to the window. It might get cold and die. Oh, yes, did you enjoy your headache this morning?"

The Russian chuckled to himself and walked away, turned and with a slight goodbye gesture began down the path toward the music. Johnny thought about following, but knew the Kursalon would be full of tourists. Their energetic dancing would make it almost impossible to follow the Russian.

As he watched, Collins was surprised to see the man and child, who had been sitting on the first bench, and the lady with the baby carriage walk down the path behind the Russian. Johnny smiled to himself and wondered who was following who.

The only thing that Johnny knew for sure, was that the man was Russian and well informed. Johnny was positive the man was the same man who had been the passenger in the blue VW that had driven by the Embassy several times since he arrived.

Glancing at his watch, he realized it was too late to do anything. He decided he'd check the files at the Embassy in the morning and then send a report to Langley.

Johnny walked the path back to the hotel more relaxed than he'd been since his arrival. Although he was thinking of everything that was ahead for the next day, he couldn't help but wonder why a computer shipment was so important that it would bring out the opposition.

He was sure Chief-of-Station Greenly would know something of the shipment if anyone within the Embassy did. Suddenly, he began to feel the strain of the day, and his stomach rumbled from lack of food.

CHAPTER TWENTY SIX

Meanwhile, across town from the Hilton Hotel, in the nineteenth district, three men prepared to enter a restaurant. Each arrived in his own car. One drove to the meeting in a red Ford, another was parked across the street in a white Mercedes, and the third was parked down the block in a gray Audi. They had agreed to meet at the restaurant entrance at exactly eight-thirty.

The red Ford arrived first, and the driver watched the other two cars arrive within minutes. Haddah sat in his red Ford, not wanting to be exposed any more than necessary. He hated meeting out in public, but knew this was probably the best place in town not to attract attention.

The restaurant served an international cliental. It was located on Billroth Strasse, in the middle of the nineteenth district. Over ninety-five percent of the Vienna diplomats lived in this district.

The restaurant was known for its Middle Eastern cuisine, and was frequented by the Arab community. On any evening, a passerby could easily count twenty or more expensive cars, with diplomatic license plates, parked in front. The chauffeurs or bodyguards usually waited out front.

All three of the men, meeting tonight, were in Vienna without families and lived in or near the first district, the heart of the city. However, all three men were frequent visitors to the nineteenth district for various reasons.

At exactly eight-thirty, all three car doors opened, and the three gentlemen got out, as if the scene were part of a movie and had been carefully rehearsed. They looked around the area.

The man who got out of the red Ford was tall and thin with a ruddy complexion. He was dressed in a very expensive tailored blue suit, and glanced from side to side as he walked. He appeared to be very sure of himself. His dark hair was stylishly cut, with a slight wave. Women found him attractive, and he took complete advantage of their admiration.

He was a native born Lebanese. His features were dark, but extremely handsome. His name was George Haddah. The occupation listed on his passport was businessman. However, throughout the Middle East underground, he was Colonel Haddah.

He was an international terrorist and leader of the militant Democratic Front for the Liberation of Palestine, the DFLP, and a supporter of most anti-US terrorist groups throughout the Arab world.

Another Middle Easterner stepped from the new white Mercedes. He was considerably shorter and heavier than the man from Lebanon. This man was born in Syria. He was not as handsome, nor as wealthy as the Lebanese man, but more deadly. He walked with the grace of a fighter. Born an only child, big for his age, he learned to take care of himself with his fists. His name was Mehmet Gadhafi. He was no relation to the famous Colonel Gadhafi.

Mehmet Gadhafi had been trained in all forms of guerilla warfare and self preservation. He was, at the present time, the chief assassin for the Syrian government. He had been sent to Vienna to mix with the terrorist groups, keep abreast of the latest international developments, and report back to his country on the Lebanese man, George Haddah.

The GRU Colonel got out of the gray Audi sport car, and brushed dirt from his trousers. He lived in Vienna under the cover of an under secretary to the Russian Economic Section and an Assistant Military Attaché. His position was a definite advantage for the Russians, because he could ask questions about arrivals and departures of personnel, shipments, companies, and businesses.

The two men with whom he was meeting didn't know what the Colonel's true mission was in Vienna, nor did they know his position within the GRU, but they suspected. As in this matter, and all international diplomacy, things were not what they seemed.

All three men walked into the restaurant within seconds of one another. They looked at the customers already seated.

The room was dark, lit only with small hanging lanterns and candles on the tables. The entire restaurant smelled of garlic, coffee, and strong cigarettes.

When the waiter saw the men enter, he nodded. The men walked through an arched doorway, filled with hanging beads, into a back room.

The room in which they entered was not as noisy and bright as the main room. They sat at a large circular wood table with large wood upholstered comfortable chairs. This room was only used for special meetings.

A small lamp, hanging over the table gave an eerie appearance to the room. There was a pot in the middle of the table with three bottles of mineral water in it. Without looking at menus, the men ordered something to eat from the waiter who followed them into the room. When the waiter left the room, the older man from the Russian Embassy motioned with a nod of his head. Before he began to talk, he looked around the room to see if someone could be listening in on their conversation. Taking a small portable transmitter from his pocket, he walked to the window on the other side of the room.

Turning on the machine, he placed it near a plant on the windowsill. The small device had very limited range but would send out a screeching sound that would discourage anyone who might be listening from directly outside the window. In the room, he trusted his comrades and knew they would not have any listening devices with them.

He never was a man to take chances, and this evening was no exception. Convinced this would work, he walked back to his seat and smiled at the other two men.

"Well, gentleman, it's unfortunate, but Barr didn't live long enough to give us all the information we had hoped. Have you found out anything since our talk this afternoon?" Golodin asked turning to George Haddah.

The tall, thin Lebanese man spoke, "First, I found out that the satellite computer intelligence shipment will be arriving in Vienna in a couple days, possibly over the weekend. I haven't been able to find out where it will be stored until it is shipped to Israel. Earlier today, the Colonel and I discussed activating our plans all at the same time to create mass confusion. That would give us more time to take possession of the satellite equipment. I called my Hamas friends. They're willing to help for fifty thousand dollars. I told them I'd be in touch later tonight or first thing in the morning. They know I'll be their only contact. I don't want any of you in touch with them. Is that understood?"

"Yes, that is fine," Golodin said. "Do we furnish the equipment or do they? How many men does the fifty thousand buy?"

"They said they'd prefer using their equipment which will be remote devices. They said they are the easiest to control." Haddah rubbed his injured hand and looked at both of the men. He continued, "They said they could get as many men needed for the projects. They'll plant the bombs over the weekend when the guard is the weakest. I've been assured the bombs won't detonate until they're triggered. There will be no accidents such as the one that occurred recently in Cairo. Shall I tell them to start with the arrangements?"

"Whose cars will be chosen? When and where will this happen?" Gadhafi whispered. He leaned forward in his chair with a big smile on his face.

"Who do any of you suggest?" the Russian asked, really not caring who was targeted.

"I say we try for the American Ambassador. He's such a lover of the Israelis," Gadhafi answered.

"That's fine with me," Haddah said. "But, I think we should also target someone outside the diplomatic community, more of a common person. Do either of you have someone in mind?"

When no one answered Haddah continued, "Well, we plan on having all the bombs coordinated to go off during the British reception early next week. It's scheduled for Monday night. I'd imagine they would invite some of their most respected businessmen to the reception. How about the Director of British Oil? He's to be in town for a meeting with OPEC members."

"That's fine with me," Golodin said. "He would be ideal. Targeting him would send waves through the business community. Is everyone in agreement? Are we sure he's going to be at the reception or at least somewhere in the city on Monday?"

"Yes, I have it on good source that he's due to arrive Monday morning on the direct BA flight from London. He's invited to the reception and I think he'd be present. It should not be difficult to get his travel arrangements and what vehicle he'll be using. The British Oil office here should know it. I imagine between one of our countries, there's someone that could have the information within minutes."

Gadhafi spoke, "I will find out his travel plans. I know someone that works for British Air that owes me a big favor."

Haddah nodded. "May, I tell the Hamas to go ahead with the bombs? That would be a bomb for the American Ambassador, one for the British Oil Director and at least one in the British Embassy. That will be three altogether."

Golodin answered, "That sounds fine. When do they want their money?"

Haddah smiled. He turned and looked directly at each of the men.

"I will find out, but I will tell them that they will get it when the computer shipment is in our hands. Now, what kind of damage do you want? Do you want to send a scare or do you want people killed?"

Gadhafi answered quickly. "We want to send a warning. Don't plan to kill anyone, but should someone get in the way, it's too bad."

"Tell them the bomb inside the British Embassy should be only a warning," Golodin said. "The car bombs are to destroy the intended cars as well as any parked cars beside them. That would be enough damage. We don't want a massacre on our hands."

Both men answered, "We agree."

Golodin leaned back in his chair and sighed. "Now, let's get back to the satellite computer shipment. Haddah, you said you know when the shipment is due to arrive, but we still don't know where it will be stored."

"I know that answer. They're storing the shipment in a warehouse in the area outside the Prater near the Danube," Gadhafi answered.

"Very good," Golodin said. "Our main goal is to make sure the shipment doesn't reach Israel. When I came to you both about this matter less than a month ago, I thought maybe the Americans would change their minds but it is not to be. The rich Jews in America have pressured Washington and succeeded. How is the shipment to arrive?"

Haddah reached inside his jacket pocket and took out a typed piece of paper. He turned toward the lamp and read, "The shipment left by ship from Minneapolis on the fifteenth of this month. Everything is in wooden crates marked "farm machinery." The Americans have somewhat altered their plans. Barr told us the shipment was coming under the disguise of "building supplies." My sources informed me, the out of the way route was taken so as not to attract attention. It will come to Vienna and then be transport to Israel. I've not been able to get a bill of lading. Rumor has it, that the crates might also contain surplus American tanks and jeeps. I've been told the Americans have included some type of desert uniform, similar to what they used in the attack on Hussein."

Golodin shook his head in disgust. "I wouldn't be surprised. We will plan on taking the shipment at the same time. Do any of you have any questions?"

"What will happen to the computer shipment?" Gadhafi asked.

Golodin smiled. "I know both of you would like to have it shipped to your countries, but it is going to Moscow. I already have two railroad cars ready that will be used as decoys. There is a plane waiting at Ferihegy right now. It will be used to ship the computers to Moscow."

Gadhafi smiled. "At least it won't be used against my country. That is all I care about."

"We could always blow it into a million pieces," Haddah said.

Golodin stared at Haddah. After several seconds, he said, "That would be the last resort, and only as a last resort. Is that understood?"

Haddah replied, "Yes." He poured himself a glass of mineral water from one of the bottles in the middle of the table. He looked at the two men and without speaking offered them each a glass. They both declined his offer.

Mehmet Gadhafi looked at both of the men and said, "Since we're going ahead with the abduction of the school bus, I found out that the warehouse which will be receiving the shipment is privately owned. The owner has a son about ten years old. It just happens that the son attends the American International School on Salmannsdorfer Strasse. Also, he rides a school bus to and from school. I suggest we take the school bus that the warehouse owner's son rides."

"I know we discussed this before, but we can't harm children. Some of our Embassy staff have children attending that school. If we harm the children, we'd be hurting ourselves!" Haddah blurted out in disgust.

"Wait! Let us hear what our friend from Syria has to say," the Russian interrupted, playing the role of the peacemaker.

"I personally watched the boy being picked up by the bus in the morning and have watched him get off the bus in the afternoon about three-thirty. I've not watched the security at the school, but I will. I propose we take the bus hostage, drive it outside of town for a couple hours, park it and turn everyone loose. No one would be injured. I think in that period of time the parents would be worried enough. We could call the American Embassy and demand a large sum of money just to cover our tracks. We know they will not pay it, but it will give the police something to worry about. What do you think?" Mehmet asked, looking to the others for some sign of approval.

The Russian was the first to answer. "I think it would be great. It will keep the police busy. We take the bus after school and then bomb the British embassy later in the evening. Then, sometime during the two incidents, we steal the satellite computer shipment from the warehouse. It is wonderful. We'll have to work out a thousand and one details ahead of time. Do you know if the buses are equipped with radios?"

Haddah sighed, "I agree as long as none of the children are hurt. The car bombs would be threats to the adults and the school bus to the children. No one would be safe."

Gadhafi smiled. "I don't know about any radio system, but they probably carry cell phones. I'll work out the details with the help of my friend here." He pointed to Haddah.

The Russian noticed for the first time that the waiter was standing by the door. "Yes, you may serve us now," he said and motioned to the waiter.

The three men observed silence until the meal was served and partially eaten. When he noticed they were almost finished eating, the Russian began reviewing the plans they had discussed earlier in the evening.

As the men finished their meal and pushed their plates to the side, they agreed to meet the next night. They decided that Gabrielle would be responsible for taking over the bus.

She was already established in the school and the children would have a tendency to trust a woman, especially someone they had seen around the school during the past couple weeks.

All three men left money on the table that would more than cover the cost of their food and the privacy of the room. They shook hands inside the building, and said their farewells.

The Russian stopped to pick up his small transmitter and was the last to leave the room. On the way out, he asked the waiter to reserve the same room for the next evening at the same time. The waiter smiled and nodded his approval to the request.

After the men left the restaurant, the waiter began to clear up the room. When he removed the dirty dishes and cleaned the area, he also removed the brass pot that was sitting in the middle of the table holding the mineral water bottles.

He took the dishes and the pot into the kitchen. He was alone in the kitchen, and quickly removed the small tape recorder from underneath the pot. He carefully put the tape in his pocket, took out a new tape and inserted it in the machine, replacing it back underneath the pot.

Taking a cloth as if he were doing some cleaning, he took the brass pot and walked back into the room which the men had just left. Quickly, he placed the pot back on the table, and checked to see that everything was in order.

After all the customers were gone, the waiter and the cook remained to prepare for the next day. With almost all the work finished, the waiter turned to the cook and told him to go home.

Once the cook left, the waiter went to the telephone, dialed a number and spoke briefly. He walked once more through the restaurant, making sure all the equipment and lights were turned off. Glancing at his watch, he walked to the door and looked out.

He saw a car pull up in front of the restaurant as he stepped out and locked the door behind him. The car parked. The waiter walked over to it.

The passenger side window was down. He tossed the tape through the open window, without stopping. He continued up the street toward his apartment.

The driver shifted into gear and drove down the street toward the first district. The car was a small blue Volkswagen. The streetlight reflected off the driver's bald head.

CHAPTER TWENTY SEVEN

Yuri Rubin returned to the Russian Embassy after his evening activities. He had listened to parts of the tape from the meeting at the Middle Eastern restaurant. He had mixed emotions about using bombs. They often caused more damage than expected. But, he had to agree with the men. The satellite shipment to Israel had to be stopped.

As he sat thinking, his telephone rang. With a tired voice, he answered, "Yes."

"Push your switch," the other voice said.

Rubin reached across his telephone for the black box sitting on his desk. He pushed a switch that he knew would distort and scramble his words.

Only two people had similar boxes. One was the GRU Colonel Golodin and the other was the Director in Moscow. There were no clicks signifying the call was long distance. Rubin knew it was Golodin.

"It's done," Rubin answered, leaning back in his chair, putting his long legs on top of his desk. He felt very American, just like the scenes from the western movies.

"What did you learn from Collins? You did meet with him, didn't you?" Colonel Golodin questioned.

"Yes, I met with him. He appeared not to have known anything about the shipment. I don't think Langley told him. However, he knows about it now and I'm sure he'll question Hubert."

Golodin answered, "Yes, I agree."

Rubin smiled and asked, "How was your meeting?"

"The meeting went fine. We're going forward with our plans. Hopefully, we will be successful and have the computer shipment on the way to Moscow before this time next week. But, if not, we'll have to blow up the shipment ourselves."

Rubin sighed and felt a cold breeze. He answered, "Let's hope not. Those computers are the latest state-of-the-art and worth billions. They could help our country."

"Yes, I know," Golodin answered. "We will do everything we can to keep the shipment safe. Tonight, I heard that the shipment might also contain some tanks, uniforms and jeeps. I may just give those items to my men. It would help their causes."

Rubin was surprised at Golodin's remark. He didn't want to make any decisions on those items now. He replied, "I'm tired. I'm going to bed. Is that all you wanted?" He made a loud yawning noise directly into the phone.

Golodin asked, "Did Collins suspect Barr of being one of my agents?"

"No," Rubin answered. "He never said anything about Barr. We just talked about the shipment. That was my main concern. Now, I'm going home and to bed. Good night."

Rubin hung up the phone and flipped the switch back to manual. He was too tired to talk about anything. It had been a very long day.

CHAPTER TWENTY EIGHT

It was almost seven-thirty when Johnny arrived at the Embassy. He was surprised to see so many Embassy cars. Pushing the door bell, he waited for the door to open, knowing the receptionist wouldn't be in for another thirty minutes.

The Marine on duty released the lock and Johnny went up the stairs and through all the gates to sign the before duty log. He flashed his diplomatic passport and the State Department Identification card he had in his suit jacket.

After checking Johnny's papers, the Marine checked the visitor list for official verification of Johnny's clearances. Seeing that everything was in order, the Marine handed Collins a yellow badge which authorized him complete unescorted access to all of the Embassy buildings.

The Marine checked a pad on the desk in front of him and then said, "Sir, I've been asked to tell you Mr. Swartz is waiting for you in his office. He came in about thirty minutes ago. Shall I buzz him that you're in the building and on your way?"

"Yes, please do," Johnny answered.

The Marine reached for the phone and looked back at Johnny and asked, "Do you know the way, sir?"

"Yes, thanks. I was here all day yesterday. I'll be fine. Thank you."

The walk to Swartz's office gave Johnny a few more minutes to decide what to tell Swartz. During the taxi ride, he decided he wouldn't tell anyone but Greenly about his evening rendezvous with the Russian. He wanted to find out what Greenly knew about a computer shipment. "Good morning, Jim. You're looking much better today than you did last night," Johnny remarked walking into Swartz's office.

"You're looking better yourself. Did you have a good night's sleep?"

"Yes. I went back to the hotel, ate, and slept like a baby. It's amazing how much better one feels after a good night's sleep. Have you had any feedback on any of our questions?"

Swartz dug though a pile of folders on his desk. He put one on top of the file and opened it. "You're to cable your home office as soon as you can. You have a couple messages that arrived just minutes ago. We called the hotel, but the hotel switchboard said there was no answer in your room. You must have already left."

"Great," Johnny said reaching for the file. "Thanks. Who's working this morning?"

"Mason's there now. The two couriers are due in today. Karl Jennings from the Moscow run will arrive this morning. Kay Blackburn will be in later. She'll be taking the rest of the pouches to Frankfurt. Will you want to talk to them?"

"Yes, I will. What time is the memorial service again?"

"It's at ten. That gives us plenty of time to go over things. Blinksdale will be in soon. Greenly's been in and gone. He plans on running by the Barr house first. Mrs. Barr was to leave on the Delta flight this morning at seven, and her sister is due in about eight this morning. Greenly was going to have his driver take Mrs. Barr to the airport while he stayed in the house until the driver got back. He thought the sister would arrive by then. He also has a man with him at the house in case he needs to leave and she hasn't arrived. I think they're going to give the apartment a once over this morning. If you need him, you can call him there."

"No, that's alright," Johnny answered. "I'll just wait until he gets back to the Embassy, but I do want to go to the service. Could you be sure and get me when you're ready to go? I think I'll go ahead and go into the center now and send a cable back to Virginia."

Johnny walked out of the room and headed for the Communication Center. He noticed a cable on Swartz's desk and wondered why Swartz had purposely placed his arm across the message. He made a mental note to check if anything of interest had been logged in overnight.

After several moments of writing and re-editing, he decided to write a memo regarding Barr first, then include a short paragraph regarding Sue Farris, her harassment claims and close with a request to check on Swartz and his large deposits. He knew Blinksdale was checking but he wanted to be double sure.

In a second note, he wrote a detailed description of the previous night's activities with the Russian, and what the Russian wanted to know. The whole composition process took less than an hour.

Collins reread the papers, and checked the next four sheets on his pad for any indentures. He didn't want anyone else to be able to read his message. Those four pages went with him to the shredding machine.

Next, he went to one of the transmitting machines and personally sent his messages. Later, he would check with Mason to make sure the message had been transmitted and received in Virginia.

Finished, Johnny took his handwritten pages and put them through the shredder. While Mason checked on his message, Johnny checked the log book that held a listing of all the messages received in the Communication Center. He glanced down the page, checking from the time he had left yesterday, until present time. His eyes stopped on a message that had arrived early in the morning for Greenly. He saw the notation that Greenly had already read the message.

Glancing at his wristwatch, Johnny realized he just had time to stop by Blinksdale's office before the memorial service. He noticed, as he walked toward Swartz's office, that the Embassy was much quieter than normal. He met several people in the hallway who said "good morning", but with a solemn tone.

Swartz was sitting at his desk, finishing with the paperwork when Johnny returned. "I'm going over to the church in a few minutes, Johnny. Want to come with me?"

Johnny glanced at his watch. He answered,"No, since there is still a few minutes, I'm going to run past Blinksdale's office and then go over. I'd like to go out to the Barr apartment this afternoon. Do you think you could arrange it?"

"Sure," Swartz answered, making a note on his desk top calendar. "I'm not sure I'll go with you. I've got the couriers, and I want to be here when they leave. You do want to see them, don't you?"

"I thought maybe for a few minutes, before I went to the apartment. After the church service, I'll stop back here and maybe we can coordinate something."

Johnny walked out of the room, while Swartz put away the pile of folders on his desk. He walked down the stairs and into Blinksdale's Security office. Blinksdale was his desk, working his way through a stack of unfinished paperwork.

"I just left Swartz. He's buried in paperwork, and now I see you are too," Johnny said with a smile.

"I swear, for every piece we send to Washington, we get four times the paperwork back. I'm in the process of writing reports about Barr's murder. I know they'll come back and want at least a couple more things described more completely. I don't know where in the world they keep all the papers." Blinksdale shook his head in disgust when he looked at the papers piled high on his desk.

"Anything new I should know?" Johnny asked as he pulled a chair closer to the desk. The door was open, but Blinksdale nodded for him to close it.

"First," Blinksdale said, after Johnny sat back down. "Mrs. Barr left this morning on the Delta flight at seven. Her sister should be here by now. She was due in from Frankfurt between eight and nine. I personally checked on Mrs. Barr last night. She was very concerned, and insisted her sister be present when her household goods were packed for shipment to the states. Her sister has full power of attorney, and has written permission to take some of the furniture to her home in Frankfurt. I thought it was a very unusual request from Mrs. Barr, considering her state of mind. Something doesn't seem right." He paused for a moment and looked at Johnny. "Regardless, Mrs. Barr's sister, Eve Metcalf, will be attending the memorial service."

"I'd like to meet her," Johnny said.

"That shouldn't be a problem," Blinksdale answered. He searched for a file on his desk and after finding it, he said, "A similar small blue VW like the one you told me about, was parked in front of Kevin Smith's apartment last night. Kevin's apartment is next door to the Barr apartment. I wrote down the license number and had it checked. It's different from the one you gave me. This blue VW is registered to the Swiss Embassy, to a woman named Katrina Borg. It didn't have diplomatic plates, so she must be a secretary, or she could be with the intelligence department. They never have their agents listed as diplomats."

Johnny took out his notebook and made a note. "Are you checking on this woman?"

"I hadn't planned to, but I can," Blinksdale answered, making a note. "Kevin's notorious for his affairs, so she could be what she seems, or not. We both know single guys attract female agents. In his position he needs to be careful."

"I think I'll take down the license number if you don't mind," Johnny said.

"Let me see," Blinksdale answered, flipping though his memo pad about the same size as Collins's. "Here it is, W-634276."

"Now, all the "W" license plates mean Vienna, don't they?" Johnny asked.

"Yes. Also, all the cars you see with a white oval and a black CD in the middle are diplomatic cars. You can always tell diplomatic cars by their license plates. Here, I'll give you one of these plastic cards." Blinksdale handed Johnny a plastic card the size of a credit card. "On both sides are listings from one to a hundred. Beside the number is the country which they represented."

Collins studied it for a moment.

Blinksdale said, "Look at the number five. This means when you see that license number "WD-5," then a dash and more numbers, that car belongs to the American Embassy. Notice the number "54." That's the Russian Embassy. You can keep the card if you like. You never know when you might need it."

"Thanks. Anything else?" Johnny asked, after checking his watch.

"One other thing. The body is to be autopsied today in D.C. We should know the results by tonight. The messages are slowly dribbling in about Barr. Swartz, Mason, Farris, and Smith have checking and savings accounts. We'll hear more today when the branch banks open. The only thing I've found out is that Swartz has been making big deposits in his savings accounts. They're checking on the sources now. We'll know later. Also, it seems the Barr's have a savings and checking account through the military banking system in Frankfurt. It's being checked for any large deposits. I also am having them check Mrs. Barr's sister. More on that later." He glanced up at the clock on his wall, stood and started putting all of his papers into one pile.

Johnny said, "Yes, we should go to the service."

Blinksdale put everything into an open safe drawer, closed it and spun the lock several times. "The newspapers this morning didn't play it up, so I don't think they'll be a large attendance from the international community. But we'll see!"

Both men walked toward the door. Blinksdale was the last one out. He turned, and with a key from his pocket, locked the door. He smiled at Collins and added, "You never know."

When the men walked down the steps, they saw a large crowd gathered outside the church. Everyone was shaking hands and talking to each other. The scene appeared to be more like a cocktail party than a memorial service.

Johnny stepped back to watch the crowd, letting Blinksdale go on by himself. Johnny wanted to see who arrived. Several women arrived in Embassy cars, got out, and walked into the church. Another black Embassy staff car arrived, and Greenly and a middle-aged woman got out.

Greenly looked around the area, noticed Collins, nodded, took the arm of the lady and entered the church. As soon as Greenly went inside, the Ambassador, who was standing by the side of the building, nodded to the crowd and entered. The group followed.

Cars were still driving by and delivering their passengers as Johnny prepared to cross the street. He noticed there were more Austrian guards than normal guarding the Embassy.

The crowd quietly filed into the church. Collins stayed back, watching. He listened to the birds singing in the trees. He couldn't help but think it was a beautiful day for a memorial service. At least it wasn't as cold and windy as it had been the past couple days.

Just as he walked to the curb, the familiar blue VW drove directly past him. Johnny was within five feet of the car when it passed.

There was no mistaking the driver of the car. Johnny had talked to him the night before. He was alone.

The driver looked directly at Johnny, but didn't acknowledge his presence. The driver drove slowly, he looked at the cars on the street, and seemed to be most interested in the license numbers.

Johnny recognized a small black object on the VW dashboard. "Well I'll be damned," Johnny said aloud. "The bastard is video taping the scene."

Johnny watched the car move down the street past the hotel and around the corner. When the car was out of sight, he looked around. The street was quiet, he entered the darkness of the church to the sound of the organ music and took a seat in the back.

While Collins was trying to see who was attending the service, he felt a nudge on his arm. He followed the arm to the face, and saw a very attractive brunette motioning for him to move over. He did, but wondered who she was, and why she had arrived so late.

He glanced at her out of the corner of his eye as he listened to the service. Tears flowed down her face when the Ambassador spoke of Barr's good qualities.

Johnny noticed she wore little makeup, and was deeply affected by the Ambassador's words. He watched her wipe her eyes and quickly leave the church before the service was over.

CHAPTER TWENTY NINE

Realizing that the service was almost over, Johnny jumped up to follow the woman. Outside in the sunlight, she looked just as attractive as she had in the dim church light. She was a couple steps ahead and walked toward the Embassy.

Johnny heard her talk to the Austrian guards, as if she knew them. He followed behind, and when she started to open the heavy iron door to enter, Johnny rushed forward.

"It's a beautiful day, isn't it?" he said, for lack of something better to say, as he reached for the door.

"Yes, isn't it," she answered with a slight southern accent.

"Let me introduce myself. My name is Johnny Collins. I'm new here."

"That's nice. Do you like Vienna?" she asked as she nodded to the security guard and flashed her identification badge.

"I think so. I really haven't been here long enough to say. It seems like a lovely city."

"I'm sure you'll like it fine." She smiled and hurried up the steps.

Johnny kept a couple steps behind. She continued toward the Communication Center.

The door was closed, she pressed a button and spoke into the intercom system. Within seconds, the door opened and Mason let her into the area. Mason saw Johnny approaching and waited for him.

Once inside the room, the woman turned to Johnny. "I guess I should introduce myself. It seems as if you're known here. I never carry on a conversation with people I don't know when I'm at work. One never knows. My name is Kay Blackburn. I'm on courier duty, and I'm posted in Frankfurt. I came in early to pay my last respects."

"Nice to meet you, Kay. Jim Swartz told me you were coming. I'm from Washington, and I would like some time to talk to you later today. Would that be all right with you?"

"Sure. I've time now. Kevin Smith is getting my pouches ready. My flight doesn't leave until five this afternoon, and I need to leave for the airport around three or three fifteen."

"Fine. Let's go see if Jim is back yet. We can talk in his office."

They walked out the door and down the hall together in silence. As they approached Swartz's door, Jim Swartz turned the corner coming from the other direction. He was headed toward his office. He stopped to wait for them.

"Glad you could come in early, Kay. Did you arrive in time for the service?" Swartz asked. He reached into his pocket and unlocked his office door.

"Yes, thank you. We received your message yesterday, so I changed my flight right away. I arrived just in time to catch the Ambassador's words. I thought they were very touching." She dabbed at her eyes.

"Yes, so did I. The service was well attended." Swartz stated simply, then entered the room and pointed to chairs for Kay and Johnny.

"I thought we might like to ask Kay a few things," Johnny explained, as he pulled a chair closer to the desk. He took his notebook out of his pocket and reached across Swartz for a pen.

Swartz nodded and looked directly at Kay. From his expression, it was obvious he knew Kay had been crying.

"Would that be all right with you, Kay?" Swartz asked in a fatherly tone.

"Yes, I'd like to ask you both some questions, too," she answered. She looked at each of the men in turn.

Johnny started to explain what they wanted to know. He told her they would try to answer anything they could which she might like to know. She had to remember, however, if it was considered confidential, they couldn't tell her. Johnny explained some things were on a need-to-know basis.

When Kay heard his remark, she looked at Johnny. It was obvious by her expression that she knew Johnny wasn't a State Department official.

For the next hour, Kay told how she had met the Barr's. She described dinners she had shared with them; activities she had attended with them and the times she had gone to their home bath in Moscow and Vienna.

"Kay, have you ever seen the Barrs other than in Moscow or here in Vienna?" Johnny asked hoping to learn more.

"Yes," Kay said. "Just recently, I saw Mrs. Barr and another lady in Wiesbaden shopping. I'm not sure of the exact date. Mrs. Barr was making a purchase at the same counter."

Johnny made another note in his notebook. He asked, "What did you talk about?"

"Oh, my!" Kay exclaimed. "That was over a week ago. It was idle chatter. Now, I remember. Mrs. Barr told me they had just finished a hiking trip to Switzerland and a bit of sightseeing in Italy. Mrs. Barr mentioned she had broken a tooth, and was going to Munich for care."

Swartz looked at Johnny but didn't say anything.

Kay continued, "Now, it's my turn. I was surprised to hear about Alan. How did he die? Was it a car accident?" She looked directly into each man's eyes, searching for an answer.

Johnny got up and walked over to the coffee pot and poured a cup. He asked the other two to see if they wanted any. Swartz didn't say anything. He sat looking at the palms of his hands as if he had just discovered he had two of them. Johnny took the coffee and walked back to his chair, blowing on the cup as he walked.

After he sat, he turned toward Kay "Kay, I'm sorry but we aren't able to tell you a great deal about how Alan died. It's still under investigation. Now, just to make things clearer in my mind, explain for me in simple terms how the courier system works."

"Couriers are assigned to a certain city. That city is usually a regional office. Couriers live and work out of that city. For instance, I'm assigned to Frankfurt's regional courier office. On Monday, I go to London and back the same day. I usually get to the London Embassy in the morning, leave after lunch, and am back in Frankfurt about four or five in the evening. Usually on Fridays, I leave Frankfurt in the morning, arrive in Vienna about ten, leave about five and fly back to Frankfurt."

"That's a lot of traveling," Johnny said, after he finished making a note. "Please, go on."

"It goes like this all week long, normally a different city each day. I always go back to the mail room, which we use for the processing of all pouches. Each city has its own bags."

"How are the bags marked?" Johnny asked.

"Say, Vienna wants to send a pouch to Bonn. They put whatever in a bag and tag it BONN and seal it. The tag has the return address of Vienna. They never put something for London in a bag tagged and sealed for Bonn. But, they might take a big bag and put lots of tagged and sealed bags, for various embassies, in it. When I get to Frankfurt, someone will take all the large bags I brought back from Vienna, open them and sort all the smaller bags. They'll then take all the bags for Vienna and consolidate them into a large bag. Sometimes one large bag may contain pouches from five or six embassies going to a specific destination. However, once a bag is sealed and tagged for a specific Embassy, no one opens it until it arrives at its final destination. Do you understand? Am I making myself clear enough?"

"Yes, I think I understand. Suppose I wanted to send something to Moscow. It would be put in a bag here in Vienna, then the courier would take it to Frankfurt, and they would put all the bags for Moscow in a bigger bag, never opening the bag I sent with the original material for Moscow. Is that right?"

"Yes. The only thing is, here in Vienna we don't send the Moscow bags back to Frankfurt. We have a man who goes through Vienna on his way to Moscow. He stops by the Embassy here and picks up the Moscow bags. On his way back he flies through Helsinki, Finland, and picks up the courier mail and takes it into Frankfurt. Moscow is the only exception for Vienna."

"Any other cities have similar exceptions?" Johnny asked.

"Some. Say for instance, Paris. Paris is a regional office. They have several couriers assigned there. Some of them fly the same route all the time, and some of them fly like the Moscow courier does. We have a courier who flies into Frankfurt once a week to take pouches for the region, and then we have a fellow who delivers pouches to Paris once a week. That way, every major city has pouch service at least two times a week."

"Now, tell me just exactly how the service works as far as local transportation is concerned," Johnny asked.

"Well, sometimes we're met at the airport and turn the bags over to Embassy couriers. Other times, we go directly to the Embassy with the bags."

Johnny thought for a moment and asked, "Are all the bags alike?"

"Not at all," Kay said. "They're a cloth bag and could be green, brown or tan, made from canvas or a very heavy material, like the mail man uses. Sometimes they're even red. The large bags have a heavy locking device actually sewn into the material. Those type of bags are locked at the embassy and opened in the regional processing office."

"Does anyone ever just come to the airport and you give them a bag?" Johnny wondered.

"No," Kay answered. "It is all regulated. Some embassies, for example in dangerous areas, give us an armed escort service back and forth to the airports. At some, like Vienna, that isn't necessary. An escort from the Embassy, who drives them back to the Embassy, meets the couriers at the airport. When we arrive, we sign a paper, and that releases us from responsibility for the pouches. Then, when it's time to leave, we sign for the outgoing pouches and are driven back to the airport."

"So there is a record all the time where you are and have been?" Swartz asked.

"Suppose to be," Kay answered. "We are always the last people on the airplane, and the first ones off. We take the bags directly to the loading area at the airport. We always ride with the pouches out to the plane and watch them loaded. After the pouches are on, we board the flight like normal passengers. The last ones on."

"It's well organized," Swartz stated, looking at Johnny.

Kay laughed. "Almost all embassies follow the same pattern such as the Brits, French, Germany, Swiss. I've been on the plane with couriers from all over. The British work just like we do. When we land, we get off the plane first, claim our bags, and then proceed to the Embassy or home base, whatever it is."

Johnny asked, "Do you always sit in the plane in about the same place and if you have special letters, do you wear a chain connected to a briefcase?"

"Yes, we sit about in the same place all the time. No, I'm afraid we don't do anything as exotic as carrying a briefcase chained to our wrists. I have, however, seen British and Russians that do. Sometimes the Russians will have two couriers together on the plane, to guard whatever it is they're carrying or each other."

Johnny looked at Swartz and said, "That's sound typical for the Russians."

"Once in a while, some agency wants to see how the courier system works, and they'll fly someone with us. Usually, they're only checking security, but sometimes just to see how efficient the service is. Is there anything else?"

"Yes. When you get off the plane at Frankfurt, do you ever stop on the way to the Consulate for any reason?" Johnny questioned.

"No. That's forbidden. We count our bags directly from the airplane, and then take them to the processing room, count them and release them, like I said before."

"Do you ever carry anything in that isn't in pouches?" Johnny asked.

Kay smiled and looked at Swartz. "Nothing illegal. Sometimes, though, we do bring back something personal for someone. It all depends on what it is and how big it is."

Kay was beginning to fidget in her chair. Johnny could see that his last question bothered her. He watched to see if she gave any further reaction to the question. She adjusted her dark skirt and brushed at her hair.

Johnny looked at her and wondered what kind of a life she had. The job had to offer a special satisfaction to make up for all the traveling. Kay was about thirty years old, was wearing a designer brown tweed pant suit with a yellow sweater. She wore large diamond earrings and a gold Rolex watch. On her right hand, middle finger, she wore a large single stone diamond ring.

"Kay, can you think of anything else you can tell us about Barr? I know you'll want to get a bite to eat before you go to the airport, so we don't want to keep you much longer," Swartz said. He checked the clock on the wall. "I have a few things to do myself before you leave today."

"I can't think of anything. But, if I do, who shall I call?"

"Either of us is fine," Johnny answered, looking toward Jim who was once again studying his hands.

"If it's all right then, I'll go back to the mailroom and see how everything is. Then I think I'll stop by the snack bar. The cook here makes the best American-style cinnamon rolls. I want to have one, and a cup of coffee while I'm waiting." She stood and walked toward the door, turned and asked,"I didn't see Mrs. Barr at the service. Has she gone back, do either of you know?"

"Yes, she left this morning," Jim answered.

"Fine. See you later, Kay. Thanks for all of your help," Johnny replied, opening the door. He watched her walk down the hall before he closed the door and turned back to Jim.

"Well, what do you think?" Jim asked as Johnny walked over to warm up his cup of coffee.

"Well, I think she might know more than she wanted to say or wants us to think she knows. I'd like to know what she's carried for people that wasn't in pouch bags. Don't you think she overreacted to that question?"

"Yes, I think she definitely knows something. She made a point of saying "not illegal." None of us even mentioned anything like that. Strange comment, I think. I think we need to check into that."

CHAPTER THIRTY

"Did the Moscow courier check in yet?" Johnny asked. He glanced at the coffee and decided to make a fresh pot. He wondered why Swartz had the coffee pot in his room, he never seemed to keep it fresh.

"I don't know, but he should have. Let me call the pouch room and check."

Jim hung up the phone just as Johnny walked back in with the coffee water. "Yes, Karl arrived just before noon. They think he's in the snack bar. I left word that he was to come here when he returned. They said that he'd been gone over an hour, and thought he'd be back any minute."

Before Jim could finish the sentence, the men heard a knock. "Come on in," Jim's husky voice called.

The door opened, and a short, heavy set man walked into the room. He looked as if he had slept in his clothes for the past couple days. His slacks were baggy. The belt was hidden by his stomach overlap. His hair was turning gray, and his eyes seemed to have lost all their original color. His face was lined with wrinkles and layers of fat. He adjusted his tie, which was a solid gray and matched his solid gray suit. His suit jacket hung on him the same way a blanket would. He was definitely overweight.

"I understand you want to talk to me, boss?" Jennings asked, stretching his hand out to Swartz.

Karl Jennings was in his late fifties, and had been a courier for over twenty years. He had traveled all over the world, and looked the same as he had for the last fifteen. His voice was lively, and he had a jolly manner.

Jim turned to Johnny, sitting on the other side of the desk, and introduced the two men. Johnny looked Jennings over very carefully. Collins wasn't the type of person to form quick opinions about someone before getting all the facts. But, the first thing that crossed Johnny's mind was that Jennings was a shrewd operator.

Jennings' experience and carefree attitude made Johnny think he was more than he appeared. Johnny made a mental note to read his file.

Swartz began telling Jennings why he and Collins wanted to talk to him. Jennings took a chair, and then moved to another one.

Johnny smiled, because he knew Jennings had moved not for comfort, but so he could watch both men's faces at the same time. Jennings talked for several minutes, and told the two men almost the same thing they had heard from Kay Blackburn.

Then, Jennings turned to Swartz and asked, "Isn't that what you've already heard from everyone else?"

The question startled Jim. He looked dumbfounded but didn't answer.

Jennings smiled and then continued, "Now, let me tell you what I found out on my trips to Russia."

For the next two hours, the three men spoke behind closed doors. They all talked very honestly and openly. When they were all satisfied with the answers from each other, Jennings took his heavy frame off the chair and walked toward the door.

He said, "Well, now to get back to work. I trust you all will have a good day. Nice to have met you, Johnny. Maybe I'll get a chance to see you again on one of my runs."

Johnny couldn't help but picture Jennings as Santa Claus. He looked the part, and like Santa Claus, had given them some unexpected gifts, some of the missing pieces of the puzzle about Barr.

Johnny turned to Jim after Jennings left, and sighed heavily, "Well, how about that?"

Jim smiled and answered, "Well, someone was bound to know something. It was just a matter of time before we found it out. The only thing I don't like is the idea of another double agent. Who do you think it is? It has to be a courier. Who else would have the access that he was talking about to the Embassy in Moscow?"

Johnny looked at Swartz and really didn't want to tell him what his suspicions were. One thing he knew for certain was that it wasn't as simple as it appeared.

Johnny got up and began walking toward the door, "I think I'm going to walk around the Embassy for a few minutes. I thought I'd go up to Blinksdale's office. I also want to see if Greenly is back. Don't forget, I want to go out to Barr's apartment later in the day. It's after two now. What do you say I meet the driver out front in an hour? Can you arrange that for me?"

"Sure," Jim answered. "No problem. I've already requested one this morning. It's just a matter of letting them know when you need the car. I don't think I'll go with you. I may go over with my wife this evening and pay our respects to the sister-in-law. Anyway, my wife was going over today and offer to help."

CHAPTER THIRTY ONE

Collins left Swartz's office, and as he passed the elevator, he saw two ladies just getting into it. He had never been introduced to either of them, but he recognized the taller one as Mrs. Swartz.

She was an attractive lady, dressed in a stylish long dark blue coat, and wore a soft blue hat. She looked as if she might have just come from a church service, and Johnny knew indeed she had.

The ladies looked up and held the door open for Johnny. He had been thinking of walking, but when he hesitated by the door, they thought he was waiting for the elevator. In order not to embarrass himself or the women, he walked into the elevator.

The two women continued their conversation as if Johnny were invisible. Mrs. Swartz asked the other lady about a dinner party and reception to which they both had been invited. They spoke in low voices.

He stepped off the elevator at the lobby and held the door for them. As they passed by, he noticed Mrs. Swartz was indeed much younger than her husband. She smiled and said, "Thank you."

Johnny nodded and noted that the clothes and jewelry she wore were very, very expensive. He watched the ladies walk down the hall and out of his range of vision before he turned toward Blinksdale's office.

Finding the door partially open, Johnny knocked and entered the Security office to find Blinksdale talking to Greenly. Greenly was preparing to leave, but when Collins entered, Greenly sat back down.

"I'm going to the Barr apartment before three. Would either of you like to go with me?" Johnny asked knowing he had interrupted the conversation.

"Yes, I'll go," Blinksdale answered immediately. "I want to be able to tell my home office that I checked out their residence personally. I want to CYA myself just in case something big comes down the pike."

"No, I just got back," Greenly answered. "I left a man there, but I'm sure he'd like to get back to work. You can send him back when you arrive. Can you call me when you think you'll be finished, and I'll arrange for someone to go out and relieve you? I want to keep someone in the area."

"We can call you from there and wait until he arrives. Did you order a driver, Johnny?" Blinksdale asked. He started to clear off his desk.

"Yes, he's meeting us out front. We can have the driver bring back your man, Roy. Then, when we call to leave, we can catch a ride back with your driver. That way we won't tie up a driver all day."

"Great, that saves money all the way around," Greenly answered. He looked at Johnny and made a note in his note book. "Have you found out anything today from the couriers?"

"I don't think any more than we already knew. I need to send a memo back to D.C." Johnny turned and started towards the door. He stopped and said, "Roy, I'd like to see you for a moment if you have the time."

"Why not use this office?" Blinksdale said. "I need to go check with the Marines on something. I'll be back in a couple minutes." Blinksdale immediately left the two CIA agents to themselves.

Greenly got up from his chair and walked to the desk, and sat down in Blinksdale chair. Johnny was tired of sitting, and paced the room as he told the Chief-of-Station everything he had learned from his talks with the couriers.

Greenly sat through the long report and didn't say a word, but made a few notes in his notebook. After Collins finished, Greenly took the time to explain to Collins what he knew about the satellite computer shipment which was coming through Vienna on way to Israel.

"So, what do you think, Roy? Why do you think Barr was killed?" Johnny asked.

Greenly shrugged. He thought for a moment and then answered, "I think it had something to do with the Communications Center and the articles printed in the papers. I doubt if it had anything to do with the upcoming computer shipment. Barr wouldn't have anything to do with it other than simply reading a message which might have arrived while he was on duty."

"Do you think the Russians could be interested in the computers?" Johnny asked, still not having told Greenly about his meeting with the Russian in the city park.

"No, I think that would be more a Middle Eastern concern. The Russians supply the Syrians and the Lebanese with military weapons. Now, if one of the those countries could get their hands on the computer shipment, that would be another story. But, I doubt that Moscow would let them. I understand the computers are the most sophisticated ones available today. This is a system that our President negotiated when he was talking to Israel about Middle Eastern peace. It was his bargaining tool."

"But, the peace talks fell through," Johnny answered.

Greenly smiled and answered, "That didn't matter. All the Jews in the US united and forced the issue. Hence, the shipment was shipped. Will you be stopping by the Embassy when you get back from the Barr's?"

"Yes. I plan to stop by before going back to the hotel. I want to check if I have any messages. Say, did you hear anything from the fingerprints on that note card I gave you?" Johnny asked.

"Oh, yes, I forgot about that," Greenly answered. He flipped through a couple pages in his notebook and said, "The note card held a set of your prints and a thumb and middle finger from a Yuri Rubin. Rubin was a top notch KGB agent in the late 80's. He is also a senior agent with the Mokrie Dyela and one of their "wet" men. Virginia didn't know Rubin was in Vienna."

"Well, he is," Johnny smiled.

"The last description we had on him was that he is quite tall, over six feet, big stature and thinning brown hair. Does that ring any bells with you?" Greenly asked.

"Everything except the thinning brown hair. Now, he is completely bald. He either shaves his head or has lost it all. That's the exact description of the man that I saw driving by the Embassy in the blue VW. Why do you suppose Rubin is in Vienna?" Collins questioned trying to put the pieces together in his mind.

"I don't know. Maybe, they have him based here now. Whatever he's doing here, is big. Rubin is a bad dude. He has the same reputation among the terrorist groups as Carlos, and he is just as deadly. You might want to keep a lookout for him. Although, it would be interesting to see what he wants to know. Maybe he's in town regarding that computer shipment." Greenly scratched his head and looked around the office. "Boy, I hope not. Then again, he might have been Barr's controller, if Barr was a double. That makes more sense."

"I can't quite picture someone like him, if he is that important, as a controller. It seems like a waste of manpower," Johnny answered.

"Just imagine. Barr gave Rubin classified information. Rubin pressured him for more information and Barr refused. Rubin, an expert in torture tactics, gave Barr the once over. Things went too far and Barr died. It fits the picture. But, Collins, I doubt if we'll ever be able to prove it. The only thing we can hope for is a clue in the Barr apartment showing Barr was a double agent. If we can find that, the pieces will fit perfectly. Don't you think so?" Greenly said, glancing at his watch.

"Well, one thing we know for sure is that he knows I'm in town. He also knows where I'm staying. No secrets there," Collins answered. He turned toward the door. "I'm going to find Blinksdale. It's almost three."

Collins knew Rubin would be waiting for an answer regarding their exchange of information. Now that Collins knew who Rubin was, he felt Rubin could wait. The waiting would make Rubin nervous or angry, Collins didn't know which, and at the present time, Collins really didn't care.

CHAPTER THIRTY TWO

The afternoon sun was bright and warm. The two men sat in the white Mercedes and complained of the heat and inactivity. For over three hours, they parked on the corner of Salmannsdorfer Strasse and Keylwerth Gasse and watched the activities at the American International School.

Although, they had chosen the Mercedes for its luxury, they were still uncomfortable. Part of the morning had been spent following the school bus as it made the rounds in the twenty-third district.

They followed the bus from UNIDO headquarters, across the Danube all the way to the American school. They watched the driver park in the parking lot directly behind the school.

Making notes as they watched, they saw the bus driver unload the children. They followed him as he drove a different bus to a bus garage twenty minutes from the school. It was obvious to them, the driver was a mechanic. He drove the bus route in the morning and evenings, and went back to the garage in between times.

They watched the garage and the driver until they felt they knew the driver's schedule. Their legs were cramped and their stomachs growled. Neither man had eaten since their evening meal the previous day.

Since school wouldn't be dismissed for several hours, they drove through the Vienna Woods to Grinzing. For two hours, they relaxed in a small wine cellar on Grinzinger Strasse. There, they talked to the owner, and discussed the world situations while they ate pastry and drank espresso coffee.

They returned to school, to await the dismissal of classes. They saw no one go near the buses once the buses were parked on the school grounds.

All buses looked alike. They discovered that each bus had a small number painted on its front door. Each number was different. Now, they knew which bus they would capture.

While they discussed the hijacking and the jobs each person would do, several children filed out of the school and passed near their car. The two men watched with interest.

A teacher supervised the children. While the children marched to the buses, more buses pulled into the parking lot. The bus driver they had watched in the morning arrived, walked over to his bus, and opened the door for the children.

The men were glad to see that the bus driver didn't arrive too early. Nor, did he check the inside of the bus before he allowed the children to enter it. They could see that all the buses were equipped with some type of a short wave radio, not cellular telephones.

In just minutes, the school doors flew open, and several older children ran toward the buses. Now, there were twelve buses parked in various places around the school, not just in the parking lot. Within fifteen minutes, the buses were loaded and the children were on their way home to their families.

Mehmet Gadhafi followed behind their special bus taking care not to be noticed. He drove slowly and carefully. Children were all around him. Some were getting into private automobiles and others walked in the streets. His partner kept his eyes on the bus, as Gadhafi concentrated on his driving.

They kept a safe distance until they were well into the residential area. They followed the bus for an hour and a half. The children got off at various stops. Some children moved closer to the front as the seats emptied. The driver drove as if it were routine. He never paid any attention to any cars following.

The two men noticed older people on the bus. They decided they must be mothers, who were helping at the school, or teachers. If they were correct, that would give Gabrielle the perfect reason for being on the bus. Who would question her? She would have to do some research at the school to see if any paperwork needed to be filed before the trip. But, since she already worked at the school, and several of the children knew her, the children would feel she belonged on the bus. She would fit in perfectly.

As they followed, they found the perfect place to take over the bus. It passed over an autobahn bridge before turning into the twenty-third district. Rather than going across the bridge, the bus would simply turn left and take the Autobahn toward Budapest.

Gabrielle would instruct the driver to drive out into the countryside. The two men would follow in two cars. After they drove for several miles, she would instruct the driver to park the bus at a pre-arranged spot.

The men would leave one of the cars in that place. Gabrielle would take the driver with her in that car. They would leave the children locked on the bus. The men would park a distance from the bus and watch to make sure that everything went as planned.

In the meantime, Golodin would telephone the American Embassy and the American School. He would reveal the bus had been hijacked. In his statement, he would explain that taking the bus was only a sample of what could happen if the Americans did not pay a ransom of $2 million dollars.

The men went over and over the arrangements. They wanted to be prepared for Golodin when they met later in the evening. After the bus phone call, and before the newspapers went to press, a message would be delivered to the KURIER.

The message would state simply that the Freedom Group did the bombings at the British Embassy. There would be no mention of the bus hijacking or the computer shipment.

No one would get hurt either at the British Embassy or on the school bus. The men just planned to distract the police and take the computer shipment without any problems.

They would take precautions not to be followed or recognized. The men would wear stockings over their faces, and would use a stolen car.

Gabrielle, already wearing her disguise, would be out of the country before the children would be back in their homes. It would be an easy drive for her to the Hungarian border where she would leave the driver.

She needed a vacation, and the Balaton in Hungary would be the perfect place. The mineral baths always catered to foreigners. She would blend in perfectly.

It would possibly take hours for the police to locate the bus. To be on the safe side, the men decided to slash the bus tires before they left the scene. That would cause further delay.

It was almost dark when the bus driver finished his route and headed back toward the city. The men watched until he repeated the routine as he had in the morning. Then, they headed for the first district.

Mehmet Gadhafi stopped his Mercedes by Schottentor, leaving George Haddah out near his apartment. Haddah lived in the corner apartment building across from the Schottentor Church.

George Haddah needed to rush to make his daily report before the close of the day. He hurried to his apartment and put a call in to the laundry where his Controller worked. The Controller, in turn, reported straight to the Embassy, and from there, to Lebanon.

Haddah gave complete details of his day, and his plans for the evening. It was coded. The average person would have thought he needed his laundry ready by the following day.

All finished, Haddah relaxed in his recliner and spent the next few hours in quiet meditation. He needed time for himself to recall his purpose in life. Recognizing his weakness of being materialistic, he prayed for strength to ignore all the merchandise and opportunities that were available in Vienna.

Mehmet Gadhafi also lived in the first district. He liked his apartment location, for it was near all the things he loved most: restaurants, coffee houses, disco bars, and the lovely women. He was more materialistic than his friend, George Haddah. He insisted on driving a Mercedes, he loved the style and wealth that it represented.

His idea of being really living was living in the first district, where he could walk to everything he wanted. It made it easier for him to attend the operas and ballets. Now, he went home, called his latest girlfriend, and reported that he'd be free for a couple hours.

CHAPTER THIRTY THREE

The Moscow headquarters of the SVR - The External Intelligence Agency and the Federal Security Services at one time was a depressing sight. However, in recent years, the huge building, with bars covering the ground-floor windows, had taken on a new look. It is located on the corner at Number 2 Lubyanka Square (the former Dzerzhinski Square), the end of Okhotnyi Ryad (the former Karl Marx Prospekt).

A statue to Felix Dzerhinsky, a Soviet revolutionary and founder of the CHEKA, the KGB's forerunner, once stood in this square. Today, only the pedestal remains. The statue was toppled in the aftermath of the failed August 1991 coup. However, after the coup, the streets were renamed to their pre-Revolutionary names.

Over the years, the majestic structure had additions added that expand on two sides, connected by a building in the middle. The sides, or wings as they are called, remind one of a huge hospital. In the middle, between the sides and behind the front of the building, is a big empty space.

One of the side wings holds several offices, including the office of the chairman of the SVR. The other wing and front section holds offices and living quarters for the top SVR and FSB officials. The center is known and feared by all Russians as "The Complex."

The building connecting the two wings in the rear was once a dreary building. Before the 1990 revolution, it was the home of the infamous Lubyanka Interrogation Center and Prison. Today, it contains a museum, a laboratory, a disco, a clinic and several offices. The empty courtyard between the buildings acts as a buffer, keeping its activities from the eyes of those passing.

Visiting government officials always arrive with drivers and bodyguards. They never enter through the front doors. The visitors park in the courtyard, leave their cars and drivers safely out of the range of the street vision.

The SVR Chairman's office is on the third floor of the largest wing. It is an extensive suite of rooms elegantly decorated for a man with that position. When Andropov was chairman, during the days of the old KGB, he had these spaces completely refurnished.

He replaced all the simple, stark furniture with impressive, expensive comfortable leather pieces and chosen antiques. The furniture gave the suite a look of power and dignity. The Chairman's desk, a large dark oak, was the most impressive piece of all. Andropov insisted on such a large desk to be able to hold all the telephones and paperwork which he controlled.

The walls are covered with wood paneling removed from a royal mansion, and on the floors are some of the most valuable oriental carpets in all of Russia. Pictures of famous Russians and Russian scenes hang on the walls.

Over the years, the office began to show signs of wear and decay. Although, recent Directors thought the impressive office fit their style, they didn't have the money to give the rooms and building a needed facelift.

A door on the right, behind a massive desk, lead to a large conference room. Several top officials gathered for a meeting. They had been called for a briefing on the latest SVR/FSB reports from Austria. During their last meeting, they had learned of the satellite computer shipment scheduled to go through Vienna on its way to Israel.

The men sitting around the table, many in their military uniforms laden with medals, were GRU. Those in street clothing were either SVR, FSB, or Kremlin security. Some were attending in order to inform the President. Others were attending so they could inform their field agents in the Middle East, especially Lebanon and Syria.

As the meeting progressed, the men discussed and agreed with the plan to take the computer shipment while it was in Vienna. However, for their image, they also agreed to issue an order to every Russian consulate and embassy around the world, to send a protest to Washington in regards to the shipment.

They would also make an official protest through the UN. The same protest would be presented to the UNIDO delegation, and other international organizations throughout the world in which they were members.

The men also approved the kidnapping of an American International School bus coordinated with the car bombings and small attack on the British Embassy. They agreed that these two events would give their men time to steal the computer shipment.

If they managed to take the bus successfully, the bombings were simply icing on the cake. Hopefully, these two actions would relieve interest in the double agent's death and any further questions regarding more double agents.

Unanimously, the attendees acknowledged that taking the American communicator and allowing him to die had been a tragic mistake. It had cost them a prized double agent. Silently, with a simple nod, they voted to eliminate those responsible for the double agent's death, when they were no longer of use.

They insisted all evidence regarding the Barrs kidnapping and death be linked to a Middle Eastern terrorist group, eliminating any Russian connection. The meeting adjourned after all details were discussed.

Silently, the men filed out of the room and went down the back stairs to their cars. They left at timed intervals, so as not to call attention to the activities inside the building.

When all the men departed, the Director of the SVR returned to his office. Once behind his massive desk, he reached for one of his many telephones. This phone was a direct link to the SVR/FSB office in Budapest, Hungary. It was the closest, secure direct contact to his SVR/FSB Vienna agent.

"Good day, Mr. Director!" the voice in the Budapest office answered immediately.

"Yes, let me talk to Arkady," the Chairman replied in a weak voice.

Within seconds, a husky, raspy voice came across the wire, "Yes, Mr. Director?"

"I want you to do something for me personally." The Director spoke slowly for several minutes and ordered Arkady to personally deliver his message to Rubin in Vienna.

As he talked, he looked around his office proud of the luxury and comfort the position had given him. He finished with the phone call and rested his head in his arms on top of the desk.

Ordering someone's death bothered him even after all the years he'd been a "wet" agent working with SMERSH and the Mokrie Dyela groups. The old SMERSH organization, dealing with spies, and the Mokrie Dyela, nicknamed the death squad, were the two most infamous organizations within the Russian intelligence system.

It was from these groups, the FSB agent in Vienna had been recruited. He had been selected personally by the Director to handle anything, even murder, at the Director's order.

After several moments of reasoning with what he had just ordered, the Director reached for another phone and told his secretary that he would be going back to his quarters in the opposite wing of the building.

His wife would be waiting with the boiled potatoes and beef that he loved. He hurried, not to keep her waiting, but, smiled as he thought of the Americans running in the wrong direction.

CHAPTER THIRTY FOUR

Blinksdale and Collins arrived at the Barr apartment and relieved Greenly's agent. Ultimately, they decided not to have a driver and Blinksdale drove one of the Embassy cars which Greenly's man drove back to the Embassy.

During the drive, they discussed their plan once they arrived at the apartment. They decided they would ask questions first and then look through Barr's personal belongings. Blinksdale was to do the talking and introduce Collins as just another man from the Embassy, not revealing his CIA identity.

Silently they walked to the door, while looking over the neighborhood. Blinksdale pushed the bell. The door opened immediately. Collins and Blinksdale recognized the woman from the church service.

"Come in! I'm Eva Metcalf, Mrs. Barr's sister. She's already left. Can I help you with something?"

Mrs. Metcalf was dressed in a plain cotton floral print house dress. She wore no makeup, was about five-foot six-inches tall, and carried several extra pounds for her height. Her graying brown hair was pulled back from her face in a tight bun. She wore heavy bifocal glasses which didn't compliment her face, but gave the appearance of being someone's mother or grandmother. Both men thought Mrs. Metcalf, definitely didn't look the role of the wife of a successful business man, or of a diplomat, as her sister had.

"Yes, we're from the Embassy. We'd like to talk to you if we might. My name is Bob Blinksdale, and this is Johnny Collins." Both men extended their hands.

Mrs. Metcalf shook their hands and exclaimed, "Oh, I'm sorry. My, how rude of me. My, yes! Do come in. How nice to meet you, Mr. Blinksdale and Mr. Collins. Do you mind if I call you Bob and Johnny? Mr. sounds so impersonal and formal. I'm just sitting down to a cup of coffee and some cake that nice Mrs. Fisher, from next door, sent over. Won't you join me?"

"Yes, I think that would be nice. We'd love to join you," Blinksdale answered.

Collins followed last, looking all around the apartment to see if there were any expensive personal items that would not fit the salary of a man in Barr's position. They went through the living room to the dining area, rather than taking a short cut through the kitchen.

Johnny noticed one entire wall in the living room was devoted to electronic equipment. He recognized the brand names, and knew they were the very best that money could buy. All the components were new, or at least within the past year. He roughly estimated the equipment would have easily cost over thirty thousand dollars.

The apartment was much like any other government apartment built by the Embassy. It contained a living room, dining room, kitchen and powder room on the first floor. All the rooms flowed into one another. The kitchen was the only room with doors.

The furniture was new, but standard issue from the Embassy furniture warehouse. The only pieces giving the room personality were the numerous accessories.

The rooms were full of pictures, extra pieces of furniture, and little dust collectors on end tables and in the china cabinet.

Johnny looked at the china cabinet. It contained a complete twelve place setting of crystal. From where he was sitting, it looked as if the set consisted of both red and white wine glasses, champagne, water, and sherbet goblets. He didn't recognize the trademark, but they were either Waterford, Baccarat or Reidel. All three kinds he knew were extremely expensive.

On the shelf, below the glasses was a complete china dinner set for twelve. He wasn't sure of the brand, but judging from the crystal, it was the finest and undoubtedly expensive.

Several original oil paintings, in various sizes, hung on the walls. Johnny wasn't familiar with the artists, so he had no idea of the value of the pieces. They were a mixed assortment of landscape, modernistic and figural.

Mrs. Metcalf played the role of hostess perfectly. She poured the coffee and had them all eating cake within a matter of minutes. Her motherly manner gave the room a warm feeling and made the men feel comfortable.

She looked at Blinksdale with a matronly look, smiled and asked, "Come now, you men tell me what it is that you want from me. I know you didn't leave your offices just to come and see if I need help?"

Blinksdale smiled at her directness, "No, Mrs. Metcalf. To tell you the truth, we came to see if you could tell us anything about Alan that might help us find out why he was killed."

"I wondered who was going to ask me about what I know," Mrs. Metcalfe answered with a smile. "Greenly was here all morning. He acted as if he were afraid to come out and ask me what was on his mind. He walked through the house, looked in Alan's desk drawers, and even went through all the drawers in his bedroom. The only thing he didn't do was come right out and ask me what I thought, or what I know. He did ask what my sister was doing in Frankfurt when Alan was killed."

"Well, I'm sure Greenly has a lot on his mind. He probably didn't want to upset you any more than you were," Johnny answered, still looking around the room, wishing he had brought a camera with him.

"Posh! I never really cared for Alan anyway. He would have known that if he would have asked me."

"Well, Mrs. Metcalf, what can you tell us?" Collins asked. He helped himself to another piece of cake while he talked. "We'd like to know your opinion of Mr. Barr. We'd also like to know why you didn't really like him. Do you have any idea if they were getting an income from some other source, other than his salary? Some of the things I've seen here are very expensive, such as his stereo and video equipment."

"I really like that. Johnny, you're all right. Go ahead and help yourself. At least you're honest about what you want from me. Not afraid to say what's on your mind. I like that in a person. Not mealy mouthed like that Greenly person." Eva

Metcalf wiped her hands on a kitchen towel that was on the table and poured the men fresh coffee.

"Thanks," Blinksdale said. "I think you've pegged Greenly wrong. He was only looking out for your welfare."

"Hogwash!" Mrs. Metcalf answered with a shrug. "Anyway, now to tell you about my sister and that horse's ass she married. It all began when they were in Moscow. My sister met Alan when he was in the States before he went on an assignment to Turkey. They were both assigned there for two years, and then when they transferred to Moscow, they got married."

"What did she do?" Johnny asked.

"She was an airline hostess and then when they went to Moscow, she quit and worked for the embassy," Mrs. Metcalf answered.

"Is she younger than Alan?" Blinksdale asked.

"Hell, I don't even know how old Alan was, probably mid forties. My sister is in her early forties."

Johnny said, "Do you mind if I made notes as you talk?"

"Not at all. Anyway, I was with my husband in South America when she wrote and told us all about this wonderful man she had met. I didn't get a chance to meet him until they had been in Moscow for a couple months. My husband got transferred with his company from South America to Frankfurt. I went to see them in Moscow. Then, when I planned on making another trip, Alice called and told me she was flying into Germany for a commissary run. She graduated from college with a business degree, so when she arrived in Moscow, they wanted her to help with the commissary and buy supplies for the Embassy. It was just down her alley. She loved organizing and managing things like that."

"Did she travel a lot?" Johnny asked, making another note.

"Some. They never had any children. I think Alan might have children from his first marriage, but I never really knew for sure. I guess I never really cared enough to ask either of them. I couldn't tell you squat about his first wife. I only heard him talk about her a couple times. She might live in Woodbridge, Virginia, but hell, what do I know or care now."

"Did you know she was black?" Johnny asked.

"No, and really don't care," Mrs. Metcalf answered, with a shrug. "Anyway, Alice flew in and stayed with me. When she arrived, she was carrying a suitcase full of Russian Icons. She had met some man in Moscow who was supplying them for her. Also, she had made arrangements with someone she had known in Turkey, and sold them to that person. That person is now living in Frankfurt. That accounts for any extra money they had."

"Did she make a great deal of money?" Johnny asked.

"I think so, but I don't really know, I never asked. Anyway, every time she came to Frankfurt, she had more Icons, and art treasures with her. As far as I know, she never kept any of them for herself. She was only interested in the money she could get from selling them. I asked her one time wasn't this all a bit illegal. She just laughed and said the man who was supplying her was taking all the chances."

"Did her husband know about this?" Blinksdale asked.

"Probably, she told the old bat everything. She held a black diplomatic passport, and usually flew on military runs. No one ever stopped her and searched any of her suitcases. The money was deposited in a military bank account in Frankfurt. She and I both have accounts there. In fact, I took her the first time to open her account. I'm not sure if she had Alan's name on the account or not."

"Did you ever go back to Moscow?" Johnny asked.

"Well, for two years she came in every couple weeks or so. My husband and I went into Moscow after a couple months for him to meet Alan. Alan was more interested in my husband's business, than he was in the family aspect of our relationship. As I said earlier, Alan was a real horse's ass." She got up and walked into the kitchen for some fresh coffee, when she returned she continued.

"My husband is with an electronic company. He's an engineer, and works with various governments and private companies. As I explained, Alice made trips about once or twice a month while they were in Moscow. Then, last spring they told us they would be transferred to Vienna. I thought that was great. I'd be able to see Alice more. My husband and I have three children, and she is my only living relative. Then, they moved to Vienna. Alan never once came to Frankfurt to see us. They seemed to have a thousand and one reasons not to come to Frankfurt together. Alice still came, and some man was always calling her while she was in Frankfurt."

"Did she still sell things?" Johnny asked.

"I don't think so. She seemed to be nervous all the time, and had lost some weight. I began teasing her about the spy world in Vienna. She got violently angry with me. I don't know what was going on, but from the bit I could see, the man who supplied the icons in Moscow had gotten transferred to Vienna. I think he was trying to get repaid for all the money he had made available to her. I know it had something to do with Alan's work. You know, don't you, Alan was one of the communicators who handled all the secret and top secret material that came into and out of the Embassy?"

Both men looked at one another and nodded.

"So, that's all I know." she continued. "I told the other men in Frankfurt that Alice broke a tooth at my daughter's birthday party and had gone to Munich to have it fixed. Why, Munich? I don't know. She said an old friend was a dentist there. I guess your men checked it out and found it to be true. I think there was more to it than she said, but I thought she would tell me if she wanted me to know. She usually told me all that was worrying her anyway."

Johnny shifted in his seat. He opened his mouth to ask a question but decided against it and let Mrs. Metcalf continue.

"When she called and told me about Alan's death, she insisted I be here when the household goods were packed. There are some things she wants me to ship to Frankfurt. Some are things that belonged to our parents. She left me a list. Now, how about a glass of wine, guys? I think it's late enough in the day for a drink. What do you think?"

Both men looked at each other and agreed to a glass of wine. Neither man wanted to leave the room for fear Mrs. Metcalf might remember more about Alan and his wife, her sister, Alice.

Mrs. Metcalf rejoined the men with an opened bottle of white wine. She walked to the china closet, took three crystal goblets out and placed them on the table. "Might as well use them since they're here, don't you think?" she asked the men, referring to the crystal white wine glasses.

"Yes, that's fine with us," Blinksdale answered, with a bewildered look.

"Mrs. Metcalf, is there anything else you can think of that might help us? Do you think the person who helped your sister in Moscow was with the American Embassy, or a Russian?" Collins asked. He wanted to get the conversation back on track.

"I really don't know. I think, with all the items they brought out, it would have had to have been a Russian. But, a Russian with strong connections. Someone who had unlimited access to such treasures. Many of the pieces were worth several thousands of dollars. I don't think an American would have had that access. I don't know anything about the items, but with the money Alice was depositing, they either had to be real, or very good copies."

"Do you think any Americans knew what your sister was doing?" Johnny questioned.

"I really don't know. I think one of the couriers might have known. I'm not sure. I remember Alice saw someone she knew one day in the PX in Wiesbaden, and was very frightened. I don't know who she was. Alice didn't introduce us. I only saw Alice talking to another woman for a few minutes."

"Where are your children now?" Blinksdale asked.

"We have an *au pair* girl living with us. The children are all in school, and my husband is home in the evenings. They'll manage nicely. They'll call every night and catch me up on all the happenings of the day."

Collins finished his wine, stood up and stretched. "Do you mind if I walk around the house and go upstairs to the bedrooms?" he asked, taking a step away from the table.

"Not at all. Make yourself at home. Alan's desk is in the spare bedroom. His computer is still connected. I don't think any of the desk drawers are locked. I'm in the bedroom, on the left, when you first go up the stairs. The master bedroom is toward the back. Just wander around."

Blinksdale remained sitting with Mrs. Metcalf while Johnny left to explore the rest of the apartment. Blinkdsdale asked, "Mrs. Metcalf, may I see the list of things that Alice asked you to take back to Frankfurt with you?"

"Surely. Let me get my purse." She went into the kitchen and returned in a moment with a new Louis Vuitton leather purse. She withdrew a matching wallet from the purse, and handed Blinksdale a folded sheet of paper.

Blinksdale took the paper and memorized the list as he read. The list contained several pictures, some personal papers, a reading table, a china cabinet, some linen, books, camera equipment, and specific video tapes. Blinksdale finished the list and handed it back to Mrs. Metcalf.

Before Mrs. Metcalf put the list back in her wallet, Blinksdale asked, "Was there anything on the list that you thought might be a bit strange?"

"Come to think about it," she answered as she looked at the list again. "Books. You know, neither one of them read at all. My husband doesn't read anything that doesn't relate to science or engineering, and I read only romance novels. Alice knew that. Why she would be giving us the books, I couldn't understand? I haven't had time to look over the books, but she mentioned several times that I was to take them all. I guess she's referring to those over there, and I did see some more in the master bedroom upstairs."

Mrs. Metcalf pointed to a shelf of hardback books that were stacked in a bookcase. The other shelves were full of video tapes, records, CD's, and stereo tapes. Without saying a word,

Blinksdale walked to the books. He opened a bank and flipped through it. Mrs. Metcalf joined him. She also began to look through the books, beginning from the opposite end of the shelf.

Collins checked the upstairs and didn't find anything out of place. He glanced at his watch and went back down stairs carrying two telephone books. One was the latest copy of the American Embassy Employees phone book, and the other was a copy of the American Women's Association telephone book.

"Find anything?" Collins asked as he walked into the living room.

Blinksdale looked up and answered, "I asked Mrs. Metcalf what it was that her sister had wanted her to take back to Frankfurt. The only thing she found unusual was Alice's request to take all the books with her. Neither of the Barr's read much, and Mrs. Metcalf confesses to only reading romantic novels. She said her husband reads only things to do with science and engineering. We've gone through the books here to see if anything might have been in them. We came up empty. How about you?"

"Nothing from me, either. I noticed various things, but nothing unusual. I'd like to have permission to take these two telephone books back to the Embassy. Would it also be alright to come back sometime over the weekend and go through the apartment again?" Johnny asked as he sat in one of the easy chairs in the living room. "To tell you the truth, my body is really getting tired and I'm afraid I might overlook something if I continue today."

"Sure, you can take the two telephone books. If I need to call someone special I can get the number from Mrs. Fisher next door. Tomorrow's Saturday, and I'll be here all weekend. I thought I'd begin cleaning the kitchen things out tomorrow. You two are welcome anytime. Don't bother calling first, I'll be here."

"Thanks, we appreciate that. If it's okay with you, Bob, let's plan on coming back tomorrow morning about nine-thirty or ten, and we'll see how things go." Johnny stood up and walked back into the dining room.

"Great. I'll be looking forward to your company for the weekend. To tell you the truth, I wasn't very excited to be here by myself all the time anyway. Why don't you both plan on staying for lunch tomorrow and we'll eat up some of the things left in the freezer? We can't let all this wine go to waste either, can we?" she winked.

"Fine with me," Blinksdale teased back. "I was only going to do some things around the house."

"Bob, why don't you call Greenly's office and get a man out here to watch the house for Mrs. Metcalf. I don't want anyone bothering her, or have her frightened in any way." Collins added as he smiled at Mrs. Metcalf. "Also mention to Greenly that he get someone out to check Alan's hard drive, in case he hasn't done that yet."

Blinksdale went to the phone to call the Embassy, while Mrs. Metcalf freshened Johnny's wine glass. "Might as well have one for the road, as they say."

While waiting for their relief to come, the men drank another glass of wine. Then, a knock came to the door and put an end to the afternoon visit. The relief man had arrived. After introductions were made, Collins and Blinksdale left with a promise they would return around nine-thirty in the morning.

"Nice lady, isn't she?" Blinksdale asked as they drove back to the Embassy.

"Yes, she is. But she knows more than she's telling us." Johnny answered, sitting in the passenger seat, watching the late afternoon traffic on Wahringer Strasse.

CHAPTER THIRTY FIVE

The Friday evening rush hour traffic was unusually heavy. Johnny Collins and Bob Blinksdale rode back to the Embassy in silence.

Driving down Nussdorfer Strasse and crossing Wahringer Strasse was an adventure in itself. The streetcars had the right of way, but the small cars and the taxi drivers tried to out distance them with their speed.

Horns blared, and the streetcars continually rang their bells. Drivers made obscene gestures to one another, and called each other names behind the privacy and safety of the closed windows and locked doors. Johnny hadn't seen traffic as heavy since his trip to Cairo. When Blinksdale turned off of Wahringer Strasse and turned onto Boltzmangasse toward the Embassy, Johnny said, "It's like a Formula One race track in this city."

After Blinksdale finished parking the car, Collins jumped out. He was glad to be standing on his own two feet on solid ground, out of the hectic rush traffic.

"To say the least!" Blinksdale laughed. He waved to the Austrian guard, and followed Collins into the Embassy.

It was Friday evening and the normal week duty hours were over. Collins rang the bell to notify the Marine at Post One to push a button to release the big steel door and let them enter. They both went to the desk and signed in. He noticed his briefcase was still resting against the coat rack by the main desk. He reminded the Marine that he would pick it up in a few minutes when he was on his way back out of the Embassy.

The Marine guard told Collins that Kevin Smith wanted to talk to him if he came in before six. Collins checked his watch and was surprised to see it was almost six.

Both men walked toward Blinksdale's office. Kevin Smith stepped off the elevator.

"Mr. Collins, may I talk to you a moment?" Smith called when he saw Collins.

"Sure. Bob, go on. I'll join you in a few minutes. What can I do for you, Kevin?" Johnny asked.

"I wondered, sir, if you wanted to go to the Dubrovnik restaurant tonight?"

Hesitating for just a moment, Johnny answered, "Yes, I'd like that. I planned to get in touch with you earlier in the day, but to tell you the truth, I got held up. Why don't you bring a girl and I'll meet you there. I think I can walk to it from the Hilton, can't I?"

"Yes, sir. It's just a few minutes walk. I'd love to bring my girl friend. She's Swiss. I'll call and make reservations. How about eight?"

Johnny glanced at the clock at the end of the hallway. He answered, "Yes, that's fine. See you there. Oh, by the way, what's the dress?"

"What you have on is fine. Sports clothes, suit, whatever. Usual wear for Vienna. I just wouldn't wear jeans. See you at eight."

Collins watched Smith sign out and walk down the steps to the entrance door before he headed back toward Blinksdale's office.

"Damn, I forgot those two telephone books I found at the Barrs," Johnny said, as he entered Blinksdale's office. "I put them down by the easy chair on the end table when I had the wine. Don't let me forget to pick them up in the morning. Some of them had notes beside the names. I wanted you and Greenly to look at them and see if you might know why. I think I'm going to call it a day. I just made plans to go with Smith to the Dubrovnik restaurant this evening at eight. He's going to bring his Swiss girlfriend. It looks like it might be a long night. What do you say I meet you back here at eight in the morning? We can go over anything we think of overnight, and check on incoming messages?"

"Fine with me," Blinksdale answered. He stuck a paper in his desk drawer. "I think I'll go home, too. One of the kids has a play at the American School tonight. If I miss it, she'll never forgive me. See you in the morning. I'll let the Marines know where we'll both be for the night, if it's okay with you?"

"Fine. I'm going to head out. May I use your phone to call a taxi. No, on second thought, I'm going to walk back to that hotel on Gersthofer and pick one up there. I could use the fresh air anyway. See you in the morning."

CHAPTER THIRTY SIX

Friday evenings were the most hectic night of the week at the Hilton Hotel. It was the night when most tour groups, incoming or outgoing, held their banquets and social hour get-to-gathers.

The first floor conference center was filled to an overflowing capacity with a variety of cocktail parties. Viennese music filtered through the stereo speakers. Numerous tables were filled with an assortment of tempting appetizers, ranging from imported caviar sandwiches to pates, and mouth-watering varieties of "finger foods." Everything was colorful and expertly displayed.

Because the elevators weren't running to the lobby, Collins found himself in the middle of a large cocktail party on the first floor. Realizing immediately that this was not a function to which he was invited, nor belonged, Collins turned to correct his route. When he turned, two men in the corner of the room caught his attention.

Instantly, he recognized Chief-of-Station, Greenly, talking to the Russian bald headed man, Yuri Rubin, whom he had encountered in the park. Collins was surprised to find the two men together in a public place.

Not wanting to be discovered, Collins turned and moved to a table where cocktails were being served. With a glass of white wine in his hand, he stepped behind a tall potted plant. From there, he could watch the two men without having them see him.

A waiter with a large silver tray, offered him a snack. Collins smiled, studied the assortment and took one of the small bits of pastry. He felt better, knowing he had blended into the scene, although he had no idea who was sponsoring the event.

Several women started toward him. The closer they came, the more insecure Johnny felt. He saw two men, just feet away from where he was. They looked lost but were talking to one another.

He approached the two men, introduced himself using his first name and his mother's maiden name. He talked to the men as if he had known them all of his life. Before long, he knew who the two men were, why they were in Vienna, where they were from in the States, and small incidental facts about their families.

Continuing with his conversation between the two men, Johnny watched Greenly walk down the stairs, and Rubin vanish through a door at the end of the room. Johnny glanced at his watch and excused himself.

He moved up the back stairway and saw Rubin going up the stairs to the next floor. Silently, Collins followed. The door opened to the fourth floor landing.

He followed as closely as possible, and stepped out just in time to see Rubin enter the room next to his. The room where the young couple had been.

Johnny tiptoed down the hall, stopped for a moment by the door that Rubin entered. He leaned his head against the door. There was music playing. He could hear people talking but couldn't make out any words.

Now, he realized Rubin was monitoring his actions from the room next door. Collins opened his room and checked his room again. He found no new listening devices. The two old ones were still intact. Knowing he had nothing to fear for the time being, Johnny prepared for his night on the town.

CHAPTER THIRTY SEVEN

The couple in the room next to Johnny Collins was completely unaware their cover had been blown. They had stayed in their room all day, listening to the silence from the room next door. Each had gone for a walk for a change of scenery, and to keep themselves alert. Their training in Russia, had taught them that staying alert, and keeping the mind free from outside distractions was the only way to stay alive. It was also the answer to keeping a dull surveillance from becoming a weary ordeal.

The couple were professional SVR agents. They loved their chosen career. Through years of training, in the little American community in the heart of Russia, they had studied hard and learned all the tricks of surveillance and espionage. Over the years of working together, although they had never actually had a marriage ceremony performed, they lived as a married couple. Their lives together had been good. They enjoyed the same things, and each other's company.

They had been contacted for the Vienna assignment after having completed an assignment in Zagreb. In Zagreb, they had a surveillance assignment of an American business man and an Embassy employee. Both men, the Russians felt were easy targets for blackmail.

It is known that the Russians as well as the Americans and most foreign countries have experienced teams that only do surveillance work. These are trained agents who play various roles such as tourists, and follow people throughout the world. Usually these agents play the part of wealthy international citizens, who live in the heart of the international business, diplomatic and social scenes.

These agents are trained to watch for any sign of weakness in their subjects, but they never make decisions for themselves. They stay buried in the background, keeping low profiles, and not attracting attention.

Also, these agents are totally loyal to their countries. In Russia, they are directly supported and assigned by the Federal Security Service. They are rarely given classified information, and are only assigned to watch, report, and do as they are told. In America, the agents could be working for any number of government organizations: Defense, Intelligence, State or Federal.

Yuri Rubin, acting as the joint SVR/FSB Resident Agent in Austria, was with the young Russian couple. He had just praised the young couple on having done an excellent job. He told them, they would leave Vienna as soon as their subject left.

He ordered the couple to become friends with Collins suggested they all go out to eat one evening. However they did it Rubin didn't care. They were specifically instructed not to question Collins. They were to listen, record and report.

However, if the occasion should arise, they could ask basic family questions. Rubin stated they would probably not be told the truth, but Collins may slip in just enough of the truth to help them form a more complete portfolio.

After Rubin left, the couple returned to their assignment feeling very pleased with themselves.

CHAPTER THIRTY EIGHT

The street lights went on as Johnny left his room and began his short walk to the restaurant. As he walked from the hotel, he looked around and watched the evening stars blazing in the cloudless Austrian sky. The air was calm and had a clean freshness after the rush hour traffic.

The sound of music and people talking flowed through the night air. A full moon had just cleared the horizon. The city displayed the magical look of the tourist postcard. Calmness seemed to give everything the look and feel of past centuries.

Johnny walked along as casually as possible. He stopped when he crossed the cement bridge leading to the city park, and looked down at the small flow of water running smoothly under his feet. He gave the outward appearance of being an American tourist enjoying the sights and atmosphere of the city, totally unaware of what was going on around him. No one gave him a second glance. Nothing stirred his feelings of being watched, that experienced agents develop. Listening to the sounds of the city, he paced himself so he would arrive at the restaurant fashionably late, hoping Smith would be on time.

The restaurant, located only a short block from the city park exit and across the street from the Inter-Continental Hotel, was ablaze with lights. The streets around the Inter-Continental hotel were filled with buses. People were out in the night air, walking their dogs and enjoying the tranquility of the city.

Johnny played the tourist role completely by spending a few minutes looking at the menu, which was posted in a glass display case directly outside the entrance. He checked to see the various foods and wines available. The international menu consisted of a variety of dishes from Europe, including Austrian, as well as Serb and Eastern European specialties. Convinced he wasn't being followed, he opened the door and entered.

"*Guten Abend,*" the waiter, dressed in a black suit and black tie, greeted Johnny.

"*Guten Abend.* I'm joining a friend. Mr. Smith. Kevin Smith, from the American Embassy," Johnny answered in English, for his German was limited.

"Mr. Smith and his date have already arrived. Would you like to check your coat, please?" The waiter pointed with his outstretched hand.

"Yes, I believe so. Thank you," Johnny answered. He followed the man's point and glanced to the area on the other side of the room where an elderly lady was.

The white haired coat check lady was sitting behind a small counter, alert and aware of all around her. In front of her was a small tip dish. No sign was posted as to the price for checking coats, so Johnny decided he would wait to tip her when he picked up his coat.

"Please, follow me," the waiter ordered, talking over his shoulder as he led the way through a large room. He walked toward the back of the restaurant into another room.

Johnny studied the Eastern European decor of the rooms. Most of the large, wall size murals were old scenes of Hungary, Czechoslovakia, even Russia. It was hard for Johnny to distinguish what was what, for they overlapped in their designs.

A small group of roving musicians, dressed like gypsies, played the zither and made visits to the tables upon request. The soft lights and music gave the whole room a relaxing effect.

"Good evening, Johnny," Kevin greeted, standing when he saw Johnny approach the table. "I'd like you to meet my date, Katrina Borg. She is assigned to the Swiss Embassy, but does translations for several embassies."

Katrina was a very attractive brunette. She had large brown eyes and a very thin face. Her hair had been cut short in one of the latest styles. She had her chair pushed very close to Kevin's and leaned toward him as she spoke. Her bright purple dress had a low cut neckline and long sleeves. She wore gold button earrings, a heavy gold necklace and a feminine gold Rolex watch.

Johnny thought she was about twenty-five years old and wondered how tall she was. After shaking hands, Johnny moved to the empty chair behind the table.

He was pleased Smith had left that chair empty. That way he would be able to keep his back to the wall, and watch those that entered and left. After everyone was seated, the waiter rejoined the table with offers of cocktails and hor d'oeuvres.

Johnny looked at Smith, "Kevin, I'll leave the appetizer ordering to you. Let's have something a bit different. After you're finished, you can help me decipher the main courses. Is that all right with you?"

"That's fine," Kevin answered, and placed an order with the waiter.

For the next several minutes, the trio reviewed the English language menu, and listened to Kevin as he explained the selections. Johnny was amazed at how well informed Kevin was with the various dishes. Following the advice given to him, Johnny decided on a dish he felt was well balanced with spices.

"So, tell me about yourself, Katrina. How long have you been in Vienna?" Johnny asked with curiosity.

"I've been here just about six months. I was previously posted in London. And yourself?" she asked, turning her head slightly so that her dressed gapped just a bit in the front.

Johnny was impressed how she used her body and easily answered the question, and then skillfully turned the conversation back to him.

"I'm only visiting," he said. "I've been here almost a week. I love the city. Don't you think it holds somewhat of a magical charm? Can't you just see the Kings and Maria Theresa riding in their carriages down around the Ringstrasse?"

"Oh, yes," Katrina replied. She leaned slightly on the table and placed her hand on the table near Johnny. "I think this city is a pure tourist delight. There are so many things to see, and such lovely places to visit. Do you have any special place you plan to visit?" She smiled and fluttered her eyelashes as she waited for an answer.

Kevin watched the couple and smiled. He didn't say anything.

Johnny had become completely engrossed in the conversation, and was unaware of a couple approaching the table. He saw Kevin stand and shake their hands before the faces of the couple came into view. He was surprised, but he hoped the shock wasn't apparent when he recognized the couple.

It was the couple in the room next to his at the Hilton Hotel. The room he had seen the Russian enter earlier. His mind raced to the ingenious organizing of the evening. It had taken careful planning to bring all parties together, and still make it appear as if it were a chance meeting.

"Mr. Collins, I'd like you to meet the Van Gelders. Johanna and Kurt. They're also from Switzerland. Katrina and Johanna are old friends. In fact, they tell me they both went to school together," Kevin explained with a proud sense of familiarity.

"Good evening," Johnny said politely. He glanced at the couple and smiled. "Are you also visiting Vienna? I believe I've seen you at the Hilton Hotel, where I'm staying. I think I saw you in the hall or lobby last evening."

Johanna Van Gelder smiled, glanced at her husband and replied, "Yes, I believe that's correct. We are at the Hilton. We are here playing the tourist role, seeing the sights, taking in a few concerts, and doing some shopping. We love to visit Vienna in the Spring. It's such a lovely time of the year. Good evening, Katrina. How are you this lovely evening?"

Johnny was aware that the conversation was getting a bit awkward. He decided he might just as well go along with the role and invite the couple to join the table.

After the usual excuses, the Van Gelders were finally persuaded to join the group. The waiter was called and two more table settings were added. Within seconds, the usual confusion of adding extra drinks and appetizers was completed.

Johnny smiled to himself. He had been seated between both of the ladies. Now, he knew deliberate planning had gone into the seating arrangement. He was determined not to let on what he suspected about the Van Gelders, or that he knew the Russian agent had visited them earlier in the day. He was certain that Katrina Borg was also a Russian agent.

It amused him when he thought how easy it was to assign an agent to a single man. He was sure Kevin Smith was completely unaware of his date's Russian connection. With the look in Kevin's eyes, he knew Kevin had fallen into the trap willingly. It was an old Russian trick, developed during the former KGB days, to take an experienced agent and assign her to capture a single unsuspecting male's attention.

Johnny remembered his days at the Farm in Virginia, where he heard the rule repeated over and over: "Never believe that things are as they seem." How true that saying was.

CHAPTER THIRTY NINE

George Haddah had just parked his red Ford. He sat in the car for a few minutes watching the people walking by the Middle Eastern restaurant in the nineteenth district. His mind wasn't on the faces of the strollers because he was still deep in thought about the message he had just received concerning the computers shipment to Israel. His orders were explicit; under no conditions was he to allow the shipment to leave Vienna.

He and his Syrian counterpart had spent all day planning the kidnapping of the American International School bus. Even though it had been decided earlier there would be no violence, his latest orders took priority. Now it looked as if he may have to take matters into his own hands if he were to follow his government's directive.

He knew what would happen to him if he failed. He was covered with sweat just thinking that again he could be facing death, not in glory, but in disgrace. He would go ahead with the bus plan as planned. With the grace of Allah, he hoped the Americans did not offer resistance and no blood would flow.

Within minutes, he watched the GRU Colonel park his gray Audi and enter the restaurant. Haddah knew he had to join him quickly before the Russian had time to plant any listening devices at the table. He didn't trust the Russians, no matter how sweet they talked, or how nice they appeared to be, for he had learned the hard way that nothing was as it seemed.

Mehmet Gadhafi drove past as George Haddah was walking into the restaurant. He found a parking place without any difficulty. Pretending to busy himself in the car for a few minutes, Gadhafi allowed time for the car to park that had been following him from the first district. He had become aware of the car as he turned onto the street that led into the nineteenth district.

The car was a small VW. He wasn't able to see the driver, nor was he able to see if the driver was male or female. But, he was sure the driver was alone. Mehmet had been taught that nothing was a coincidence everything had a meaning and a purpose. His teachings stressed one had only to follow one's way, things that happened were meant to be.

All three men were seated at the table in the rear of the restaurant as they had been the previous evening. They were served strong coffee, and had just ordered a dish of lamb and rice.

The two men explained to Golodin what they had learned about the bus. They agreed their plan would begin Monday evening after school was dismissed.

Golodin smiled. The two men didn't know he and Gabrielle had already discussed the attack. Golodin hadn't told, nor did he plan to tell, the two men about his relationship with Gabrielle. He didn't feel they needed to know anything further about Gabrielle than what was public knowledge among the terrorist crowd. Golodin knew that Gabrielle lived alone and had devoted her entire life to terrorism. She was one of the best.

She loved the action and needed it to keep a balance in her life. The bus attack was perfect for her, it would give her fresh attention within the terroristcommunity. It would take her out of her present world of being a covert agent and into the open.

Golodin waited until the food was served and then said, "I'll place my calls to the American Embassy and the American School around four-thirty Monday. We want the car bombs and the bomb inside the British Embassy detonated around five. I will attend the reception and that allows me time to get out of the building and away from the area. I'll call from a pay phone near the British Embassy. The police will have no way of finding out who made the call if it's discovered later that the call was made from the pay phone. Don't you think it will take that long for them to become alarmed that the bus isn't following its normal schedule?"

Haddah answered. He pulled out a sheet of paper and checked the bus time schedule. He said, "I don't think the parents will start calling the school until later maybe even five-thirty or so. It'll take them some time to realize the bus is missing. I think if you plan the call about five, the timing will be perfect."

"I agree. We should be way out of town by then. I don't think any notice will be made of the bus driving down a road. It doesn't have any signs on it saying it's a school bus. It looks just like the hundred other tour buses you see around Vienna every day," Gadhafi added.

Golodin pulled out two pieces of paper from his inside jacket pocket. He said, "I have written out my warning to the American School and the American Embassy. Would you like to read it? Oh, yes, I also have the message to be delivered to the Kurier. Do we agree that the newspaper message is not to be delivered until later in the evening, about nine? I was told they schedule the paper to go to press about ten. That should give them time to run it."

"Yes, let me read them," Haddah replied, reaching for the papers. The soiled papers had been folded several times. Several words had been crossed out and new ones inserted. As Haddah read the first page, he smiled.

"WE HAVE TAKEN AN AMERICAN INTERNATIONAL SCHOOL BUS HOSTAGE. NO ONE WILL BE HARMED THIS TIME. WE DEMAND THREE MILLION DOLLARS IMMEDIATELY. IT IS TO BE IN SMALL BILLS AND PLACED IN A BRIEFCASE. I WILL CALL LATER WITH THE DELIVERY INSTRUCTIONS. IF OUR WISHES ARE NOT MET, WE WILL REACT BY MAKING ANOTHER MOVE AGAINST THE AMERICANS, THE AMERICAN COMMUNITY, THE AMERICAN SCHOOL, AND THE INTERNATIONAL DIPLOMATIC COMMUNITY."

Taking the second paper and unfolding it, he read. "THE FREEDOM FIGHTERS OF THE WORLD CLAIM THE RESPONSIBILITY AND TAKE THE CREDIT FOR THE BOMBINGS WHICH TOOK PLACE EARLIER TODAY AT THE BRITISH EMBASSY."

Both men read the messages and nodded their heads in agreement. They liked the idea in the school bus statement that another incident would occur should the money not be paid. Although, they knew the car bombs were scheduled for minutes later.

Haddah spent the next several minutes discussing how they would take the computer shipment. He explained that the Hamas were really to act. However, he didn't say anything about his orders from his government.

The conversation switched to small talk as they concentrated on the food in front of them. Everything had been decided for the three attacks. They were ready.

The restaurant was again closing for the evening. The men decided to meet Tuesday morning in their favorite coffee house in the First District, just to the North of the Rathaus. They would discuss and review the reaction of the world to their acts.

In European custom, the men shook hands and waited to leave at separate intervals. This gave them the chance to watch one another.

The Russian left first and was in his car when the Lebanese followed. Gadhafi wanted to be last. He looked from the door to his car. Quickly, he ran to his Mercedes and sped away. He watched the traffic behind him. When he was certain no one followed, he drove back to the first district. He parked his car at Schottentor, and walked the remaining several blocks to an all night disco.

Yuri Rubin sat in the VW that had followed Gadhafi earlier in the evening. Valentina Sergio had driven the car to the restaurant, parked the car and hid around the corner. Rubin took public transportation to meet her. Neither of them could see the door to the restaurant, but both had a good view of the street and the white Mercedes.

Valentina Sergio had eventually been sent to watch the Barr house, and Rubin took over the responsibility of the VW and watching the Mercedes in her absence. As soon as the Mercedes drove away, Rubin waited for a few minutes and started his car. He drove slowly so he could watch the lights in the restaurant.

As the waiter walked out the door, Rubin pulled up to the entrance and rolled down the passenger window. Within seconds a cassette tape landed on the empty passenger seat. Rubin had the car in gear and was gone before anyone could have noticed an exchange. The waiter walked on toward his home. The VW turned left on Billrothstrasse and drove off into the night.

CHAPTER FORTY

The last glass of wine for the evening had been drunk and the bill for the dinner had been paid. Johnny Collins felt that he had been under a microscope for the past couple hours. He even had his picture taken with the two couples, and wondered where the photo would eventually end up.

After bidding farewell to the two couples and thanking them for a pleasant evening, he decided to take a long walk to clear his head and think over what had happened. He turned down the Ringstrasse and took his time walking back in the direction of the Hilton hotel by the Graben.

No one asked to join him on his way home. Johnny gave a sigh of relief and strolled through the heart of the city. The evening had been full of pressure. He knew he was being followed and watched.

He kept thinking of the couple in the room next to his, and how like tourists they appeared. He must remember to run a check on Kevin's Swiss girlfriend. Undoubtedly, he would discover she was Russian not Swiss, and probably a SVR or FSB agent.

He glanced at his watch. The day had passed swiftly, and the bald headed agent hadn't contacted him again. Smiling, he remembered the day was not yet over. The stars were twinkling above his head as he headed down toward St. Stephen's square. After walking around the church and looking in the store windows, he stopped and listened to the bells chime on the hour.

He turned down Kartner Strasse and walked pass the Sacher Hotel. A sign in the window caught his attention. He glanced in and saw that the gift shop was still open. He hurried in and ordered a torte to be shipped to Sue back in Virginia.

Back on the street, his thoughts turned to his family. He wondered what the night was like there. He missed his wife and kids. It was times like these when he realized how lucky he was.

185

In the distance he could see the Riesenrad, the largest ferris wheel in the world. He watched the lights go around. The magic and charm of the city impressed him.

The Hilton was ablaze with lights shining from all of the windows. Taking just a moment, he made out the floor and room he was occupying. Blinking, he stared up at his room. Was he mistaken? Was that his room light that had just been turned on? He stood, glued to the spot.

He waited and watched not wanting to walk in while someone was there. He wanted them to finish whatever it was they had come to do. But, maybe it was the maid turning down his blanket and leaving a piece of chocolate on his pillow. In his business, he wasn't allowed to be careless. That was a luxury he couldn't afford.

Walking slowly, he kept a watchful eye on his room. Ready to walk into the building, he looked up for a final time. As he looked up, the light went out. Humming to himself, he went to the reception desk and asked for any messages.

He was told his phone had rung several times, but no one had left any messages. He picked up a copy of the latest USA Today from the counter, and again took his time. He purposely took the long way, through the gift shops.

He glanced at his watch as if he were meeting someone then walked to the restaurant on the first floor. He took a moment to check the diners. Turning, he shuffled toward the elevator. If someone were watching, he would have given the appearance of someone who had been stood up. Shrugging his shoulders for lack of something else to do, he talked aloud to himself, and took the elevator to his floor.

With the room card in hand, he reached for the door. Just as he stepped inside the room, the telephone rang. Closing the door tight, he hurried to answer.

"Hello," he said, pulling a chair toward the phone and throwing his jacket on the bed.

"Johnny, glad I finally caught you. I've been trying to call you for the last hour," the voice on the other end said.

Johnny recognized Swartz's voice.

"I just got in this very minute. I was at the restaurant with Kevin and his girlfriend. What's happened?"

"I got called back to the Embassy. My wife and I went out to dinner and stopped by Mrs. Metcalf to see if she was doing all right. I'd left a message with the office when I thought I'd be home. Anyway, I received a message from Frankfurt. Kay Blackburn became ill with a case of ptomaine poisoning on her flight back to Frankfurt. It's believed the airline served some tainted food. There were three other cases. An ambulance met the airplane at the airport, and she was whisked off to the hospital."

"How is she?" Johnny gasped.

"Not good. The biggest problem is, that by the time the Consulate was notified and someone went to get her courier bags, they were one short. Frankfurt immediately called us. I've begun a review of the missing bag from this end. We think it was the one that held all the classified information for the Middle Eastern embassies. I didn't want to bother you, Johnny, but I thought you'd want to know, especially after Barr's death."

"Thanks for letting me know. Do you think I should come in?" Johnny asked. He had already put his jacket back on.

"No. Not yet. I notified Washington. I'm sure they'll advise us. It's still working hours there. I'm waiting for a report from Frankfurt. They're to cable us with the list of the courier bags. They gave me a makeshift list, but I wanted to wait for the official one. I think it will be a matter of minutes. They promised to keep us notified on Kay's condition, but from the first reports, it doesn't look good. I hope she pulls through. If not, that would make two deaths within a week. That certainly is more than a coincidence. Are you going to be in your room for the rest of the night?"

"Yes, call me if you need anything," Johnny said. "No, call me as soon as you know anything at all. I'll decide then if I should come in and cable Langley. I'm sure Frankfurt will notify them. They get ticked off if they aren't told what's happening. Be sure and call, no matter what time."

"I will. I'm going to stay until I know something more definite. I'll keep in touch."

Putting the receiver back on the cradle, Johnny sat and stared. Kay's illness was too much of a coincidence to be anything but deliberate. Who else was on the plane? Could this have anything to do with the computer shipment or the missing courier bag?

Glancing around the room, Johnny had almost forgotten someone had been in his room earlier. He gave the room a quick check to see if any new listening devices had been added. He smiled when he found a new transmitter on the underside of his bed stand. The original two were still in place. He spoke aloud, "Guess it's time to go to bed now. Oh, I see the maid has been in and left a piece of candy on my pillow. Now, wasn't that nice of her?"

He didn't want anyone to lose sleep staying awake for him. Now, he was going to bed himself. If Swartz called, he could be dressed and on the way to the Embassy within minutes.

CHAPTER FORTY ONE

The night seemed endless. For some reason the sheet and blankets kept wanting to strangle Johnny. He continually tossed and turned. No matter how he moved the bed felt full of lumps. The sheet he was laying on felt as if it were covered with cracker crumbs and sand.

The claps of thunder woke him with a start. He jumped out of bed, stood dazed, looking around the room. He wasn't sure what had startled him, but for a moment all time seemed to stand still. With another flash of lightning so bright it lit up the whole room, he was jolted to the realization that it was morning.

He walked barefooted to the window and looked out into a sheet of rain. The sky was pitch black and the sounds of thunder and lightning filled the room. Looking at his watch, he saw it was almost seven. He couldn't believe his eyes. He felt as if he hadn't slept at all, but by his watch it was already morning.

He hadn't heard any more from the Embassy. He wondered if Swartz was still sitting in his office waiting for the Frankfurt police report.

He ordered breakfast, showered, and dressed for the day. Checking the temperature, he chose warm clothing. Within thirty minutes, he was in a taxi and on his way to the Embassy. As he rode down the Ringstrasse, he noticed several trees and branches had fallen during the night.

He passed by the Parliament building and saw several police cars and maintenance crews cleaning away a very large tree that had blown directly onto the steps at the entrance. He wondered why he hadn't heard the wind. As he looked closer, he saw it was the lightning hitting the tree that had caused it to fall, not the wind.

The driver continued past Schottentor and down Wahringer Strasse. Johnny saw small rivers of water flowing in the street. The cars were barely moving.

The people walked and battled with their umbrellas. He watched several umbrellas turned inside out. Owners were struggling to keep their umbrellas from being blown out of their hands. Turning onto Boltzmanngasse, approaching the Embassy, he was amazed, for a Saturday morning, to see both sides of the street lined with WD-5 Embassy cars.

When the taxi stopped, Johnny had a great deal of difficulty opening the door. The wind was blowing like a small tornado. First it pushed the door, making it almost impossible to open. Next, when the door was open, it pushed with equal force causing problems closing it. Finally, Johnny found himself inside the shelter of the Embassy. Since it was Saturday morning, the after hours logbook was full with names.

He asked the Marine why so many people were in so early. The Marine explained that during the night the electricity had gone off. Most of the offices had computers and sensitive equipment. When the electricity came back on, which was about seven, everyone came in to reset their computers and alarms.

"Modern technology," Johnny commented aloud, walking down the hallway. Upon entering Swartz's office, Johnny found Swartz sound asleep on the floor in a sleeping bag.

"Say, been a long night?" Johnny asked softly as he entered.

"What in the hell time is it?" Swartz answered, trying to get to his feet. Staggering, he stumbled and almost fell. Quickly, he grabbed a chair for support, moving his legs back and forth trying to restore their circulation. Slowly he regained feeling, and took a direct path toward the desk chair.

"It's almost eight now. We're having one hell of a storm outside. The wind and lightning have caused real havoc all over the city. On the way here in a taxi, I noticed trees and branches down all over. Water is running in the streets. Looks like a great Spring weekend," Johnny said.

"Well, I feel like hell," Swartz said. "I waited all night for Frankfurt to call back. Earlier in the evening, they had storms. In fact the Delta flight was late leaving here because of the storms there. When the weather finally cleared up in Frankfurt, the electricity was off here. Our emergency generator went on and then it died after a short period of time. By then, I decided I'd rest for a bit. Finally, I scrounged up a sleeping bag from some Marine who had just come back from camping in the Alps. Hell, it was better than nothing. If I'd known it would take all night, I'd have gone home and slept in my own bed. What a job!"

Swartz sat at his desk and yawned. He started rubbing the stubble on his face. He was wearing a suit when he had come in earlier, and now the jacket was thrown over a chair near the coffee pot. His tie was hanging over the front of the desk. His shirt and slacks looked relatively presentable, considering he had slept in them most of the night.

Johnny looked at Swartz and thought that his clothes were made from an expensive material not to show that he had slept in them all night.

"Should I make some fresh coffee?" Johnny asked hoping it might help Swartz wake up.

"Yea, go ahead," Swartz answered headed for the door. "I'm going to go wash and get cleaned up a bit. I want to see if someone will go get us some sweet rolls or semmels. I'll be back in a few minutes."

Johnny busied himself with the coffee making and then rolled up the sleeping bag and straightened up the room. Swartz had papers and empty Coke cans scattered around the room. Johnny had spent many nights like that and knew those kinds of nights were a good way to test a person's patience, endurance, and job dedication.

After a few minutes, a refreshed Swartz returned with a bag of fresh sweet rolls he had gotten from the Marines. The coffee was ready. They both took some food and began to discuss the previous night.

"So, did Frankfurt ever call back?" Johnny asked after he finished his jellyroll.

"Yea, I just picked this message up on the way back to the room from the Communication Center. Frankfurt says the list of bags received matches the ones we sent. The only one missing is

191

the one that was destined for the Middle East. They must have a listing of information it contained by now. I had it compiled and sent late last night, or early morning, whatever time it was. I had to call in Greenly. He had to call the office in charge of the computers being transferred to Israel, to provide duplicates of some of the information. We relayed it to Frankfurt as soon as we were able."

Johnny said, "Was all the material in the bag from Vienna?"

Swartz shrugged. "It's hard to tell, several of the offices give us information to transfer, but I would think most of it was."

"Then, that should make it easier," Johnny said.

"It might," Swartz answered. He poured himself another cup of coffee and freshened Johnny's. "Can you believe what happened to that back up generator? The wind blew something against it, the Marines just told me. So damn upsetting. Several of us sat here from about four to five waiting for the damn thing to start working. I finally came in to rest at about six or so. I think the other guys went on to their offices. If we would have had any sense at all, we would have all gone home."

"How's Kay, do you know?" Johnny asked.

"They don't think Blackburn is going to make it. She's still critical. Her family in the states has been notified."

"Wow! That's too bad," Johnny replied.

"Anyway, the messages were all re-transmitted again this morning, just in case. Sue Farris just came in a little after seven to relieve Mason. Mason's been here since yesterday at eight. He was really bushed. I never could get hold of Kevin Smith. We finally gave up trying to call him about two this morning."

"I left him around ten-thirty or so," Johnny said.

"It really doesn't matter now anyway. What the hell, we transmitted everything we could and Frankfurt should be reviewing it as we speak. By the way, Frankfurt still believes it was food poisoning, but all the tests hadn't been returned."

"That's too bad," Johnny stated. He could still see Kay Blackburn's face. "Has anyone gotten a list of the other passengers on the flight? Are they checking to see if this was simply an accident, or if someone could have put something in her food?"

"Yes, we called Austrian Airlines last night. They sent a list of the passengers over after midnight by courier. They were running their own investigation. It seems four passengers became ill. They couldn't say for sure where the problem was. They were going to have the food analyzed. They should know more today. None of the others became as sick as Kay. The other three were released last night after a couple hours. Sounds a bit fishy to me, doesn't it to you?"

"Sure does. Any names on that list that we should know about? Were the others that became ill sitting anywhere near where Kay was sitting? Where any of them also couriers?"

Swartz shrugged. "I gave the list to Greenly last night, but made myself a copy, too. Greenly is having his office check on the nationalities. Then, he was going to run the names through their computer. He has one of those computers that have all the aliases and junk in it. I'm not sure where any of the other sick passengers were sitting. From talking to the airline, I had the feeling they all ate the same thing, but for the life of me, I couldn't tell you what that was. Greenly was calling his people in when I was trying to round up a sleeping bag. We'll call him in a few minutes and see if anything has developed."

"Let me glance at the list. Never know, I might find something." Johnny took the list from Swartz. Sitting back in his chair, he began reviewing it.

The airline had provided a comprehensive list. It contained not only the name of the traveler, but the nationality, the passport number, the address where the ticket was purchased and the assigned seat number. He saw that Kay Blackburn had been sitting in the front row of the plane. She was correct there. All couriers were to sit in the front if at all possible. She was in seat 1A. In 1B was someone with a Japanese passport. That didn't appear to be unusual.

2A, directly behind Blackburn, contained a man with a Swiss passport. Johnny's mind whirled. The couple at the Hilton held Swiss passports, so did Kevin Smith's girlfriend.

At the CIA Farm, he had been taught that most coincidences were man made. He was sure there was a "red" connection, but he wanted to talk to Greenly first. He also wanted to ask Greenly about his meeting at the Hilton.

"I think I'll run up to Greenly's office and see if they've found anything out," Johnny said. "I'm supposed to go with Bob Blinksdale to Barrs apartment this morning. If he comes in, would you please let him know where I am?" Johnny gave the passenger list back to Swartz.

"When my wife and I went to Barrs last night, Mrs. Metcalf said you both were coming back today. She really likes you and Blinksdale. I'll bet you sat and drank coffee or wine with her, didn't you?"

"Yes, she really likes her wine," Johnny answered. "She's a nice lady."

"My wife is going over this morning to help her. They seem to hit it off. Personally, I got tired of sitting around and talking about nothing. It was as bad as some of the cocktail parties I have to go to. A big waste of time."

"I'll run up to Greenly. Anything you want me to ask him, or any messages to be relayed?" Johnny asked.

"No, just tell him we sent out all the information about the bags as soon as the electricity came on. Will you stop back before going to the housing compound?"

"I'll check back, but you can call me if you need me. I need to send a message back to my office, before I leave the Embassy this morning."

CHAPTER FORTY TWO

Johnny chose to take the elevator to the fifth floor, which held the classified rooms for the CIA operations. Greenly also had a small office on the third floor, just around the corner from the Communications Center, but it was only a cover office. He was rarely there.

The true center of his activities, within the Embassy, was behind secure doors on the fifth floor. The hallway was unmarked, and there were no signs or names on any of the doors.

Johnny remembered the area from his previous visits to Vienna. He approached a door and rang a buzzer. A voice answered from behind the vault doors. Johnny announced who he was. A silence followed. In a few moments, Greenly spoke over the speaker.

"Step back so I can see your face," Greenly ordered.

Johnny did as he was instructed, though he knew Greenly knew who he was. Greenly didn't want Johnny going back to Langley and telling them his office was slack on security.

"Stay there," Greenly said. "A door will open. You have exactly fifteen seconds to walk through the door."

The vault door opened and Johnny stepped through it and entered another chamber. Greenly was standing beside another door. Even though Johnny had all the clearances necessary to enter the rooms, he didn't have access to the code key locks on the doors.

These were changed periodically. Each day, anyone entering had to punch in a series of numbers. Once the numbers were pushed, Greenly inserted a special card, which opened the door. After all numbers were pushed and cards inserted, they both entered the sanctuary of the CIA office.

Greenly led Johnny to a small section of the room that was partitioned off from the rest of the area. The large space looked a great deal like the Communication Center on the third floor. It was filled with all sizes and shapes of computers and shredding machines. In various corners, and along walls, were file cabinets and shelves. All the file cabinets were closed and locked. A large red magnetic "CLASSIFIED" sign hung from each drawer.

Johnny glanced around the room at the people who had been called into work. They were dressed in jeans and sweat suits. It was easy to see they had been called in after hours.

No one gave Johnny more than a passing glance as he followed their boss through the room. Although, they all knew who Johnny Collins was, and why he was sent from headquarters to Vienna, they were too busy to care that he was in their office.

"Quite a busy day?" Johnny asked as he pulled up a chair to the desk.

Johnny looked behind Greenly to the huge map of Vienna secured to the wall directly above the desk chair. The map was full of small green, yellow and red flags. Johnny instantly knew what each pin represented. The flags were stuck into the map at specific locations. Each location represented either a safe drop area, agent's address or meeting place.

Langley required each CIA American agent to control several foreign agents. By the look of the Vienna map, Greenly had agents covering the entire city. Johnny was impressed.

Greenly had already walked to the desk chair. He was meticulously dressed in a gray designer suit with soft blue silk shirt and geometric designed tie which matched the color of his shirt and suit perfectly. He kept his suit jacket on. His hair was perfectly groomed, but there were black circles around his eyes.

Finally he answered, "Yes, it's been a busy morning and night."

"You don't look too bad for a busy night. Did you stay up all night, too?"

Greenly rubbed his face and twisted his neck. He said, "I came here about five or so and have been working since. I thought you might be in earlier. What made you decide to wait until morning?"

"I talked to Swartz late last night and told him to call me when he heard from Frankfurt again. Since he never heard, he didn't call. Wasn't much I could do anyway? I didn't know anything about the courier bags. I surely didn't know what they contained."

"Have you notified Langley today?" Greenly asked.

"No, I thought I would do it next. I told Swartz I'd be down before I left to go see Mrs. Metcalf with Blinksdale."

Greenly sorted through files on his desk. He opened one and took a paper out and handed it to Collins. He said, "I sent a message off late last night to the home office regarding the Blackburn woman and the missing bag. I was waiting for confirmation from Frankfurt on which was the exact bag. Did Swartz hear anything else?"

Greenly turned toward one of his people, signaled for them and whispered something. The agent left and came back with a red folder marked "TOP SECRET". Greenly handed the folder to Johnny.

Johnny took both folders and glanced through them. He said, "Swartz told me a message came in once the electricity came back on. They're comparing the bags, but it looks as if it's the Middle Eastern bag that's missing. What can you tell me about the contents?"

Greenly stared at Collins. He stuttered, "Well, uh what have you been told about relations we're working on with the Middle Eastern countries?"

Johnny snapped back, "Damn it, Greenly. You're not talking to some young recruit. You may out rank me within the Embassy with your position, but remember I out rank you within the agency. I'm tired of your bullshit. Come off it, say what's on your mind. You don't want me to place a call to Langley, do you? I know it's the middle of the night back there, but don't think for a moment I'm afraid to call the Director himself and have him order you to cooperate with me. If your talking about the computer shipment to Israel, remember, we talked about it earlier. Is that what this is all about?"

Johnny watched Greenly's face turn a bright crimson. All he wanted to do was get on with the matter at hand. Collins really didn't care what Greenly thought or didn't think.

"Collins, I don't know what you should know," Greenly stammered trying to control his temper but still unwilling to tell any more.

"Drop the act," Collins said. He kept his voice low to avoid the other agents in the room from hearing. "If some Russian comes up to me and asks me what I know about a certain computer shipment, I believe I should have some working knowledge of what the hell is going on. If Barr's death is connected to this computer shipment, then I know damn well I should know all there is to know about it. I didn't get my G-Man badge out of a cereal box!"

"Well, all right," Greenly answered with a loud sigh. "I know you know something about it. But understand, if anything comes back to me about this, I will swear under oath that you pressured me into telling you, and that you pulled rank."

"Fine," Collins said, "Just get on with it."

"Yes, we have spoken about the computer shipment. The shipment arrived this morning in the middle of the storm. It's stored in a warehouse out in the twenty-first district on the other side of the Prater, along the Danube Canal. It's going to be shipped to Israel via EL AL, Israeli airlines. We're still working out the details. The Middle Eastern governments don't want the shipment to go through."

"Have you actually gotten warnings?" Johnny asked.

"Yes," Greenly answered. "We had initially planned to ship by trucks, but after receiving threats, the Israelis suggested flying it in on specially arranged flights." Greenly stopped for a moment to collect his thoughts, then he continued, "Johnny, the complete details regarding the shipment were in the missing courier bag. Also, in the bag was a complete inventory of the shipment. The shipment contains several computers, some are satellite controlled and some are used to design missiles and nuclear weapons, warheads, as well as military supplies such as, ammunition, repair parts, uniforms, you name it. There are three huge crates. All the crates are marked "FARM MACHINERY.""

"Does Langley know all of this?" Johnny asked, shaking his head.

"Yes, they have been informed. We know the Russians and the GRU element of the Russian military is working with the Middle Eastern terrorist groups to stop the shipment."Johnny got up and walked around the small area. He turned to Greenly and said, "I was in the Hilton last evening, on the second floor. I saw you talking openly to one of the opposition. Was it about this?"

"Ah," Greenly answered. He looked at Johnny and then toward the opposite wall. "I was going to tell you about that. You had already left the Embassy when a phone call came in for you. I was at the Marine desk when it came through. The Marine told me you had left so I had the call transferred to Blinksdale's office. The caller was wanting to get in touch with you. I explained you were busy and offered to help. He was a bit reluctant, but finally agreed. We set up a meeting at the Hilton. I knew you would be there sometime. I went right down and checked to see if you had come in yet, but you hadn't. I decided I'd wait for you and tell you about the meeting but you never came back, and it was getting late. I finally decided to meet with him. I had a feeling it was the Russian SVR agent, Yuri Rubin."

"Did you ever think of calling Barr's apartment for me?" Johnny asked. He stared at Greenly.

"I tried but wasn't able to get through," Greenly answered. He glanced at Johnny and back to the wall. "I already knew what he looked like from our conversation yesterday. So when he came in, I walked up and talked as if I knew all about what he wanted. He said he had talked to you in the park about trading information. He wanted to know about the computer shipment. He wanted to warn us that someone would try and stop the shipment from reaching Israel. He didn't say who. He was attending a social function at the Hilton so it wouldn't appear out of line for him to be talking to someone from the western world. We chatted for just a moment, and then I left."

"What time was that?" Johnny asked.

"I'm not sure," Greenly answered. "Somewhere around six or after. I drove back to the Embassy and reviewed the files on the computer shipment."

"Sure sounds like it," Johnny answered. "He must know something. Did you alert the warehouse? Are they prepared for any type of attack?"

Greenly made a face and said, "Not exactly."

"What do you mean?" Collins questioned.

"I've talked to the Ambassador and the warehouse owner was told to take some security precautions, but the owner doesn't know exactly what is in the crates. He only knows they are ours."

"Whose bright idea was that?" Johnny asked.

"Actually, Ambassador Latham's. He believes the fewer people that know the details the better."

"Is he willing to take the responsibility if something goes wrong?" Johnny asked.

Greenly snickered. "I doubt it. He'll pass the buck. At the present time it has been decided not to put on special guards. They're afraid it would just attract attention and maybe even the media."

"Whatever," Johnny answered in disgust. "Did you get a list of the passengers?"

Greenly dug through the stack of loose papers on his desk. He pulled out one and handed it to Johnny. "Yes, they just finished the list when you arrived."

Collins didn't tell Greenly that he had already seen the list. He glanced at it and asked, "Did you find anything strange?"

Greenly took the list and looked it over. He answered, "There were no nationals from the eastern block countries using any aliases that we're aware of. We did find out that the man sitting behind Kay had visited Hungary recently. He's listed as a Swiss national, traveling on a Swiss passport. He sells electronic equipment. He's been in the Middle East and Hungary within the last month. That's the only one we thought might be suspicious. How is she, do you know?"

"Not good," Johnny answered. "It's such a shame. It's some kind of poisoning. Her family has been called. They are on their way over from the states. She's even too ill to make the plane trip back to Walter Reed. She might not make it."

Greenly looked concerned. He said, "We've asked the German police to see if they can locate this Mr. Henri Curiel. They're to let us know through the Frankfurt office when they locate him."

"Looks as if all we can do now is wait. I think I'll send a cable to Virginia. I'll be at the Barr house later in the day if you need me. Blinksdale and I are going to help Mrs. Metcalf. Say, did you get someone to check Barr's hard drive?" Johnny answered. He knew there was nothing further he could do in Greenly's office.

"Yes, I had everything copied and sent back to Virginia," Greenly stood up and started toward the door. "I'll probably be here for a couple more hours. I want to see what Frankfurt has to say on that passenger. If you need me over the weekend, I'll be in town. We don't have anything big planned for the weekend. We'll be at a big reception at the British Embassy on Monday evening. By the way, would you like to come with me? It starts at four and lasts until seven-thirty. We'll have one of the drivers take us straight from work. At least think about it. You might enjoy it."

"Sounds fine for now, but I'll wait and see what develops," Johnny answered. "Sometimes those receptions are so boring. I'll probably do some sightseeing tomorrow. But, I'll give you a call if anything comes up. Thanks for asking, we'll decide for sure on Monday."

CHAPTER FORTY THREE

Bob Blinksdale and Johnny Collins were getting out of Blinksdale's car as Mrs. Swartz came out of the Barr apartment. She was carrying a cardboard box full of discarded household items.

She was wearing jeans and a sweatshirt. She glanced at the two men and nodded as she walked from the door, heading toward the dumpster trash bin.

"She's really into the neighborhood spirit for a Saturday, isn't she?" Blinksdale commented as they both walked to the door.

"Her husband's been at the Embassy almost twelve hours now, so she might as well do something to keep busy. I'm sure my wife would be doing the same thing if the roles were reversed," Collins remarked just before Mrs. Metcalf answered the door.

"Good morning. The coffee's on." Mrs. Metcalf greeted the two men as if they were long lost friends.

"Good morning," they both answered together.

"So, quite a storm we had, wasn't it?"

"Yea, I'm glad it finally stopped raining," Blinksdale answered.

"Well, April showers bring May flowers, so they say," Mrs. Metcalf answered as the men took a cup of steaming coffee.

"Come, let's sit and talk about what you big husky men want to check out first. Mrs. Swartz and I've begun on the storeroom in the basement. Next, we're going to attack the kitchen. The packers will pack on Monday, and pick up on Tuesday. I've made arrangements to have my things shipped Tuesday. I'll finish up the apartment and hopefully be back with my husband and kiddos Tuesday evening, or Wednesday at the latest."

Bob Blinksdale looked at Collins, waiting for him to give a sign of what they should answer. Collins took another drink of coffee and replied, "Mrs. Metcalf, I set those two books down that I was going to take with me to the Embassy last night. I don't see them sitting on the table where I left them. Do you know where they are?"

"You are the forgetful one." Mrs. Metcalf teased. "Kay Blackburn stopped in last night on her way to the airport. In fact you must have just passed her. You two had just left when she arrived."

"Kay was here in the apartment?" Johnny asked. He would have to ask Greenly why his agent that was watching the apartment hadn't said something about her visit.

Mrs. Metcalf laughed. "Yes, here in this apartment. I haven't been out of here since the service. Her plane was delayed leaving Vienna due to bad weather in Frankfurt, so she had a couple extra hours to kill. She came by to express her sorrow over Alan. Kay is that lady that I told you about. You remember the one my sister saw the time we were shopping in Frankfurt. Well, Kay wanted to tell me how sorry she was and she stopped in to pick up a couple books that Alan had borrowed from her. I asked her was she going back to the Embassy and she said she'd be glad to drop the books off that you forgot to take with you. Didn't she give them to you?"

Collins looked at Blinksdale with a puzzled expression. They both knew Kay Blackburn was on her deathbed and she had never returned to the Embassy to deliver any books.

"What books did Alan borrow from Kay?" Collins asked.

"Oh, I'm sorry I didn't mean Alan borrowed the books, my sister borrowed them. One was the latest Tom Clancy book and one was that book about the bridges in Iowa. It's a best seller, although I have to admit I haven't read it. Kay told me it was quite good and offered to leave it with me if I wanted to read it. I told her I wouldn't have time now. Kay told me they made a movie from the book. I'll probably see the movie before I get around to reading the book."

"Did you look inside the books before Ms. Blackburn took them?" Collins asked, hoping Mrs. Metcalf had the insight to check the books first.

"Heavens, no. I've looked at so many books, I was glad to get rid of those. We had a hard time finding her two books. My sister had them upstairs in one of her suitcases in her closet. Kay said my sister probably put them in a suitcase so she would have them with her the next time she went to Frankfurt." Mrs. Metcalf thought for a moment and then added, "But, now that I think of it, it's funny. They were in a suitcase my sister rarely used. Oh, well, it's just something less for me to think about now."

Johnny was disgusted with himself for leaving the two telephone books that he wanted checked. He never even thought of checking the suitcases. Knowing there wasn't anything else he could do now about the books, he said, "I think I want to go over the rooms upstairs again. We talked about the things your taking back with you. Do you have them ready? Would you let one of us go through them?"

"My heavens, not at all," Mrs. Metcalf said. She smiled and pointed to the far corner of the room where several boxes and pieces of furniture had been moved.

Johnny nodded. He said, "The rest of their household goods, from what I've been told, will go into storage for a while. Is this right?"

A buzzer rang in the kitchen and Mrs. Swartz entered the room. "Nice and fresh outside since the rain has stopped, don't you think?" she said.

"Yes, I think spring is on the way. Say, Mrs. Swartz, have you ever met Johnny Collins? He's here from Washington," Blinksdale answered, motioning toward Collins who was sitting on his left.

"No. I'd never met him, but I believe I saw him at the Embassy the other day. My husband told me about your being here. Nice to finally meet you. How do you like Vienna?" Mrs. Swartz answered as she extended her hand toward Collins.

"Nice to meet you, Mrs. Swartz," Johnny answered as he stood and shook her hand. "I like Vienna very much. I haven't had too much time since I've been here to do any sightseeing. I thought I might do a bit tomorrow. I left your husband a few minutes ago. He told me to tell you he'll be at the Embassy for the better part of the day. He said he'd call you later."

"Jim's so devoted," Mrs. Swartz answered. "He works all the time. Oh, well, I have plenty to do here to keep me busy. What should I be doing next?" She smiled and directed her question to Mrs. Metcalf.

Mrs. Metcalf jumped up and rushed to the kitchen door. She said, "I think we're finished in the storeroom. What do you say we begin going through the cupboards in the kitchen? Since things will be going into storage, let's box up some of the items we won't be shipping, and take them to your apartment. No sense in throwing anything away, like the flour, sugar and such. We need to clean the refrigerator." The words faded as the two women walked into the kitchen, leaving the two men sitting around the dining table with their coffee.

"I'm going upstairs. What do you think you should check, Bob?" Collins asked as he stood and walked around the living room.

"I'm going to go over these books in the bookcases again. Mrs. Metcalf said she was going to take all the books with her. I see she has some in piles and in boxes, in the area with the stuff she is taking back to Frankfurt."

"I noticed books upstairs. While I'm looking, I'll give them the once over, too. Were you surprised to hear about Kay Blackburn stopping by last night?" Johnny asked, leaning toward Blinksdale and speaking in a low voice.

"Yes, I wonder if anyone else knows about it?" Blinksdale said. "I don't think she had any intention of taking those two books you left back to the Embassy."

Collins nodded, "Neither do I."

Johnny walked up stairs and left Blinksdale on the first floor. What only seemed like an hour soon developed into three hours.

Blinksdale watched as Mrs. Metcalf set food out for lunch. "We must break for some lunch. You men must be starved," she commented as she walked to the stairway to call Collins.

After a quick lunch of cold cuts and foods supplied by the neighbors, the men hurried back to their searching. So far, neither man had found anything of interest.

The day sped past. Mr. Swartz called his wife early in the afternoon to tell her he was still at the Embassy and planned on being home before six. Mrs. Metcalf left Mrs. Swartz busy in the kitchen and went to begin cleaning the bathrooms.

While Mrs. Swartz was packaging up the flour and sugar, she found a plastic bag in the bottom of the flour canister. She took it out and carefully wiped it off. Without opening the bag, she examined it. Her husband had told her to look for anything suspicious while she was cleaning. Realizing the bag contained a tape cassette, she looked carefully around to see if anyone was watching. Cautiously she placed the bag in with the box of things she had for her house. Then, she returned to her cleaning as if nothing had happened.

Johnny checked the master bedroom in the late afternoon. He was beginning to think there was nothing hidden in the apartment. He remembered being told never overlook the obvious. Things were usually in plain sight.

Recalling this, he took a new approach to the search. Sitting on the bed, he reached for a book lying on the nightstand. He had previously noticed the book, but hadn't thought anything about it. The book contained a bookmarker, as if someone had been reading it and had just put it down. Picking up the book, he turned to the page where the marker was.

There was nothing unusual. Finally, ready to put the book down, he turned to the Table of Contents.

"Well, I'll be damned," he said. Running to the top of the stairs, Johnny called for Blinksdale to come see him in the bedroom. The ladies heard Collins and ran to the steps.

"Just Blinksdale if that's okay with you," Johnny said when he saw everyone at the foot of the steps.

"Bob, let me show you what I've found," he whispered as they walked into the bedroom and shut the door. He handed Blinksdale the book he was holding with the Table of Contents exposed.

Taking the book from Collins, Blinksdale glanced through the pages Johnny had opened. "It's about time one of us found something," Blinksdale commented with a big sigh as he read the Table of Contents.

The book had various pages circled and, beside each, was a number. The book had been converted into a codebook. When they checked the page that was circled, and the number, they found that each number meant a certain word. The words ran from train, bus, car, and various forms of communication to places in a city, such as park, zoo, etc.. The men suspected this was the way communication between Barr and his controller was made. It would have been easy to follow. As they checked it further, they found it could also suggest a day of the month, and a different meeting place. It was so simple, but very effective. The book didn't give a name of a specific hotel or cafe. They were sure Barr had that part memorized.

Both men began searching the bedroom with a renewed interest. They looked for two hours steady without talking. Finally, they decided there wasn't anything else.

When the men went downstairs, they found Mrs. Swartz had already called it a day. She went home with a care package to fix dinner for her husband. She planned to return in the morning after church.

Mrs. Metcalf was sure that with Mrs. Swartz's help, they would be ready for packers on Monday. Blinksdale and Collins agreed they also would call it a day.

Collins would have liked to stay longer, but Mrs. Metcalf was beginning to look exhausted. He didn't want anything to turn her against him, so he asked if he could also return in the morning, if she didn't mind. She smiled and agreed. Blinksdale added he would stop by later in the afternoon after he had spent some time with his family. Neither men mentioned anything about what they had found upstairs, and Mrs. Metcalf didn't ask.

When the men walked out the door, they saw an Embassy car pull into the parking lot. The men turned and told Mrs. Metcalf good evening as an agent from Greenly's office arrived to offer his assistance, if needed.

"Do you still have the book with you?" Blinksdale asked as they rode down Peter Jordan Strasse toward the Embassy.

"Yes, in my pocket. I want to look at it closer, and then I'll turn it over to Greenly and have it sent back to the States by courier. I don't want it to leave our hands until it's on that courier flight. I still think there's more in that house. What do you think?" Johnny asked as he patted the book safely in his jacket pocket.

"I agree. Barr met someone the evening he was taken. It was someone that either called or sent a message. It must have been a routine meeting. His wife wasn't home. He wouldn't have gone to any bank, it was late Friday or the weekend. They were just arriving back from a vacation. Unless, he had money stashed in the house, he would have been low on cash. I'll bet his wife knows. I don't know why she didn't take the book with her on the plane when she went back to the states. Unless, she was afraid she might be searched. If she were found with it on her person, she would probably be in a federal prison now. I think they were in it together, just like twins. Gemini twins. Almost like your typical spy story." Blinksdale commented as he stopped the car for a red light and almost hit the car in front of him.

Collins answered, "I agree but I can't figure out how Kay Blackburn figures into this, except she was doing courier runs to Moscow when the Barrs were there. Do you suppose she knew about them bringing icons out and selling them? What do you think, Bob? Should we go to the Ambassador and the Administrative Officer and have the packing delayed until we are positive we don't have anything else to check in that apartment?" He braced himself as the car missed a near collision on the passenger side with a streetcar.

"I don't know, Johnny. Let's wait until we finish tomorrow. The packers are coming on Monday. We can always put a hold on it Monday morning when they arrive."

When the men got out of the car and started toward the Embassy, John turned back toward the traffic. He watched a VW with the license plate W 634276 pass.

It was turning dusk and the street lights had not been lit. Although, Johnny wasn't able to get a good look at the driver, he sensed it was Kevin Smith's Swiss girlfriend. He needed to check the license number of her car again just to be certain.

Blinksdale went back to his office, and Collins took the elevator to the Communication Center. He read the list of messages that had arrived while he was gone. Greenly had received one from Langley and Swartz had received several from Frankfurt.

He was told Swartz had gone home. Johnny glanced to a sign posted on the wall. It stated: "We will be sending flowers to Kay Blackburn's funeral on Wednesday. All those willing to contribute, please sign."

He signed his name, and decided he, too, would call it a day. That made two deaths. He felt his pocket and remembered the book. Bidding the Communicators a good weekend, he left for Greenly's office.

The fifth floor was just as busy as it had been earlier in the day. The ritual of him entering the CIA office wasn't as strict as it had been earlier in the morning. Greenly allowed one of the men to open the door and escort Johnny to his desk.

Johnny noticed how tired Greenly looked. Choosing an upholstered chair in the corner, Johnny pulled it closer to Greenly's desk. He told Greenly about his visit to the restaurant the night before and explained about the book and the afternoon at the Barr house. Greenly listened attentively, making a couple notes as Collins talked.

"Have you sent a message to Langley about the restaurant and your suspicions about the couple you met?" Greenly asked as he consulted his notes when Johnny stopped talking.

Stretching his weary arms over his head, Johnny answered. "I sent a short message early this morning but thought we could send a longer one now. I want you to include comments regarding this book in the cable. Do they know about Kay's death? Has an autopsy been ordered?"

"Yes, I'm sure they'll do an autopsy," Greenly answered. He made a note in his notebook. "But, I'll send a message just in case. I want one of my people to look over the book over the weekend. We won't be able to send it back until Monday anyway. You don't have any objections, do you?"

Johnny was thankful Greenly's manner had mellowed because it made it easier for the two men to work together. Collins really didn't care who examined the book. "Whatever is fine with me. I only want the lab to check it over eventually."

"I'll have a report ready by morning." Greenly answered, thumbing through the book.

Johnny noticed Greenly's hand shake as Greenly fingered through the book. Johnny didn't know who of the clerks would be working all weekend, and really didn't want to know.

"Anything else we should add?" Collins asked as the two men sat after finalizing their message to Virginia. Johnny felt they had explained a great deal, but knowing Hubert, whatever they wrote still wouldn't be enough.

CHAPTER FORTY FOUR

The ringing of the telephone was constant. The sound blended in perfectly with the dream. The dream shifted, but the ringing kept on and on. Slowly the sense of awareness awakened Johnny. He bolted upward in his bed. The ringing of the phone continued. He reached for the telephone by his bed.

"Yes," he whispered, for fear he was still dreaming.

"Johnny, is that you?" Greenly's voice echoed across the wire.

Fully awake now, Johnny answered, "Yes. I'm awake now."

"How soon can you come into the Embassy? I'm at the Communication Center."

"I think in about thirty minutes or so," Johnny answered quickly. Then he remembered it was Monday. "Wait, this might be a long day. Is that reception still on for this afternoon?"

"Yes, around four."

"Give me no more than an hour. I'll need to shave and get respectful. Something tells me I won't be back here for a while. Do I go right to the Comm. Center?"

Greenly answered, "I'll meet you there in an hour. Swartz was here but he went home again. He'll be back by then too."

The shadows of the dream, Johnny had were fresh in his mind. He had called his wife last night after spending most of the day with Mrs. Metcalf. When he called home, he was feeling low. His wife had a way of cheering him up, even from a distance of thousands of miles.

Within forty-two minutes, Johnny walked into the Communication Center at the American Embassy. It was just barely seven, and already Mason, Smith, and Farris were busy in the room. Johnny wondered when these three slept. They always seemed to be at work. He spied Swartz and Greenly talking in the corner.

"Early today, aren't we?" Collins asked breaking into their conversation.

"Let's go into my office," Swartz said and led the way out of the center and down the hall to his office.

"Close the door, will you Collins?" Greenly ordered as he pulled a chair closer to the desk. Swartz had already walked to the desk and unlocked a drawer and removed some papers.

"Well, Johnny, we had several cables arrive late last night and more already this morning. What it boils down to is Kay Blackburn was a double agent. Frankfurt combed her apartment yesterday. They found a codebook exactly like the one you found at Barrs. They found thousands of dollars hidden all over her apartment. But, they never recovered the books you said she took from the Barr's apartment."

"Mrs. Metcalf said she left with them. Could she have left them at the pouch room or such in Frankfurt?" Johnny asked. Then he remembered she hadn't gone to the pouch room. He added, "Maybe they are in her purse or suitcase."

Greenly said, "In fact we haven't recovered any personal suitcase or purse she had with her on that flight from Vienna to Frankfurt. She either didn't take them along or someone beat us to them. We're checking with the airline to see if she checked any baggage in before the flight or if they have any unclaimed bags. Often couriers carry their bags aboard. She might have done that and if she did we won't have any record."

Johnny looked at Greenly and at Swartz. He said, "Someone has to have taken them. Who drove her to the airport here in Vienna?"

Greenly answered. "We are checking on that. It seems she was driven out by one of the Embassy drivers and he is on vacation for a couple days."

Johnny sighed, "Can't they get in touch with him?"

Greenly snapped back, "We are trying. She evidently thought her bank accounts would be checked, so she believed in keeping cash in the apartment. We found she had a couple savings accounts but neither of them were over ten thousand dollars. That amount isn't suspicious."

"No," Johnny answered. "Most people have about ten thousand in savings somewhere."

Greenly shifted in his chair. "We have reason to believe she was paid to have that courier bag stolen. We don't know how they did it. They must have thought she was becoming a threat."

"Who?" Johnny asked.

Greenly answered, "We have a couple leads but not sure who just yet. Probably someone from the Middle East."

"Do we have a name or group?" Johnny questioned.

"Not for sure, but my people are working on it," Greenly answered. "The medical examiner ruled she was poisoned by some exotic toxin. Something called ricin. I had never heard of it. Frankfurt said they had to run several tests to determine exactly what kind of poison it was. They thought at first it was some type of botulism. It seems this ricin was popular during World War II. We sent a message to Washington for more information on it. The doctor in Frankfurt said he thought the poison was from a castor bean, but he wasn't sure either."

"How did they discover it?" Johnny asked.

Greenly sighed. "The weekend doctor, an elderly man, analyzed it. He had seen it during the War. It's not your most common way of killing someone. The hospital performed the usual stomach pumping but they were simply too late. She grew weaker and weaker. Nothing worked, and she eventually died. From what I've learned the poison is quite deadly. The caffeine was probably the only think that was fighting to keep her alive. Caffeine seems to slow the reaction."

"Maybe our lab can find out more when the body gets back to Washington?" Johnny said.

"Maybe so," Greenly answered. "From the books and all the other evidence we've found in her apartment, it looks as if she has been with them for some time. Maybe ever since she became a courier. Which could have been several years. We're debriefing anyone who has had any contact with her in Frankfurt and along the routes she held. Without a doubt, there's a connection between her and Barr and maybe even Mrs. Barr.

Although we have no evidence against Mrs. Barr. The fact that Kay had two books that Mrs. Metcalf says her sister borrowed from Kay is not evidence. It could be perfectly innocent."

"I doubt that," Johnny laughed.

"We may never find out to what degree Kay was connected to the Barrs," Swartz said. He spoke for the first time in the conversation.

"Do either of you have any idea where the computer shipment fits into this?" Johnny asked.

"I think information was leaked about the shipment, and some factions are trying to stop it. I don't know much more than that. I thought I'd drive out to the warehouse later today and check to make sure that all was going along according to schedule. We should have a definite report soon on when it will be shipped out of Vienna," Greenly answered, with the best attitude Johnny had seen since his arrival in Vienna.

Swartz stood and said, "Well, I'm going to finish some reports and try to get things back in order here. My wife is back with Mrs. Metcalf this morning. They'll have all the things packed and ready for pick up tomorrow. I believe Mrs. Metcalf is having her things shipped, too. Did you get a chance to go through the things Mrs. Metcalf is shipping back to Frankfurt, Johnny?"

Johnny stood and stretched. "I spent most of the day with them yesterday. Blinksdale joined me later in the day. I couldn't find anything else in the house that gave any clues. We didn't cut up the mattress or the furniture. Someone could do that after the household goods are packed if they think it's necessary. Since it's all government furniture, I didn't think it was necessary. I suggest we notify Frankfurt to keep a watch on the things Mrs. Metcalf is having shipped. One never knows if something might show up later. I think Mrs. Barr needs to be debriefed in the states."

Greenly stood and walked a few steps with the men. He said, "Yes, I agree, but we have very little control on Mrs. Barr. Alan was the employee, not his wife. Legally, she could make hell for the agency if we insisted she undertake any type of debriefing. Maybe when you send a report this morning you might suggest it to Langley."

When Greenly and Collins prepared to separate at the Comm. Center door, Greenly added in a whisper. "I wanted to tell you this, but I didn't want to say anything about it in front of anyone else in the Embassy. When they were doing the autopsy on Blackburn they found a mole on her."

Johnny's eyes grew wider, "Let me guess. It was on the underside of her knee on her left leg. Am I right?"

"How in the hell did you know that?" Greenly questioned, pulling Johnny by the arm into a supply closet.

Collins smiled and said, "I saw Barr had one in the same place on his body."

"Well, I'll be damned. Why wasn't I told?" Greenly demanded.

Collins shrugged. "I believe it's in the report that the Embassy doctor made when he first examined Barr in the warehouse. I just remember the Doc mentioning it. Until now, I never thought anything about it. Did they cut off Blackburn's mole?"

"Well, he not only cut off the mole, but he found out it was man made. Can you believe that?" Greenly added.

"Those slimy bastards. Was it checked to make sure it wasn't a tracking device or such?

"They have sent it back to Washington and it will be tested," Greenly said.

Johnny smiled. "Isn't that something. Just think about it. They have branded their double agents. They think it's a game. I bet if we were able to check others we would find more people with a mole in the exact same place. A mole for a mole. Actually, it's pretty clever. Everyone knows a double agent is called a mole." Greenly answered, "This whole business is making my stomach churn. What a mess! No one will be able to find out how long those two have been working for the Russians."

215

Johnny pushed against the door. He laughed and said, "Well, the first thing we're going to do is get out of this damn closet and go to your office. We have to send a message back to Hubert right away. He'll be really pissed."

Collins tugged at Greenly's arm as he opened the closet door. Stepping back out into the hallway was like a breath of fresh air. As the two men rushed to Greenly's office, Johnny kept taking deep breaths of fresh air to clear his mind.

The remainder of the day flew, and it was time for Johnny to meet Greenly before he knew it. They had agreed to meet for the British reception. Collins kept busy with reports and meetings with Blinksdale and Swartz.

Around four, Greenly walked down the steps looking like a million dollars. He had gone home and showered and changed clothes. His suit was a proper dark blue, almost hard to distinguish from black. He had spent time getting everything to perfection without being too showy. Johnny was impressed. All Greenly was missing was a ribbon across his chest, like the diplomats wore when they were in formal attire.

"Glad to see you haven't changed your mind, Johnny." Greenly remarked as they walked out the door to a waiting Embassy car. "I've decided to drive us to the reception today instead of using a driver. This way we'll have more flexibility in case we want to deviate and follow someone after the reception. It's rather hard to do that when you have a driver."

Collins nodded his head in agreement. He was glad to see Greenly was thinking the same way he was regarding Rubin and where the evening might eventually lead them.

CHAPTER FORTY FIVE

The more George Haddah stayed in Vienna, the more he dreaded going back to the Middle East. The weather was beautiful as he and Mehmet Gadhafi sat and watched the children file out of the school building, and into the waiting school buses. They had already activated a device that would create interference and make the radios inoperative before the children began to leave the school building.

As they watched, they observed Gabrielle looking very much like a mother boarding the school bus with the children. Earlier, she had gone with them and parked her car at the site. They had rehearsed her role in the bus hijacking before she returned to school. She had told the two men, that if anything seemed suspicious to anyone at the school, she would walk out early and wait on the school grounds.

Everything went like clockwork. She took a seat on the bus, directly behind the driver and shared the seat with a small child.

The men watched her talk to people as if she belonged. They didn't anticipate any problems because the children came from various backgrounds, and speaking English was just one of the requirements. Gabrielle's having an accent didn't matter.

The two men waited in their stolen car after confirming the car bombs had been placed in the cars of the American Ambassador and the Director of British Oil. They also re-confirmed a bomb had been placed in the guest bathroom on the first floor of the British Embassy.

The Hamas followers guaranteed they would detonate the bombs at the British Embassy, within minutes of each other, starting at four fifty-five. The Hamas also agreed to meet later in the evening to receive pay for their services.

The two men looked at their watches. The first buses began to pull away and begin their trip homeward. They followed their bus at a safe distance. The remainder of the buses turned off on their appointed routes. As their bus crossed the canal, the men could see Gabrielle talking to the driver. The bus turned and followed the route that had been planned by the men. They followed closely behind the bus, but kept a couple cars between the bus and their car. Nothing seemed unusual. As they drove further out of town, children could be seen looking out the windows.

Some of the children realized the bus wasn't following the normal route. They didn't seem to be frightened. They just looked to see if maybe there might be a detour sign. Some of the children got up and walked around.

Finally, the bus arrived at the designated spot. The men watched as Gabrielle stood up inside the bus. They could see a gun in her hand. Control came to the bus immediately. All the children sat down in their seats, and the men heard a loud cry come from inside the bus.

CHAPTER FORTY SIX

The American School was almost deserted. One of the teachers had invited the rest of the teachers to an after school barbecue. Most of the teachers left for home as soon as they cleared their desks and saw the buses leave.

The janitors were busy cleaning and heard the phones ringing, but never paid any attention. The ringing was a little heavier than normal, but that didn't seem to concern the janitors.

Parents began to worry when their children hadn't arrived home on their normal schedule. They called one another. It didn't take long for the families to learn one of the buses hadn't kept to its regular route. Mothers who usually didn't panic were suddenly afraid something had happened to the children. Some upset mothers called their husbands at work when they were unable to contact the American school. Parents called one another, asking if anyone knew if the school bus had broken down.

Several parents called the School Director at his home. They were told the Director and his wife were attending a formal reception at the British Embassy. Having no idea of diplomatic procedure, the mothers decided to wait a few more minutes before calling the police.

Some mothers got into their cars and drove the bus route looking for the bus. Other parents called the bus company, asking if the bus had broken down. The bus company said they had not heard anything from the bus driver and were unable to contact him on his radio. Uneasy, concerned parents could only sit and watch the minutes tick pass.

CHAPTER FORTY SEVEN

Colonel Nikolai Golodin was at the reception at the British Embassy. Occasionally, he glanced at his watch. His fellow Russian representative, Yuri Rubin, had listened to all of the tapes from the meetings at the Middle Eastern restaurant. He had forwarded the tapes to SVR/FSB headquarters in Moscow.

That very morning he had been given specific orders, direct from Moscow, not to interfere with Golodin's plan. Rubin watched as Golodin disappeared down the hall toward the men's restroom. Rubin had to control himself not to follow.

He knew it was time for Golodin to make the call to the American Embassy and the American School regarding the school bus. Rubin also knew Golodin would be able to leave by a back door through the hallway. Rubin was sure Golodin had enough foresight not to make the call from within the British Embassy.

Rubin walked around the building. He talked to everyone as a good Russian representative. Off in a corner, he spotted Greenly and Collins.

For a split second, he considered telling the two men to leave immediately. Instead, he stepped to the side and watched. He knew the call was being made. If one thing the GRU stressed, it was being punctual.

Glancing at his watch, Rubin decided it was time for him to leave. He wanted to wait to see the reaction but feared for his life. As he walked out the door saying his farewells, he saw activity center around the Americans.

Greenly had been called to the telephone. He rushed back and whispered to Collins and the School Director who were standing nearby. Rubin moved to a corner, observing all the excitement, but out of view of the casual eye. He knew what was causing the excitement. He was amazed to see that the Americans were following protocol, and made the proper farewells before leaving.

Rubin looked at his watch and noted it was almost four-fifty. Walking as fast as he dared, he hurried to his car, which he had purposely parked two blocks away from the British Embassy.

Just as he started his car and turned down the street toward the Russian Embassy, he heard an explosive sound, then another and by the time he turned onto Ring Strasse, he heard the third blast. His hands were sweating, because he knew what had made the noise.

CHAPTER FORTY EIGHT

The taking of the American school bus driver and the children on the bus went exactly as planned. Gabrielle had taken the trouble to lock the door when she got off the bus. She told the children the bus driver was going to get someone to come and help them.

She warned them about trying to leave the bus for fear they would get lost. She stressed it was almost dark, and little children could get lost, kidnapped, or hurt if they wandered around in the dark by themselves.

When the driver and Gabrielle were out of sight of the children and hidden by her car, she told the driver to put his hands behind his head. She pulled a roll of white surgical tape from her purse and bound his hands securely. She also placed tape over his mouth.

His eyes filled with tears. He was a man in his late forties and shorter than most Americans. He was dressed in a gray shirt and gray slacks. His arms were muscular from years of repairing automobiles. He offered no resistance.

Gabrielle put the driver in the back seat of her small car. He was cramped. She glanced out her rear view mirror and saw the two men parked on the road behind her. They hadn't interfered or made themselves known to the children or the driver. After she left, they would be free to go back to Vienna and not fear exposure.

She would be heading for the Hungarian border, and she knew she wouldn't get caught nor recognized. As she started her car, she hummed to herself. She pulled out on the road as the two men left their parked car and crept toward the bus. They were slashing the tires on the bus as she sped down the road.

After several minutes of driving, she pulled off into an area frequented by tourists during the summer months. On the side of the road was a restaurant built into the side of the hill, like a cave. No one was around. The restaurant was closed until June.

She stopped the car and told the bus driver to get out. Leading him to the cave, she forced the door open and motioned for him to enter. She took more tape and bound his legs together. He did exactly as she wanted. She pulled the door closed behind her and promised to call the police at the border and give them instructions on where to find him.

The driver sat quietly until he heard the car drive away. He waited several minutes for fear she might return to check on him.

When he felt it was safe, he rolled from the chair. With his feet, he pulled open the door and rolled out toward the highway. He knew few cars would be on the road so late in the evening and could have a long wait for help. He started praying.

CHAPTER FORTY NINE

After slashing the bus tires and making sure the children were safe inside the bus, George Haddah and Mehmet Gadhafi followed Gabrielle as she drove away from the bus. They watched as she returned to her car from putting the driver in the cave.

They watched as she headed directly for the Hungarian Austrian border. They parked on a side road and waited until she was in the traffic line and ushered to the Hungarian side.

She had already taken off her blonde wig and was waiting for her passport check on the Hungarian side when they turned their car around and headed back toward Vienna. They purposely avoided taking the same road back to the city. Once back in the city, they drove to the bus barn where some of the buses were kept and serviced.

The area was fully lit. There were police cars everywhere. Turning down Heligenstater Strasse, they drove down to Nussdorf and turned up Wahringer Strasse toward the American Embassy on Boltzmanngasse. It was now after eight. Several WD-5 cars were parked in front of the Embassy. They commented to one another that the Americans must have called in all their reinforcements.

Pleased with themselves, the men decided to drive up to Salmannsdorfer and past the American School. When they approached the area, they were amazed at all the police cars. Parents were standing in the parking area that earlier held the school buses. Police were talking to the parents trying to calm them.

Several truckloads of military men, dressed in combat fatigues, arrived as the men parked their car. The uniformed men immediately began roping off the school and blocking the traffic into the schoolyard.

George and Mehmet decided to ditch the car they were driving and come back and wait for the bus load of children to arrive. They got back in the car, drove past the school down the Hohenstrasse, and parked the stolen car on a dark side road. They left the keys to the stolen car in the ignition.

They walked through the woods, following a path that led to the tramline that would take them back into the city. As they walked, they both removed the light weight gloves they had been wearing since early morning. Walking past a tree, the two men took the gloves and buried them deeply under one of the roots.

Then, they continued on their way toward the city. They had already parked Haddah's Mercedes near the school and headed back toward it.

CHAPTER FIFTY

Greenly and Collins had talked to the Director of the school before walking toward their car after leaving the British Embassy. Greenly had advised the Director to go back to the school and keep the parents informed about their missing children. They would call the police from the Embassy. Greenly promised as soon as they could, one of them would go to the school and help.

Greenly was pulling out of his parking place when the first car bomb exploded. Startled, the men knew immediately what the noise was. He pulled the car back toward the curb and stopped. They sat silent, looking around.

Although, they knew the explosion came from the direction of the British Embassy, they spent a moment deciding whether they should go to the American School or back to the British Embassy. Suddenly, the second car bomb exploded.

Without hesitation, the men decided to go back to the British Embassy to offer assistance. Greenly drove the car onto the sidewalk.

The third explosion rocked the area. It caused the streetlights near them to shake and their light bulbs to explode.

"What in the hell was all of that?" Collins quizzed looking toward the British Embassy. He could see clouds of smoke and dust rising above the huge structure.

"It sounds as if someone has declared war on the British Embassy. Come on, we'd better hurry," Greenly answered running down the street.

As the men arrived on the scene, the reception guests were filing out of the British Embassy in the state of shock. Several were bleeding and their clothes were torn and shredded. They walked dazed.

Collins looked at the scene. He knew instantly that two of the blasts were the result of two car bombs. He could tell by the twisted metal in the parking area that the bombs had been carefully prepared to destroy most of the cars nearby.

"Looks like a battle zone," Collins yelled to Greenly who was standing beside him.

Instantly, the entire area filled with screaming people and people rushing to offer assistance. Horns were blowing and smoke filled the air.

"Is that the Ambassador's car?" Greenly shouted, running toward the American flag which was still flying proudly over the armored car.

"They did some damage, but not as much as they would have liked to, by the looks of things," Collins added, pleased to find that the armored car was battered but not destroyed.

The Embassy driver was smiling as he touched the vehicle. "Really strong old babe, isn't she? She came through that blast a bit shook up but she still runs. I'm proud of her."

"Looks as if she has had some damage. Will you be able to drive her back to the residence?" Greenly asked when he saw the American Ambassador, Robert Latham, run toward them.

The driver smiled and said, "Yes, she'll get him there safely. She was especially designed to ward off such attacks. She'll be all right. Ambassador, do you want to go right home?"

"Yes, in just a moment." The Ambassador turned to Greenly and asked, "What is this all about? Do you know? I was talking to the British Ambassador about the school bus incident when I heard the blasts. The British security had us both under chairs while they investigated. I just now was allowed to get up. What's going on, do you have any ideas?"

The Ambassador spoke as his eyes took in the devastation around him. He stood away from his car and surveyed the damage. His hand went up to motion to someone he saw approaching from the other side of the lot.

Greenly leaned toward the Ambassador and said, "I really don't know. A message came to the British Embassy that a school bus from the American School had been hijacked. The group behind the bus hijacking wants several million dollars.

Collins and I were on our way to the school when we heard the three blasts. We came back to see if we could help. It really looks as if everything is under control now. We're going to go to the Embassy and then to the school."

The Ambassador answered, "Keep me informed. I'll be at the Embassy as soon as I know what's going on around here. I have a reception tonight that I have to attend, but I'll go to the school if at all possible." The Ambassador turned and said a few words to the man to whom he had motioned. Turning back toward his car, he took a cell phone out of his pocket and checked his watch.

Greenly and Collins stopped for a few moments to offer assistance before heading back to their car. On the ride back to the Embassy, Greenly told Collins of the phone call that had come to the Embassy and his short talk with the Ambassador.

Greenly explained the terrorist message had been read over the phone to him. But, as he related the message to Collins he only touched on the main points.

"They want millions of dollars?" Collins asked as Greenly parked the car in front of the Embassy. "How soon do they want this money?"

"I don't know all the details," Greenly answered. "Let's check here at the Embassy before going to the school to make sure someone is manning the control centers. The British are capable of handling the car bombings. We need to concentrate on the bus situation."

In the Communication Center, several of the agents from Greenly's office were sitting with Mason and Smith. Swartz was off in the corner reading a file. Collins and Greenly walked toward Swartz. While the men stood talking, they saw the Ambassador arrive. Instantly, the Ambassador began briefing everyone in the room on the situation at the British Embassy.

"I called from my car as you men were leaving the British Embassy and sent Blinksdale up to the school to see if anything developed there. The Austrian police have been notified. They're at the school now. I have to attend a formal function tonight, but do let me know if anything develops. I've called the school and offered any help that we can give."

The Ambassador pulled Collins and Greenly aside. "Don't forget, that computer shipment must go to Israel. It's scheduled to leave within 48 hours. I've a cable into Washington now. We expect an answer from the White House any minute. Is everything ready on our end?"

Greenly answered, "We just finalized the plans today. It leaves by plane on Wednesday evening. Should be in Israel in a matter of hours. All the clearances have been approved. It's just a matter of getting it out of Vienna and on its way."

"Good. Pray none of the children are hurt. What kind of men would harm children? I'm sure reporters will catch me at the reception. I'll only comment about the type of people who would make such an attack on defenseless children. Thanks, gentlemen, for all of your help. I know times like these put a strain on everyone. Let's hope no one is hurt. A prayer might be called for at this time."

The three men stood and watched the Ambassador being shown out the door by Mason. Mason had been on duty and had taken the call. He insisted on staying until Greenly and Collins had arrived.

Swartz said, once Mason had left. "The school called the parents of the children on the bus. They asked parents if they wanted, they could go to the school and wait. They felt being part of a group would be more comforting. Mason has a son on the bus. His wife called and said she wanted to go to the school. He agreed and said he would pick her up as soon as you two arrived here. He's been very calm. Smith is here, and I'll stay until the bus is returned safely. All we know is what we were told in the message. But, there was something else we found out from the School Director when the names of the students were given to us a few minutes ago. It's the strangest coincidence. The man who owns the warehouse that's storing the "farm machinery" has a son on that bus. Isn't that something?" Swartz shook his head.

"Someone did their homework!" Collins remarked.

"I'm going to go back to my office and get a message ready for Langley. If they hear about this over the wire service, the shit will hit the fan. Collins, are you going to send anything back now?" Greenly asked almost running out the door.

"No, I'm going to wait a while. I think I'd like to go to the school. Do you think I could get a ride up there? I want to watch the people and the cars. I believe the kidnappers might be watching the area. I also think we should check the warehouse. Have we any guards there?"

"No," Greenly answered. "I hope we haven't made a mistake in judgment on that one. We didn't want to cause any undo concern for the warehouse. If you're going to the school, you might get a chance to talk to the owner. Tell him things look as if all is going according to schedule. I talked to him earlier today. He'll be very concerned."

"I'll search him out," Johnny said.

Swartz walked back into the room. "A driver will be assigned to you for the rest of the evening. He's waiting out front now."

"Great," Collins said. "I'll get back in touch if anything happens. I'll take a cell phone with me. Jim, can I use the same one that Bob and I took to the warehouse? "

After picking up the phone, Collins bolted down the stairs for the waiting driver. The Marine intercepted him and had him sign the logbook both in and out. Collins told him he borrowed Swartz's cell phone. Collins knew it was procedure for Post One to have a list of names and numbers of all Embassy cell phones.

HAPTER FIFTY ONE

Collins recognized the driver from his days at the Embassy. The driver drove carefully, but faster than normal. Within minutes, he was parked near a police car on a side street before the entrance to the American International School parking lot.

"I'll stay by the car, just in case I have to move it. Just look for me when you're ready to leave," Kurt, the driver, told Collins.

"Thanks," Collins answered. He instantly headed toward a group of parents who were standing near the school theater.

Collins saw the Director, and signaled to him. As Collins walked to meet the Director several reporters ran toward the Director.

The Director saw the reporters, raised his hand and walked toward Johnny. He whispered, "I haven't given anything to the reporters yet. What do you think of having all the parents go into the theater, and I'll talk to all of them at one time?"

Collins nodded and walked to the Director toward the High School Principal. They talked for a few minutes, then, Johnny left to talk to Blinksdale who was surrounded by a circle of policemen.

Johnny could hear one of the policemen telling Blinksdale the Americans shouldn't make any decisions regarding the case. They had no right to agree to any type of ransom. It was strictly an Austrian police matter and a simple case of kidnapping.

"Sir, I think the Director wants to make an announcement to the parents and the press in the theater," Collins said, knowing he was breaking into the conversation. But, he wanted to take the pressure off Blinksdale. He looked directly at the policeman and said, "I think you should go talk to him before he does."

"I agree," Blinksdale added, nodding to Collins. After the policeman left, Blinksdale continued. "Thanks, he was really getting on my nerves and he has no authority. He is just a street cop."

The men stood and listened as the announcement was broadcasted over the speakers regarding the meeting, which was going to be held in the theatre. They both stood back and watched the parents rush into the theater anxious to hear the latest news regarding the bus and the children.

"Thanks for that!" Blinksdale sighed. "All of these Austrian police have been a royal pain in the ass ever since I showed up."

"I could tell that last one wasn't your best friend. So, what's happening here?" Collins stood to the side of Blinksdale so he could see the policeman talking to one another.

"Really not any more than you know," Blinksdale sighed. He pointed to the area where the cars were parked. "As you can see, the police are everywhere. See all those men in the combat uniforms? They're the Austrian SWAT team. Look, they're on the roofs of the buildings near the soccer field. I don't think anyone would try anything here now. They have set up roadblocks all over the area. Were you stopped on the way up?"

"No," Johnny answered. "I didn't see any road blocks. I noticed several police on the corners of the streets when we drove up Krottenbach. They didn't stop us, though. But, remember I was in an official Embassy car with dip plates. I'm sure that had something to do with our not being stopped."

"Yes, that probably had everything to do with it," Blinksdale answered with a chuckle. "They probably thought you were some big wheel."

Johnny laughed and relieved some of the tension, "Boy, would they be surprised if they knew it was just me."

Blinksdale also laughed. "Look, more parents are still coming. I think the police have a list and aren't letting many friends pass. There were thirty-five kids listed on the bus. We did find out two students that normally ride the bus stayed after school and took public transportation home."

"Do we know anything about the students," Johnny asked. He watched two policemen escort a couple to the theatre. "Those people over there look as they are someone important."

Blinksdale watched the couple and then answered, "They probably are. Several of the students are children of diplomatic families from other embassies. The last stop for the day was at the corner of one of our Embassy housing compounds. Several of the children belonged to our Embassy. We have no idea why this bus was chosen. Did you find out anything further?"

Johnny shivered. It was beginning to get cold. The sun had gone down and there was a slight wind. He wished he had worn something over his suit jacket. He said, "The only connection we found out before I left the Communication Center was that the son of the owner of the warehouse where the "farm machinery" is being stored was on that bus. I don't know if that matters or not. If it does, whoever took the bus really did their homework."

"Too real to be a coincidence," Blinksdale shook his head and sighed. "Isn't it? That's Mason coming up the park area now?"

"Yes, he has a son on the bus," Johnny answered. "He stayed at the Embassy until Greenly returned. He said he was going to join his wife."

"Here comes an ambulance, and another one," Blinksdale called as he rushed where the ambulances were parking.

"They must have found the bus!" Collins yelled. He followed the police to the parking lot.

Within seconds the ambulances parked. Almost immediately, someone ran through the parking lot announcing that the bus had been found, and it would be in the driveway within the hour or so.

The policeman who had been responsible for checking all I.D.'s ran into the theater. Several police held a yellow rope and began roping off an area in the parking lot. They instructed that several cars be moved to make room for the returning bus.

Once the area was secure, the policeman let the parents out of the theatre. They gathered in small groups within a specific roped off area designed just for the parents and families.

The police arranged a processing area where the children would be checked first by the ambulance helpers. Then, the children would be ushered down a roped off path to the anxious parents.

Everyone waited in silence. The night was turning dark with a slight cloud cover. A full moon broke through the cover and lit up the area where everyone was standing. But, an eerie shadow still covered the corners of the parking lot.

Everyone shifted their eyes from the policeman guarding the school to the SWAT teams walking back and forth on top of buildings, and patrolling the playgrounds and surrounding streets.

The Director stood with his wife away from the parents. He looked worried and held his wife's hand. Johnny and Blinksdale walked to the couple.

Johnny said, "How are you holding up?"

The Director answered, "I'm going to hold a full school assembly in the morning to discuss the event. Since the bus contained children of all ages, we must handle their emotions on all levels. There is also a meeting planned with the police and the parents and the teachers to discuss their reactions. Arrangements are in the process to have psychologists on hand to help the students and parents deal with the situation and their reactions."

Blinksdale answered, "That's great. We will make sure the Ambassador knows about the meetings. He will want to do whatever he can to help the community."

"I so agree," said the Director. "I haven't seen Ambassador Latham, has he arrived?"

Johnny looked around and didn't see a black Buick with the American flag attached to the front hood. "No, I don't see his car. He said he would come up as soon as he could. He had an official function that he had to attend," Johnny answered.

The Captain of Police walked up to the three men and said, "It won't be long now. We just got word that they are in Grinzing." Without waiting for any comment from the group, he turned and hurried off in the other direction.

Suddenly the sirens of police cars were heard in the distance. The headlights of a speeding motor caravan moved up the hill toward the school.

Someone announced over the speakers. "Please stay back. Do not leave your rope areas." Swarms of policeman moved toward the crowd and formed a human fence.

Two police cars entered the parking area first. Everyone was silent. At the first glimpse of the school bus, the crowd roared.

The Police moved closer to the crowd, keeping their hands joined. Instantly, the SWAT team surrounded the bus. They put their machine guns over their shoulders and locked their hands to form another human barrier around the previously fenced off spaces. The remaining SWAT team aimed their guns at various places in the area.

Before Johnny, Blinksdale and the Director could walk toward the bus, parents called their child's name. "Mommy" and "Daddy" cries were heard over the roar of the crowd.

As the school bus door opened, the police barrier moved away from the bus. A policeman stepped down the steps, and ushered the first child off the bus.

A silence filled the night air as the children walked off in single file. Each gave a name to the policewoman. She checked the name against a roster she held in her hand.

A medical assistant escorted each child to the medical unit. Slowly, after the child cleared the area, one by one, a policeperson led the children to the waiting crowd.

Another policeman called the child's name, and the waiting parents rushed to claim their child. The sound of crying filled the air. Once the child was claimed, the sobbing began again, and again. Mothers, fathers, and children alike started to cry.

Collins and Blinksdale brushed away tears as they watched the faces and embraces of the families. Collins could only think that this could've have been his children.

"The children appear to be alright," Johnny said. "They don't appear to have been hurt in any way."

Blinksdale replied, "This will scar them emotionally for the rest of their lives."

Johnny turned and looked at Blinksdale, he shook his head and said, "Let's hope not."

Finally, all the children were released to their parents. The numerous reporters waited for an opportunity to question the children. Television reporters pushed microphones in people's faces asking for comments.

Blinksdale nudged Collins when he recognized a CNN television reporter headed their way. They quickly backed away and disappeared into the crowd.

Mason saw the two men. He said, "The Director wants to talk to you both."

"Thanks," Blinksdale answered. He looked at Mason and said, "How are you holding up?"

Mason nodded. "I'm doing all right, but my wife is really upset. She will probably want me to put in for a transfer tomorrow. I'll have to convince her that Vienna is probably one of the safest cities where we could be posted." He walked down the incline toward a group of people.

Blinksdale and Collins headed for the area, which was packed with press officials. The Director stood in the middle of the group.

The Director turned toward the Chief of Police and said, "He can tell you all about the discovery of the bus." He then stepped back. He worked his way toward Collins and Blinksdale.

The three men stood and listed to the Police Chief as he explained that there would be a briefing held in the theatre immediately for everyone.

When he finished, another announcement broadcasted over the speakers, inviting everyone into the theatre for a short briefing. Everyone filed back into the theatre. Collins and Blinksdale stayed outside until everyone that wanted to attend was inside. They watched the SWAT team resume their positions on top of the building and on the playgrounds.

The Chief of Police explained quickly about finding the bus. Then, a crisis specialist policewoman talked to the group. She told the parents what they could expect, such as nightmares from the incident. She further advised everyone to have their child taken to their family doctor for a complete physical.

One of the doctors that checked the students confirmed that no one on the bus appeared to have been mishandled, abused, or hurt in any way. He explained that they were hungry, frightened and tired from the long ordeal.

The School Director announced the meetings that would be held in school the next day. He warned that everyone be prepared, should they be hounded by the press for stories and interviews. They were free to talk to anyone they wished, but were told to check with their government before giving any interviews.

The Police Chief also advised, that if anyone felt harassed, they were to contact the police immediately for protection. He then offered every parent a police escort back to their home, if they wished. They were told they should call the police any time, day or night, if anyone contacted them or bothered them in any way.

After the meeting was dismissed, the parents and children left the theatre first. Some were still crying. But, some of the older children were enjoying the excitement of the moment.

The police spread out in the area. They watched as the families went to their cars.

Johnny and Blinksdale stood silently and watched. After most of the cars had left, Johnny looked at his watch. It was almost midnight.

"Has anyone found the bus driver?" Blinksdale asked the police captain as he walked toward the parking lot.

"No. Not yet. We have a network of police looking. It's just a matter of time," he called over his shoulder, as he rushed to his car to return to the station.

Collins and Blinksdale stayed until the last policeman had gone home. They and the School Director were the last people to leave the scene.

Johnny's Embassy driver was still standing by the Embassy car where he had been since arriving at the school. Blinksdale had driven his personal car. Johnny felt guilty keeping the driver when he found he could've ridden back to the Embassy with Blinksdale.

As Johnny stepped into the Embassy car, he noticed a white Mercedes parked in a small driveway to one of the adjoining homes. Johnny wasn't sure, but he thought he saw two heads in the car.

He asked his driver to drive by the car, but as he started the engine, the white Mercedes sped off into the night. Johnny blamed himself for not checking the car closer. He would mention the car when he arrived at the Embassy. Hopefully, the Austrian police had caught the license number when they patrolled the area before the school bus returned.

CHAPTER FIFTY TWO

The Embassy driver pulled up in front of the Embassy and Johnny told him to go ahead and go home. He would catch a taxi back to the Hilton. Blinksdale was parking his car just as Collins left the staff car. Collins waited on the steps for Blinksdale to catch up.

"I don't think I'll stay too long. It's been a long day and I haven't eaten since noon," Blinksdale remarked as the door buzzed open.

Collins answered, "I want to see if they found out any more out from Frankfurt. I'll probably hang around for a while. I know what you mean about eating. All I had were some of those thing-a-ma-bob sandwiches at the reception, and now my stomach is grumbling."

Blinksdale turned to go on to his office, and Collins, feeling the stress of the day, opted to push the elevator button and wait for a ride. When he finally arrived at Swartz's office, he realized just how tired he really was.

Swartz was still sitting at his desk. His suit jacket was thrown on a chair in the corner. His hair looked as if he had been sleeping, it needed combing. Two large stacks of papers and several files cluttered his desk. His computer screen had an unfinished solitary game on the screen.

"Well, it's all over except for finding the driver," Johnny said. He stood by the desk and glanced down at the files. Nothing unusual caught his attention. He added, "No one knows if he'll be found alive or dead. The kids say that he didn't know about the kidnapping, but no one knows for sure. The kids are fine. It's been a hell of a long day. Got any fresh coffee?"

"Help yourself," Swartz said, pushing his chair back on the back two legs. He rubbed the stubble on his chin and ran his fingers through his hair. "It was fresh about an hour ago. I'm going to call it a day. I've been between this office and the Center since early this morning. I know what you mean about a long day. Say, there's a message for you in the Center to be unscrambled. I took it and logged it in. It's being held in the classified area. Just get Smith to open it for you." He yawned and stood up and stretched.

"Is he still on duty?" Collins asked. He glanced at his watch.

"Yes, I have the center on twenty-four hour for the time being," Swartz answered. "The message is from your home office. There is nothing more from Frankfurt, either. They're really checking Kay's background. I suppose tomorrow's courier run will be handled by someone new. We should get a message on it any minute now. I know they are busy, but what the hell, so are we." Swartz started cleaning off his desk and walked to the file with a pile of papers. He turned back to Johnny who was pouring himself a cup of coffee, and asked, "Has anyone heard anything more about the British Embassy bombings?"

"Not that I heard about," Johnny answered. "You didn't hear anything here either?"

"The only thing we heard was that a couple people were in a hospital, but no one was killed. It appears to have been some type of a warning bombing instead of an actual attempt to kill someone, otherwise there would have been more damage. The Ambassador's car wasn't hit too badly. But then, that car is built like a tank, with all the special bulletproof armor. The other car was identified as being one that was assigned to the British Oil Director from London. He's in town to talk to some of the OPEC people. His visit was kept pretty hush-hush, but there was a small two-line bit about his meetings in the London papers. I was sure by now someone would claim the bombings for the glory, if nothing else. Maybe there will be something in the morning papers."

Johnny told Swartz he would check in at the Communication Center and then go on back to the hotel. Saying goodnight, Collins walked to the Center and pushed the buzzer. Smith answered the ring immediately.

"Been a long day for you, hasn't it, sir?" Smith asked politely.

He smiled and stood back as Johnny entered. Smith was dressed in blue jeans and a white Iowa sweatshirt, and was wearing Nike tennis shoes.

"Hell of a long day, but I've been busy ever since I arrived. But, it isn't always like this here in Vienna is it?" Johnny asked.

"No, usually the most excitement we get is when some congressmen or representatives come in on a CODEL (congressional delegation) from the states. They're always on some kind of a fact-finding mission. Truth of the matter is, they want to go shopping, and what better place than Vienna? Their wives come and buy crystal and all the things that make Austria famous. Otherwise, things are routine."

"Are you from Iowa?" Johnny asked, he didn't remember seeing what state he was from in the files. Johnny wondered if they might have missed a bank account.

"No, my mom graduated from a small college in Northeastern Iowa, not far from the Minnesota border. She was born and raised there. This sweatshirt was a birthday present from my aunt that lives there. Actually, it is perfect for work here. We have to keep the air conditioning on to keep the computers from over heating and it gets chilly in these rooms," Smith answered.

"I know, sometimes it is like a refrigerator in these Comm. Centers," Johnny answered. "Swartz said I had a message that came in from Virginia. Can you get it for me?"

"Yes, I have it in the back. You can use any of the equipment that you need."

Johnny got the message and walked to a chair by a machine. As he fed the message into the machine, his mind went over the events of the day. He was deep in thought when the machine spit out the translated words. As he read the message he sank deeper in his chair. He watched the words transform from unintelligible gobbledygook into English sentences. His eyes burned, both from the printed words and the late hour.

Completely translated, he took the message and sat and stared at it. The words were imprinted on his mind. It was the closest thing to a verbal chewing out that his boss could do under the circumstances. In plain words, Hubert wanted to know what in the hell was going on. He wanted to know everything immediately and if Johnny didn't tell him, he would send in someone who would.

He visualized Melvin Hubert sitting in his chair, rotating it, as he dictated the message. He could picture Sue reacting to Hubert's anger. Then, it would be Sue's job to re-phrase his words into a message that would be transferred across the lines. Johnny nodded. His point was received and understood.

After contemplating on just how to answer Hubert's message, Johnny reached for a pad and pencil. For the next several minutes, he wrote in complete detail everything that had happened since he arrived five days before. He was well aware that some of it was duplicated in previous messages. Taking great care to phrase each sentence just right, he read and re-read what he had written. Finally, convinced it read exactly as it should, he gave it to Smith and watched as Smith sent his message over the airwaves to be received in CIA Headquarters.

CHAPTER FIFTY THREE

The small Viennese coffee house was almost empty. It was the hour between morning coffee and the lunch group. The three men sat at a rear table, hidden from the rest of the people. They smiled and congratulated one another. Several newspapers were spread out on the table in front of them. Not to arouse any undue attention, they kept their voices just above a whisper.

"We could not have hoped for any better coverage," one of them remarked. "Look, we have great coverage on the school bus and our message regarding the British Embassy bombings was copied word for word."

"The Director of the American School explained that we had asked for millions in ransom. It makes him look good that the money was never paid," another man added.

The GRU Colonel said, "Now, is everything in place regarding the computer shipment? Are we in control?"

Haddah answered, "Yes, the Hamas are in place. As I explained last night, it would be much easier to take the shipment now, especially since we know the shipment plans." He looked at the two men, glanced at his watch and continued, "It is just a matter of time."

Mehmet Gadhafi said, "Yes, I am in total agreement. I also have some of my people standing by. We maintain a small stockpile of arms here in Vienna for just such an occasion. All we need is a truck or a station wagon. But, getting a vehicle is the least of our problems. I will go call them now and put them on alert."

The Russian Colonel smiled. "Yes, it is perfect. The few extra hours will not matter."

The Russian sat quietly looking at the Lebanese, Haddah, across the table from him. Golodin had not received a go ahead from Moscow to the change in plans. He was reluctant to act on his own initiative. But, what did he have to lose? The worst that could happen would be that he'd be sent back to Russia. That would not be so bad. He would enjoy getting to know his son and friends again. He might even take retirement.

When Gadhafi returned to the table, the waitress followed with three cups of mélange, and three large servings of hot apple strudel smothered with whipped cream.

Golodin smiled at the waitress. When she was out of hearing distance, he turned to Gadhafi and asked, "Is everything alright?"

Gadhafi smiled and reached for his fork. He said, "They are standing by."

CHAPTER FIFTY FOUR

Collins spent a restless night. His dreams were filled with terror and violence. He had awakened completely exhausted, as if he hadn't gone to bed at all. When he arrived at the Embassy, the road in front was packed with media cars and vans. Reporters were asking everyone about the bus incident.

The Ambassador stood in front of the Embassy. An Austrian policeman stood on both sides of him. He announced that a news release would be issued later in the day. The reporters shouted questions about the ransom money. They demanded to know if the money had been paid.

Austrian police had formed a human barrier in front of the Embassy. They were positioned in a circle that surrounded the entrance. They held back the mob from going up the steps to the Embassy door.

Collins could see Blinksdale and his men were trying to help the police. The reporters didn't know who Collins was, so he was able to push his way to the front of the line past the police, and finally into the building.

Once inside, the havoc continued. A privileged few, who had been admitted into the Embassy, waited for the Ambassador to finish out front. The Marine guards were watching them.

At first glance, Collins thought those waiting were reporters, but at a closer look, he discovered they were other foreign ambassadors. Johnny was sure they were there to ask about the bus incident because some of their countries children had been on the hijacked bus.

The hallway to the Communication Center was bustling. Embassy employees were running back and forth. Collins knew they were all avoiding the first floor. The various offices were sending messages back to Washington to their reporting desks.

When Collins pushed the buzzer for entrance into the Communication Center, he waited for such a long period of time he wondered if they were working. Finally, Mason opened the door.

"Sorry, sir. All hell has broken loose and we're swamped," Mason explained when Collins entered.

"I can understand that," Johnny said. "There's a crowd of reporters outside, and the reception room is filled with Ambassadors, which would be enough for several day's activities. Do you know if I received any messages?"

"Yes, several. They are all logged. When you want to read them, let me know and I'll get them for you."

"Thanks. I want to see Swartz first, then I'll be back. Where is he? Do you know?" Collins asked.

"He's in the back of this room talking to Smith," Mason pointed to the other side of the room. "Kay Blackburn's replacement is with them."

The rear of the room was darker than usual. Johnny looked up and saw the big overhead light had burned out, and in the rush of activities, no one had either noticed it or had gotten around to fixing it.

It took just a moment for Johnny's eyes to adjust to the darkness. He found Kevin Smith, Swartz, and a stranger huddle together.

"Good morning, Johnny," Swartz said when he saw him approach.

"Good morning. Seems as if there's never a dull moment here in Vienna," Johnny answered when he joined the group.

"Hell of a mess, isn't it? It never rains but it pours," Swartz answered sharply.

"Outside is pure bedlam," Johnny said. "I'm glad I'm not in the Ambassador's shoes this morning. He'll be busy for hours. What's new here?"

"This is Don Adams, Kay Blackburn's replacement," Swartz said. "I was just going over some of the things with him and Smith. As you know, Smith handles most of the courier pouch duties and this was a good time to get the two of them together.

We are just finishing up. Would you like to come with me to my office? I've some papers I want to go over with you."

"Fine, you go ahead and finish with these people," Johnny replied. He shook hands with both Smith and Adams. "I've a couple messages I want to get first from Mason, and then I'll be ready to join you. Give me a couple minutes."

Mason was waiting by the machine with Johnny's messages. Mason turned on the machine and pushed the necessary buttons to allow Johnny access to the keyboard so he could enter his special password code.

He fed all four messages into the machine and the jumbled words came out into words Johnny could read. When it was finished, Johnny pushed another button and the machine was again secure. Johnny motioned for Mason to lock it.

Johnny took the original jumbled message and put it through the shredder. He read the copies of the decoded messages in his hand. He read them again, and again. Tearing the paper in half, he took the upper part of the message and shredded it, too. The bottom half he held in his hand and headed for the door, and Swartz's office.

Swartz was already busy at his desk when Johnny entered.

"What's the latest word?" Collins asked after he entered and shut the door behind him.

"Doesn't look good," Swartz answered. "They found out more about Kay. Pull up a chair and I'll bring you up to date."

Johnny took off his jacket and pulled a wooden chair close to the desk. He took out his notebook and said, "Fire away."

Swartz nodded and said, "They did an autopsy on her. She was killed by a dose of poison that someone put in her coffee. We believe that someone was Henri Curiel, the passenger who sat directly behind her. When the stewardesses were questioned, they remembered a mix up with the coffee. Mr. Curiel had ordered plain black and Kay drank hers with cream. The stewardess had given the wrong coffee to Kay. But almost instantly, Kay and Curiel exchanged cups and the problem was corrected."

"So, an attendant gave Kay the coffee?" Johnny asked.

"Yes," Swartz answered after checking a file. "Curiel must've seized that opportunity to put it in the coffee. Small traces were found in the cup. At first, it was thought to have been in the food, but the autopsy found it in the coffee when they ran their tests."

"Did anyone else handle the cup other than the attendant and Curiel?" Johnny asked.

"No, she took the coffee out of the machine and filled the cups."

Johnny frowned and turned his head. "Are you sure the attendant didn't do it?"

Swartz laughed. "I'm sure someone checked her out."

Johnny made a note. "Well, I will have them double check. Weren't some other passengers sick?"

"Yes, it was just a strange coincidence that three passengers became ill. Now, the doctors think they were ill from the air pressure. There was a bad storm that evening. The doctors couldn't find any trace of poison with the other passengers."

"This is amazing," Johnny said.

Swartz said, "And, there is more. Upon further investigation, we discovered Kay had a very large savings account in the same bank that the Barrs use. The deposits coincided with her trips from Russia. Once, she changed to the Vienna route, the deposits were monthly, on or about the fifteenth of each month."

Johnny made more notes. He asked, "What sums of money?"

Swartz checked another file. He answered, "Anywhere from five to twenty thousand dollars. We believe she wasn't as valuable to the Russians on her Vienna route, as she was on the Moscow one. It appears to fit, but we don't have all the pieces yet. Her apartment didn't reveal anything more except the savings account book and what we discussed yesterday. We've found some neighbors who said she was visited occasionally by a very tall, bald man and a short older man. They believed the men to be relatives. Some had actually talked to both men and said one had a slight European accent and the other sounded like an American. Sounds like either the SVR, FSB or GRU, doesn't it?"

"Yea, it does," Johnny said. "I received word from my office this morning. What you just told me is about the same as they found out. They're convinced Barr's and Blackburn's deaths are connected. They believe Barr was ready to tell us everything. And, Blackburn was probably killed for the same reason. They think she was ordered to take the courier bag, or leave it for someone else to pick up."

Swartz sat back in his chair and thought for a few seconds. He said, "It all makes sense when you think about it."

Johnny answered, "Langley also believes there are no more double agents here in Vienna. They've found a few unanswered things, and their still checking them. I've been asked to have Kevin Smith's girlfriend watched. She has been identified as a Russian sympathizer. Her name doesn't appear on any Russian rosters, but she does have a history of association with known Russian agents."

Swartz made a note of her name and said, "I'll make sure that Blinksdale also knows. Maybe, I should see about transferring Smith?"

Johnny smiled, and answered, "Don't say anything. Kevin Smith will be transferred to Africa. The move will happen within the month. They feel it's best. It will be done very professionally, in the form of a promotion."

"Well, that's that," Swartz said, crossing off the note about Smith being transferred. "Anything else?"

"The Frankfurt office will continue to monitor Mrs. Metcalf and her family," Johnny continued, he look at the paper that he had carried from the comm. center. "We've not been able to find anything on her or her family. However, just because she is Mrs. Barr's sister they are concerned. They'll also watch all of the Barrs' furniture shipments. I believe everything is being shipped today."

Swartz said, "Yes, it's scheduled for pickup today. I'm sure the movers are there already."

249

"Mrs. Barr has rented an apartment in DC," Johnny added. "Several of her old friends have been seen visiting her. We're sure in time she'll adjust to her new environment and will start a new life. My office will keep a watch on her. I'll be returning to the states. I can't do anything about the bus incident, and the computer shipment is leaving tonight. Anyway, both of those problems are under the State Department. We found out what we needed to know about our people. Langley is satisfied, and so am I."

"Maybe, things will get back to normal," Swartz sighed. He rubbed his head and looked at Johnny.

"Hopefully," Collins said. "I wish we could have stopped the deaths, but the disgrace of a trial and sentencing would've cause more embarrassment to both Russia and us. Maybe everything will turn out for the best. Still, its such a shame."

Swartz glanced at his watch. He said, "My wife is over with Mrs. Metcalf this morning. I'm glad the shipment is going today, I've hardly seen my wife since she met Mrs. Metcalf. She wants to be over there all the time, helping to get things ready for the shipments."

Collins said, "Mrs. Metcalf is a very pleasant person."

Swartz stood and walked to his file cabinet. He leaned on it and said, "I never would have expected Barr or Kay for double agents. I guess it's my fault. I should have been looking for small signs that would have told me something."

"We can't blame ourselves. Hindsight is always twenty-twenty," Johnny said. "Just watch things more closely, and know your personnel. I think I'll go see Greenly and tell him what I've just told you and maybe stop by Blinksdale's office. He was really swamped when I saw him earlier this morning. He was out front with his men helping the Austrian police control the mob."

The bustle of the Embassy hadn't settled down by the time Johnny left Swartz's office near the Communication Center. He walked down the steps and into the main lobby.

The reception room was still occupied. Johnny noticed some different faces in the group. The Marines had brought coffee, and there were several dirty cups on the end tables.

Johnny stood for a few moments getting the feel of the room. He wanted to see if he could sense any resentment or anger in the room. He only felt concern. All the Ambassadors knew, that only by the luck of the draw, this could have been their problem. Johnny felt that most of them had come to offer help.

The rest of the day whirled pass. Johnny made his arrangements to return to the States. He had done what he could. He didn't feel as if he had accomplished anything, nothing more than he could have done from the States.

Johnny felt as if his days in Vienna had been carefully programmed. He hated to admit it was all a game, and no one had even given him the full set of rules.

Collins left the Embassy early in the afternoon and headed for the main part of the city. He wanted to pick up a few things for his family before returning to the Hilton hotel. He still had another day to finish all his reports before his flight.

CHAPTER FIFTY FIVE

The city was quiet. It was very early morning. The men sat in the two cars and waited patiently. They were prepared for their attack. In order to be effective, and to strike with full force, the men had enlisted four of their most trusted PLO friends.

The PLO agents were in Vienna recruiting and training new recruits. Their demolition training was perfect for the job. They agreed to drive the van with the explosives and activate them.

All the men had been briefed. They were equipped with the guns, ammunition, and other supplies they would need.

Through a string of "watchers", the group knew when the shipment arrived and where it was. Hourly reports had been sent to Haddah regarding the warehouse activities.

The computers and supplies were in crates and had been loaded onto three large moving vans. They were ready to be transported to the airport. It was just a ten-minute drive.

The "watchers" reported that after the crates were loaded into the vans, four Austrian police guards patrolled the area. The terrorists watched the guards walk their rounds, noting everything they did. They were glad there were no watchdogs to eliminate.

Haddah sat in a car by himself away from the others. He was dressed completely in black, as were all members of the team.

His face had been blackened and he wore a pair of night vision goggles so he could see the men in the other cars. Black gloves covered his hands. From time to time, he glanced at his watch.

The moon had gone behind the clouds. On Haddah's signal, the men got out of their cars and moved together. They were still a block from the warehouse.

While the guards walked their routes, the men finalized their plans to neutralize the guards. Golodin and Gadfahi agreed to take the two guards nearest the gate. Haddah and one of the Hamas members agreed to eliminate the two men who walked the warehouse grounds. Haddah checked his watch again and the four men separated to carry out their missions.

The remaining two Hamas members, as if one, moved toward the fence. They were holding small M-19-A submachine guns. The guns were the perfect small arms weapons for the job. They had a range of fifty yards and could shoot at a rate of 3,000 rounds per minute.

The four PLO recruits watched the guards through their night vision goggles. They knew they had twenty minutes to take the trucks, plant the explosives and arrive at the airport. That was the interval between routine call-ins that the guards had.

Gadhafi pulled up the antenna on his field radio and spoke softly instructing the four back up men that it was time. The van moved up to the driveway.

Although, the warehouse was in an isolated area. There was nothing within two miles of their target except more warehouses. Haddah stressed not using the machine guns unless absolutely necessary to reduce the noise factor.

Within seconds, Gadhafi opened the gate and the van drove through. The men jumped out. They had all been trained in guerilla warfare. Carrying the plastic explosives and timing devices, two men planted the explosives. The other two men and one of the Hamas members started the trucks and drove out of the area and toward the airport.

A Hamas member jumped into the van turned it around and had all the doors open, ready for their escape into the night. He listened carefully for the sound of sirens in the distance. One by one, the men finished their assigned task and ran to the waiting transportation.

Almost as swiftly as it began, the explosives were planted. All the timing devices were pre-set and hidden. They still had ten minutes to clear the area. That was the time they decided it would take before anyone would come from the police to check why the guards hadn't reported on schedule.

The men threw their weapons into the center of the courtyard. If they were stopped, they didn't want anything on them. Everyone stripped out of their dark clothing, revealing normal street wear underneath. They threw their clothing on top of the guns. A final explosive device was placed on top of the pile. With minutes to spare, they drove away from the scene with their lights off.

When the men driving the trucks rounded the corner and headed for the airport, they turned on their truck lights. They pulled into the airport area, at the same time that the van pulled into the airport parking lot.

The trucks were escorted directly to the waiting Aeroflot plane. The plane crew was in position and the flight plans had been approved. Maintenance workers were waiting to load the plane.

They had been told the shipment was for Moscow. Most workers believed it was really farm equipment, because they knew that the Russian farmers need new equipment.

The terrorists waited in the airport lounge. They were booked on the first scheduled flight. Earlier, they purchased their tickets and had placed suitcases in lockers at the airport. They even arranged for some friends to be in the lobby waiting for them, to furnish alibis if needed.

The red Ford turned back toward Vienna. George Haddah smiled and hummed to the popular song. When he entered the street leading to the Gurtel, a bright flash of light filled the sky. He pulled off to the side of the road, stopped his car, and stepped out to watch a series of brilliant explosions rock the pavement where he stood.

In the distance, he heard the sound of sirens. He watched for several minutes before heading to his apartment. He hoped to have his report transmitted before the Americans knew the shipment was missing.

In the gray Audi, owned and driven by Golodin, and with Mehmet Gadhafi as his companion, they saw the explosions as they drove down one of the streets near the Prater. They followed their instincts and stopped their car.

They stood and watched the night light up as bright as New Year's Eve. Smiling, the two men got back in the car and headed for the first district and their apartments.

CHAPTER FIFTY SIX

The GRU Colonel left Gadhafi off in front of his apartment. Golodin wished Gadhafi a good night and proceeded down Ringstrasse toward his home. When he drove the car up to the garage of his apartment, he noticed a VW parked in front of his house.

Instantly, he recognized the car as one of the cars that Yuri Rubin had assigned to his office. He became puzzled and wondered what Rubin was doing out so early in the morning.

Rubin got out of his car and walked to the doorway. Golodin parked his car and turned off the motor. "To what do I owe the honor of this visit at such an early hour, Comrade?" Golodin asked sarcastically, after he stepped out of the car.

"How did everything go?" Rubin asked.

Golodin looked around the area. He said, "Let's go inside and we can talk. It is more private."

Rubin didn't move. He asked, "Is the shipment on its way to Moscow?"

Golodin nodded and stepped on the first step. "Yes, of course. It went easier than we had planned."

"That is the first thing that you have done right in several days," Rubin said. He spread his legs apart and stared down at the older man.

"What ever do you mean?" Golodin asked, waving the remark away with his hand.

"Why did you eliminate Blackburn?" Rubin asked.

Golodin stepped backwards almost falling. When he regained his footing, he said, "I did not kill her."

Rubin laughed. He took another step closer to Golodin. "Of course not. You would not do the dirty work yourself. You would have one of your Arab friends do it." Rubin leaned forward and held on to the metal railing and leaned toward Golodin. "You are an embarrassment to my government. It was because of you that Barr decided he didn't want to work with us

256

anymore. You were the reason Kay Blackburn wanted to quit. She had grown to fear you."

Golodin shuttered. He stepped back and looked at the tall man. He muttered to himself and walked to the bench in front of his house. Rubin followed.

Golodin held his head in his hands for several seconds. He looked at Rubin and said, "Blackburn was never a serious problem. After she lost her job as Barr's controller, she asked me if I was still going to use her. I told her I would find something for her. She was not to worry."

Rubin pulled his green loden coat around his chest. He looked at the older man and chuckled to himself. He answered, "Yes, I know, I had her eliminated. You see, she also reported to me." He slid close to Golodin and whispered, "Now, I must eliminate you. You see, I could have stepped in at any time, but I decided to wait until I knew the shipment was on its way to Moscow. "

"Kay is dead?" the old Colonel questioned, with tears in his eyes.

"Yes, she's dead." Rubin had his right hand in his pocket all the time he spoke. He pulled a small Browning 9mm pistol out of his pocket. As the pistol barrel cleared his waist, he fired.

The bullet hit the GRU Colonel in the middle of his forehead. His eyes were opened and filled with confusion.

The SVR agent needed only one shot. With the silencer attached, it only made a clinking noise that blended with the early morning street sounds.

After checking to make sure the GRU man was dead, Rubin threw the gun on the front seat of Golodin's car. He carried Golodin back into his Audi and placed him in the driver's seat. Satisfied everything was in order, Rubin walked to his car and drove off into the night. He left the body and gun to be disposed of by his men.

CHAPTER FIFTY SEVEN

Johnny was sound asleep as the ringing of the phone brought him out of a daze. He was twisted in the blankets. He reached for the phone and managed to say, "Hello."

"Johnny. All hell has broken loose. Can you be ready in ten minutes? I'll pick you up in front of the hotel by the taxi stand."

"Yes, Blinksdale, I'll be there."

Johnny dressed in a flash, leaving the room in turmoil. He barely ran a toothbrush over his teeth. Grabbing his briefcase, he raced down the steps, and reached the front entrance of the hotel when Blinksdale drove up. Blinksdale slowed the car and Johnny jumped into it.

"My heavens, man!" Johnny said. "What's happened?"

"Someone blew up the warehouse and either destroyed the shipment or stole it. It's not clear which."

"Has anyone been killed? Has anyone claimed the bombing?" Johnny asked tossing his briefcase on the back seat and struggling with his seat belt.

"Yea, they killed all four guards," Blinksdale said. "Anyway, we think they killed the guards. They're dead, but it might have been from the explosion. It happened a couple hours ago. With all the confusion, it took the Austrians some time to find out who owned the warehouse. We're sure everyone responsible has fled the country by now."

"Was anything saved?" Johnny questioned. He held his breath as Blinksdale passed a tram.

"Nothing," Blinksdale answered turning the corner toward the Gurtel on two wheels.

"Where are we going now?" Johnny asked, wondering if he should change his airplane reservations.

"To the warehouse," Blinksdale answered, swerving in and out of the morning traffic. "Can you imagine what Washington is going to say? I left Greenly pulling his hair out at the Embassy."

"What's being done?" Johnny asked, wondering what was going to happen next.

"Hell, I don't know. I imagine the Austrian police have set up roadblocks and have taken all the usual precautions. I don't know what they can do. It could have been anyone. It wouldn't take a top-notch terrorist group to find out about the shipment. There were articles about it yesterday in the USA Today and such. Israel will be hopping mad. The Ambassador will be in for another bitchy day."

Johnny looked at Blinksdale and sighed. "Well, it looks as if the bastards have won another round. We will probably never know who was behind the blast unless someone claims responsibility and wants the fame. We soon will see, but I'm betting we'll be left with egg on our faces."

CHAPTER FIFTY EIGHT

Another phone rang in a large fourth floor apartment on Lubyanika Square in Moscow. The ringing stopped when the receiver was lifted.

"Yes."

"Sir, the mission is complete. The shipment should be in Moscow with hours. The plan was carried out as we predicted. Golodin has been silenced. The other two men will be recalled today. Four Austrian guards were killed. I could not prevent it. The Americans never suspected we used the shipment as a diversion against their search for more double agents. Our source, at CIA Headquarters, tells us the CIA believes all double agents have been discovered. It is exactly as we predicted. They played into our hands."

"You have done well. What about the two remaining women agents in Vienna? Are they still in place?"

"Yes, Mrs. Swartz turned over the computer tape she found in the Barr house. As you know, it contained the present and future postings for the next two years of all CIA agents throughout the world, as well as thumb nail bios of each Chief-of-Station. Mrs. Swartz is not under suspicion. Her husband has just extended his assignment in Vienna. They will be here for another three years."

"That is wonderful."

Rubin smiled and continued, "Mrs. Barr has been contacted and has been given her new orders as you directed. She hasn't been told of Golodin's death. In time, she will be told. She promises to marry again after an appropriate period of time. We have told her it must be someone of power or position. Her new case officer is not with the government, but is a journalist and has complete freedom to travel the world. It should prove to be a most efficient arrangement. We made a mistake when we assigned Kay Blackburn both Mr. and Mrs. Barr. But, all in all, it was for the best. The Americans think the Barr and Blackburn cases are solved, and the cases are closed."

"What about the other Vienna agent?" the gruff voiced man questioned.

"She's fine. She's secure. No one suspects her, and I have just given her a new assignment. We learned the new Deputy Chief of Mission is about her age and single. He also prefers tall, mature blonde women. He's scheduled to arrive at post next month. She should be perfect for him. Her identity will never be suspected. However, she's asked us to put her pay in a Swiss bank account. She doesn't want anyone checking through her accounts like they've been doing with Barr's and Blackburn's. That's not going to be a problem is it?" Rubin frowned as he posed the question.

"Not at all. I'll get someone on it right away. Have they made any connection to the mole? How are things going with recruiting the others?"

Rubin shifted in his chair and looked around his apartment. He glanced at the doorway. "I have not heard anything further about the mole. We know they removed the one from Blackburn. Barr should have been cremated by the time they found Blackburn's. Nothing has resulted from it. The others have also been tagged. As for the men, the local one is coming along nicely. We will soon see but I expect he will be more valuable than Ames ever was."

"And, the other?" the Moscow director asked.

"Don Adams, he will be fine. He will be working Blackburn's courier route part-time and in the courier processing room the other time. With all of his financial problems from a recent divorce, college students and an expensive life style, he needs the money. We will have no problems with him."

"That is good news. Then we are again one play ahead of the Americans. You have done well. A promotion will be coming your way. Where would you like to be posted next? I think an immediate change would be best."

"Washington, D.C., if I have a choice," Rubin answered without hesitation. "I'd like to watch the female agents from afar and control the journalist. I'd also like to be directly involved with our female agents in the CIA. In Washington, the possibilities are endless."

"It's yours, then. Orders will follow soon. Good night, my son. You have done Russia proud."

Rubin sighed as he hung up the telephone. He pulled a large envelope out of his desk drawer and carefully removed the pictures. He placed them, one by one, on top of his desk and grinned.

He hadn't quite decided just how he would use the nude photos of Johnny Collins. The right time would come. He whispered aloud to the empty space. "Soon it will be your turn to see if you can catch me on your turf. Collins, I'm ready to start any time you are up to it? I may even give you a wild card."

* * *

ABOUT THE AUTHOR

Elizabeth J. Jung has lived and traveled extensively in the United States and Europe, wherever her government-employed husband was assigned. In her writing, she draws on this wide variety of real life experiences to create an in-depth realistic story with local color.

Her first novel, released in 2000, was THE BUDAPEST CONNECTION. She presently is working on her next novel, which she hopes to have released in early spring of 2001.

She spends her time writing, reading, antiquing and gardening at her lakeside home in Clear Lake, Iowa. She has three grown children, two sons and one daughter and three grandchildren, two boys and one girl. The author's website is www.elizabethjung.com